TIMBERLINE

TIMBERLINE

Bernie Ziegner

Timberline

©2024 by **Bernie Ziegne**r All rights reserved.

No part of this book may be reproduced or transmitted in any form or by any means, electronic or mechanical, including photocopying, recording, or by any information storage and retrieval system, without permission in writing from the copyright owner.

Published by **Bernie Ziegner**

ISBN: 979-8-89021-526-0 Paperback
ISBN: 979-8-89021-527-7 Hardback
ISBN: 979-8-89021-525-3 eBook

Printed in the United States of America

This book is printed on acid-free paper.

1

Tom Bauer looked up and scowled as he walked briskly to his pickup truck. The starry sky of the previous evening had by dawn turned to an ominous gray. The air was damp and cold. He pulled his Stetson firmly down on his brow, tufts of unruly salt and pepper hair poking out from under the rim.

"Time for a haircut," he mumbled as he zipped up his fleece-lined jacket.

His dog leapt onto the seat when he opened the truck door. Tom again looked up at the sky, rubbed his hands together, and climbed into the truck cab.

"Hey, Bandit. We're gonna get snow. This storm is moving in quick, the temperature is dropping too." Bandit glanced at Tom but turned his attention to the window.

"I can do without it, but you know, more snow would be helpful. It's been light during the past several winters." Bandit con-tinued to look out the window.

Another summer drought would bring a marked increase in fire danger to the tinder-dry mountains of western Montana, and many of the springs that fed Elk Creek would stop running. He recalled the smell of smoke during the past summer and the haze drifting in from the Idaho fires. It had been a nervous time.

A shiver ran through his body as he pulled up the collar of his jacket. "Damn, it's cold," he mumbled to himself. He checked the outside-temperature display on the truck dashboard, 20 degrees at noon on this late April day. He reached to start the engine, antici-pating the warmth soon to come from the heater. Bandit, a mixed-breed wolf dog, sat next to him, his tail thumping on the seat. Tom reached over to pet him, running his fingers through his thick smooth fur.

"Okay boy," Tom said, "we'll have us some heat real soon."

2

The Beechcraft King Air, a twin-turboprop, sat in front of the ProAir Charter Service hanger at the edge of Calgary Inter-national Airport. The pilot and co-pilot of the charter flight stood outside the passenger entrance at the rear of the airplane expecting their passengers momentarily. They had made this run to Reno for the company countless times, and knew what was expected. Gener-ally there were only two or three passengers, couriers from the Gold Dust Casino in Reno and from the large ski resort of Skyline Lodge in Banff – both properties owned by the company. Sometimes there was a stranger from Chicago to whom deference was paid by the others.

They were paid well to make these flights in a timely and innocuous manner and not to look too closely at the passengers or their cargo. Kalispell, Missoula and Boise were places where the company had made special arrangements so that the international flight could be refueled quickly without the passengers leaving the airplane, and without undue attention from the FAA, Customs or INS. The captain had been informed that there would be four men on this flight, three new floor managers for the Gold Dust Casino and a special courier. Also at the last minute, the Gold Dust Casino had requested that a new entertainer be included on the flight mani-fest. She was scheduled to appear as a last minute replacement for an injured singer.

The captain talked to the co-pilot about the total weight and fuel load, deciding that since they had only the minimum required 30-minute margin, it would be prudent to top off the fuel tanks at Missoula.

The co-pilot showed the captain the weather information and they briefly discussed the storm layer forming over the Bitterroot Range.

"Cap'n, they're expecting that this stuff will move into lower Montana by evening. We'll probably see some spillover by the time we get to Missoula. I imagine there will be stuff backing up against the Bitterroots towards Boise later though."

"Okay, Dave...we'll have to keep an eye on this. I have us at 20,000 feet all the way. Let's see how that holds up. We'll refuel in Missoula and then get above this stuff."

"We're right on the edge on weight Bill. Missoula is a good choice."

"Okay...that's what we're down for. We might need the margin if things get shitty in Idaho."

"Ohh Cap'n, here comes that singer lady..." The copilot had focused his attention on the attractive woman just exiting the taxicab.

Karen passed the fare to the driver, then quickly alighted from the taxi. She glanced at a sign on the hanger door, ProAir Charter Service. The driver took her bags from the trunk of the car and dropped them on the pavement. He was quickly back in his cab, leaving her standing at the curb, bags at her feet.

"Thanks a lot buddy. You're a big help," she mumbled at the receding vehicle. The cab raced away, chasing another fare.

She looked about trying to decide whether to go into the hanger or through the gate and directly to the tarmac and the plane. "Awful tiny plane," she said aloud, but not loud enough for anyone else to hear, then looked at the two-man crew standing by the passenger door, and added, "Young pilots, too, but at least they look the part." She appreciated that they were well dressed and profess-sion-al, although young. As she struggled with her bags, she saw the younger of the two men hurry towards her and open the gate. He introduced himself with a wide smile.

"Hello. Welcome to ProAir. My name is Dave and I'm your co-pilot. Here...I'll take those."

She returned his warm smile and let him take the bags, not missing what appeared to be an appreciative glance toward her.

"Thank you. I'm Karen Roberts. I guess you were expecting me?"

"Yes, the Cap'n had your name on the manifest this morn-ing." He looked at her again as he bent over to pick up another bag.

He took the bags effortlessly under both arms and escorted her to the airplane. The captain, a trim man in his thirties, introduced himself and helped her aboard the airplane.

"Ms Roberts, I'm Captain Bill Richards. This is my co-pilot Dave Jackson. Welcome aboard." He gave her a generous grin and met her glance respectfully.

"Thank you, I'm glad I could make this flight...last minute thing."

The pilot, looking a little embarrassed, told Karen, "I'm sorry, Ms. Roberts, the front seats have been spoken for already. I hope that you'll be comfortable in the back seat here. At least you'll be close to the cold refreshments." He pointed to what looked to Karen like a small refrigerator.

She nodded and took her seat. "Thanks, Captain. This should do fine. It's a three hour trip?"

She felt the Captain's gaze on her as he hesitated by her seat. His gaze made her feel good, unlike the bold glances from the co-pilot. "Yes, it usually runs three hours, maybe a little more. We'll stop for a quick refueling in Missoula. We'll have to stay in the plane, though; Customs rules. Anything I can do for you before we take off?"

She met his gaze. "I'll be fine. Thank you."

He nodded and stepped back outside the aircraft.

Karen looked about the well-appointed cabin. It was small. She counted only four regular seats and her jump-seat, but felt comfortable. She glanced out of the window to see the captain welcome four men who came out of a limousine. She noticed the co-pilot and the limo-driver loaded the baggage into the cargo compart-ment. One of the passengers seemed to insist on keeping an alumi-num briefcase with him in the cabin. There was more conversation between the passenger and the captain. Then the captain shrugged and walked out of Karen's sight.

3

Tom backed the truck away from the barn and headed down the ranch road toward an old overgrown logging road that would take him over the west ridge to where a spring and stock tank were located. Even though the water tank was only about five miles by road from the ranch lodge, getting there required a 20-minute trek up and over Bauer Ridge west of the lodge on a narrow and rocky track. Heat began in a steady stream from dashboard vents. Tom began to feel comfortable and unzipped his jacket.

The year-round spring fed a rivulet, now frozen, where many wild animals watered. The now empty stock tank, filled in summer by the spring, kept water available for the Sullivan Ranch cattle that grazed on the land leased from Timberline Ranch. Tom no longer ran cattle. Instead, after the death of his father, he had sold the whole herd to the neighboring Sullivans and leased them the grazing rights to most of his land, while he prepared to convert the old place to a guest ranch. Tom knew from his inspection trip the previous fall that the stock tank had to be repaired, but he had made excuses to put it off until it could wait no longer. The welded steel frame that kept the big galvanized tank level and off the rocky ground had rusted and cracked and he knew that it would be unlikely to hold the weight of nearly 800 gallons of water. Tom turned onto the nar-row track that would take him over the ridge and geared down the truck to allow a slow and steady crawl over the bumpy trail. He enjoyed his new truck, a 2001 model 4WD Ford F-250. He had it equipped with a generator-welder and water pump, as well as a tool storage compartment. Tom readjusted the heater control to reduce the roar of the forced air since the cab had reached a comfortable temperature.

"Feels okay now Bandit, don't you think?"

Bandit responded with a couple flicks of his tail and kept looking out the windows. He flinched as tree limbs rubbed against the truck. They made their way steadily through groves of pon-derosa and up the switchbacks to the ridge top.

4.

KAREN FASTENED HER SEAT belt and wondered what lay ahead. Her agent had arranged this last minute flight to Reno to take advantage of an opening at the Gold Dust Casino. She would be filling in a one-hour segment every evening for the next couple of weeks, substituting for a popular singer who had been hospitalized after an automobile accident. A local country band would accom-pany her. She was nervous about the engagement, unsure of the band and hoping that they would have time to practice together. She was glad of the opportunity however, for it would give her much needed exposure, and if the band was supportive, it could be a successful endeavor.

She watched the other four passengers enter and go to their seats. They looked like businessmen, not the sales types she usually had to fend off. They all smiled at her and said hello, except for the last man to enter. She smiled and said hello to him, but he merely nodded. He was carrying an aluminum briefcase and struggled with it to his seat just in front of the door. He placed it on his lap and folded his hands atop it. She wondered why he hadn't put the brief-case in the baggage compartment. Three of the male passengers seemed to know each other and they quickly became engrossed in conversation. The man with the briefcase stared out the window.

The crew entered, the door was closed, and they moved for-ward to the flight deck. The engines began to turn and soon Karen could no longer hear the murmur of the crew or catch any of the passenger conversations. She had tried to call her brother in Elk Creek, Montana, that morning but got only his answering machine. She had left a short message telling him of the last minute opportunity she had in Reno and of the ProAir flight that she would be taking. The aircraft began to taxi toward the runway.

Karen closed her eyes. It had been a busy six weeks in Banff and she was anxious to get back home to Chicago, to her sick mother. First however she would do this two week appearance in Reno. She had been fortunate to get this booking and she would make the most of it to promote her fledgling career. Her mother was on her mind a lot because, she realized, all the treatments would give her - maybe - another year.

5

Tom eased the truck along the narrow road at a slow, steady pace. Rocky ledges and washouts made for a bumpy ride. Snow had started to fall, small pellets at first, but it soon became a slow fall of good-sized flakes. The outside thermometer in the dash-board still read 20 degrees. Tom wanted to get to the stock tank and finish the repairs before the storm got much worse. As the ground leveled off, he pressed a little more speed out of the truck and in a few minutes, the stock tank entered his view. The land had not yet awakened from its winter sleep, and to Tom, the early spring scene here was gaunt. The year-round spring, still encrusted with ice, bubbled out of the ground at a rocky ledge bordering a grove of mix-ed aspen and conifers. The aspens wouldn't be showing new leaves for another month. The conifers, mostly fir and larch, had not yet awakened to new growth. The gray grass lay flattened on the ground from months of snow cover, waiting for nature's signal to sprout once again into the rapid growth of the short summer season.

6

THE PROAIR CHARTER FLIGHT took off from the runway at Calgary International Airport just past noon. The flight plan indicated an IFR flight at 20,000 feet with a stop at Missoula and arriving at Reno about 3:30 in the afternoon. The King Air twin turboprop was loaded to near capacity with its five passengers and their luggage. The weather advisory had shown a layer of clouds between 5,000 and 13,000 feet with snow or rain along the Idaho-Montana border, stretching back into Idaho and western Washing-ton. The flight plan specified a route over Montana and Idaho in a direct path to Reno with a fuel stop at Missoula.

"I hope we can hold to the flight plan," said the captain.

Dave looked at him. "If the weather stays on the other side of the mountains. If not, well, we'll see."

Although the sky in Calgary had been cloudless, and the weather data hadn't indicated clouds until near Missoula, a cloud-bank could now be seen just south of Glacier National Park.

"Bill, we weren't to see any of this stuff until Missoula," Dave said nervously. The captain scowled, and muttered a profanity.

The co-pilot reset his radio to get an updated weather report from Missoula. "Cap'n, Missoula reports snow on the runway. Damn. They'll be closing in about 30 minutes."

"Shit...you're kiddin'...and Boise?"

"Boise is okay so far, ceiling at 8,000 feet. But turbulence is reported to 20,000 all along the Bitterroot Range. We'll have to get over that," replied Dave, glancing at Bill.

"Okay, we'll use the fuel now to climb out of this shit and refuel in Boise...that should work for us."

"Roger that. I'll advise Salt Lake."

He was back on the radio and gave the Salt Lake Center an update on their flight plan. The pilot increased the power to the engines and started a moderate climb. The city of Kalispell passed below them as they moved into the cloud layer, searching for the top. The turbulence increased; rime ice began to form on the wings.

"We got to get out of this, Bill." Dave bit his lower lip as his eyes darted to the window overlooking the starboard wing.

"I know...I know...Goddamn ice."

"We *got* to make 20,000."

"That the top?" asked the captain, also glancing out to the wing.

"So they say."

"Is Missoula still open?"

"Stand by."

The co-pilot set his radio to the Missoula frequency to listen to the field status.

"Damn. Missoula is closed! It just closed!" The copilot looked at the strained face of the captain, then out of the window, and then to the altimeter. He wiped his hand over his brow.

"Shit, this sucks. I sure hate to turn back."

The copilot put the microphone down and turned to the cap-tain. "Missoula said that Boise is open...not snowing there...ceiling at 8,000 feet." The copilot sounded hopeful.

"Okay...okay. Get Salt Lake again. Get a vector to Boise."

"We can make Boise...we have margin. We've been using a lot of fuel, but I calculate we have maybe 40 minutes margin for Boise." Dave caught the captain's attention and smiled. "Should be enough."

The captain looked out at the port wing. A dull gray covering of rime ice lay over much of the surface. He had flown in bad weath-er before, but not this bad. He looked at the altimeter. He was barely holding 12,000 and the engines were set too high, using too much fuel. He looked over at his co-pilot, talking to Salt Lake Center. He wondered if any of them would get to be with their families again. If they could clear the Bitterroot Range, they would get down safely.

7

KAREN WATCHED AS THE THREE male passengers gestured and looked out the windows. Their eyes darted back and forth between them, heads shaking, pointing to the window again. The man with the briefcase on his lap nervously thumbed through a magazine, his eyes often darting back and forth from the magazine to the window. Karen, too, was nervous, alarmed by the change in the pitch of the engines and worried about the turbulence buffeting the airplane and the opaque whiteness outside the window. She began to shiver, even though the temperature remained moderate in the cabin. When the sound of the engine's whine changed, her head jerked up. She was bouncing in her seat as turbulence jostled the plane. Outside, she could see only whiteness.

8

TOM STARTED THE ENGINE-DRIVEN arc welder-generator set in the back of the truck, ran the heavy cables to the stock tank, and proceeded to rebuild the support structure, cutting away the rusted angle iron and welding the new pieces in place. Lying on the cold hard ground was uncomfortable. He felt every stone and frozen nodule in his 46-year old frame. Although he was lithe and strong, he felt the years gaining on him. He completed the job by installing new plastic overflow pipes and reconfiguring the tank outlet for the summer season, to allow it to fill and the overflow to run into the natural rivulet. He was happy to stand up, and slapped his arms to stimulate his circulation.

He didn't see Bandit, but just before calling his pet, he yielded to his curiosity about what animals had been in the area. Tom walked a large circle around the spring. The new snow had not yet covered the ground and he saw deer, elk and coyote tracks in the moist earth along the rivulet. He hadn't heard any wolves for some time, but he knew that they ranged far and would be back. Although occasionally a downed calf was attributed to them, Tom was happy with their presence. He respected their social structure, their cunning, and their place in the balance of nature. He saw several paw prints of a mountain lion. The cat had come up to the tank and then probably had gone to water below in the rivulet.

The weather was worsening, and a cold wind began to blow the snow about. Tom was glad he was headed home. He started the truck engine and turned on the heater. *It will be a good afternoon,* he thought, *to build a nice fire in his fireplace,* and ask his foreman, Ralph, and wife Susan, over for a bottle of wine. Bandit abandoned his investigation of scents along the rivulet and came at a run when Tom called him with a shrill whistle.

9

BAUER RIDGE, A LINE OF mountains in the Bitterroot Range along the Idaho-Montana border, peaked at the eastern end with 9000-foot Mathew Peak. It formed the northwestern boundary to Timberline Ranch. The old homestead had been established in 1892 by Tom's grandfather and was located against the base of the ridge at an elevation of 4,500 feet. The homestead and the additional properties acquired over the decades by Tom's parents and grandparents had formed a sizable ranch of 35,000 acres of meadows and forest bordering the Bitterroot National Forest. Elk Creek, a swift running stream that drained the mountains behind the ranch, flowed through the meadows, and crossed County Road to continue its journey southward. Six miles of private dirt road led from County Road to the ranch buildings. The Sullivan Ranch to the west had been a neighbor for many decades. The small town of Elk Creek, named after the stream, and not much changed over the years, lay a few miles to the east on County Road. A high ridge of mountains beyond County Road formed the eastern boundary of the valley.

Tom's dream for a guest ranch had gotten a serious start the past season with the building of the lodge and cabins. He and his foreman, Ralph Stehling, together with a construction team from Idaho, had designed the lodge and cabins of cedar log, with all-weather metal roofing. The single-level lodge had a main room with a stone fireplace, a dining room big enough for thirty guests, a large kitchen, a few bedrooms, lavatories, and a business office. A separate cabin was constructed nearby to store all the non-food items to be used during the guest season. Ten individual guest cabins had also been erected during the previous year. The old barn had been rebuilt with a metal roof and retrofitted with new structural timbers. The County had tested the ranch well and found good quality water at a depth of 120 feet.

Timberline

In the early 1900s, when cattle had ranged throughout the mountain slopes, an old line-shack had been built high on the eastern end of the ridge, about six miles from the lodge. It had served then as a shelter for riders working the upper range and repairing fence. The cowboys had named it Timberline Cabin. In the mid-1900s, logging had taken place throughout the higher elevations and an old logging road still existed across the ridge to the cabin. Ralph had been renting the cabin in recent years to elk hunters he knew well and some effort had been made from time to time to restore the structure. Water was available at Timberline Cabin from an old hand-dug well, which sometimes ran dry in summer.

Near the lodge, his foreman, Ralph Stehling, and Ralph's wife, Susan, had rebuilt an old and long unused log cabin and it was now their cozy two-bedroom home. Tom had recently finished renovating the early-1900s cabin that had been his parents' home that also stood near the lodge. He felt a certain joy in making it his own home; it had been the place where he had spent his early childhood.

10

The Beechcraft King Air with a normal 30,000 feet operational ceiling was struggling to maintain 10,000 feet as ice continued to build on the wing surfaces.

"We're gonna be in deep shit, we don't get more altitude."

Dave glanced at the captain, then back to the altimeter. "Yeah, that new vector has us going right over the hump."

"We got peaks from 7,000 to 10,000 feet. Christ, I hope we miss them."

Dave turned away from the altimeter and looked at the captain. "If we keep 10,000, we should clear everything."

The captain nodded. "Not much margin, 10,000."

The passengers were secured in their seats, but the turbulent flight, the whiteout conditions, and the unusually loud roar of the engines had silenced all of them. Fear had replaced conversation.

"ProAir one zero niner, Salt Lake Center."

"109."

"Check altimeter setting two niner eight five. We've got you below minimums, got you at one zero thousand. Climb to one five thousand."

"Negative, Salt Lake...icing here."

"Are you declaring an emergency?"

"Negative, Salt Lake. We should be over the ridge in a few minutes. Stand by."

"We're in deep shit, Cap'n," declared the copilot, anxiously glancing at the altimeter.

"I know. How close are we to the Bitterroots?"

"Best guess is we are right over them now."

The pilot advanced the throttles to their maximum position. The roar of the engines vibrated the cabin.

11

TOM GOT COMFORTABLE IN the seat of the truck and let the engine warm, anxious for some heat from the vents while he drank coffee from his thermos.

"Bandit, this weather sucks...here, want some of this?" He pulled a trail-mix candy bar out of his jacket pocket and broke off a piece for Bandit who swallowed it in a single bite. Tom enjoyed his half of the candy bar with his coffee. He poured out a little more coffee and held the cup against the seat. "Here...have some." Bandit had it licked up in a few seconds. Tom had never heard of a dog that liked coffee, but Bandit seemed to enjoy it as much as he did.

The snow was coming down steadily and starting to accumulate on the grasses and shrubs. Although it was not unusual to get snowfall well into May and occasionally in June, Tom was anxious for springtime. He wanted to finish the construction of the guest ranch, and bad weather would delay the work. He marveled at how lucky he was that he had been able to return to the ranch, to his childhood home where forgotten dreams were reawakening.

Alone with his thoughts, Tom pondered his future. Now 46, he had been divorced for seven years, and until moving out here a few years ago, had been living an empty life of unfulfilling friendships in an increasingly unrewarding career. He thought of his mother, who had passed away just before he had come to Montana, and his father who had lived only for a couple more years before succumbing. He regretted not having seen more of his parents. Sorrow and guilt haunted him when he thought of his father's last years alone. Dad had left him a nest egg beyond anything he had expected and Tom had vowed to use the vast resources to preserve the ranch.

He realized, too, how much he owed Ralph and Susan, for they held the place together, while he had struggled to get his life in order. He mused about this while he slowly sipped his coffee. The snow was steady now; he flicked on the windshield wipers.

12

"**D**AMN!" EXCLAIMED A CONTROLLER in front of a traffic control monitor screen. He turned to his supervisor, "Stan...we have a problem. ProAir 109 is off the screen."

"I got it Bob." The supervisor, bending over Bob's shoulder to see the detail on the display, plugged his headset into the communications panel and selected the Boise connection. "Boise...Salt Lake Center."

"Boise...go ahead."

"Do you have ProAir one zero niner? We lost him here."

"We had him about a minute ago...talked to him...stand by one." The tower at Boise called ProAir 109 repeatedly, trying all of the frequencies used at that airport and finally using guard frequency without a response.

"Salt Lake...Boise."

"Go ahead Boise."

"I got no response. I tried all the frequencies...nothing... we lost him. We'll try some more, but I think they went down."

"Christ...okay...keep trying. We'll start procedures at this end...get back to you."

"Roger, Salt Lake."

The Salt Lake Center supervisor made notes from the data on the controller's screen, squeezed Bob's shoulder, and started toward his desk to work the telephone. He turned back for a moment.

"Take a break Bob...that's an order...take Jim with you... go out to the diner. I'll get Harry to take your position," he said to the distraught controller.

Bob nodded in agreement and wiped his eyes with the back of his hand as he left the room.

13

The ProAir flight 109 transponder code was last updated on the Salt Lake Center traffic control screen at 1:54 p.m. showing ProAir 109 to be at the Idaho-Montana border at just below 10,000 feet. Shortly after 2 p.m., the FAA and NTSB were notified, as was the sheriff's office in Camden, the county seat nearest the presumed crash site.

The sheriff's phone rang. "FAA here again. We got confirmation from COSPAS-SARSAT. Flight 109 is down!"

"Christ. What'd they say?"

"FAA got a report from satellite search and rescue. They received the ELT signal from the aircraft."

"Jesus, we'll have to get somebody out there," said the sheriff. "You know for sure the location?"

"Near as we can tell right now, Mathew Peak up on Bauer Ridge, near Elk Creek."

14

Tom screwed the cup back onto the thermos bottle and tucked it under the seat. The snow was melting on the warm windshield. He increased the speed of the window wipers and prepared to get underway. A call from Ralph Stehling on the truck radio jarred him out of his reminiscence.

"Tom...you copy?"

Tom grabbed the microphone from the dashboard and responded. "Yeah, I'm just starting back. It worked out well. It's all fixed."

Ralph came right back excitedly. "Okay. Hey, listen! The sheriff just called and Jeff called too. There's been a plane crash. Up around Mathew Peak...copy that?"

"Christ, on the peak? What kind of plane...how many people? Holy shit!" Tom's heart started beating faster; a chill went up his back.

Ralph responded, "Yeah, the sheriff said the peak. They had some kind of reading...ELT, GPS...I don't know what...something. It was a charter flight, a two engine prop job from some airline I never heard of. Think he said Pro Air. Anyway, the sheriff said there had been no radio communication with them since they disappeared from radar, and Jeff called from Preston's. He was beside himself, having trouble keeping it together. He says his sister is on that flight."

"Ralph...you sure...his sister? Oh God."

"He was almost hysterical. The sheriff said they didn't have anyone to send out, that they had everyone at some big wreck on the highway out past Camden. Called around, but everybody is busy in this storm. They can't even get a helicopter there in this snow... on the peak anyway. Probably won't be able to 'till the snow lets up. Tom, what do you want me to do?"

"I can't imagine what Jeff is going through. We've been friends way too long. I got to do something, even though this storm will make it slow going. Anything at all on survivors?"

"Hell, I don't know. No one was talking."

"Well, we still should try to get there."

Ralph spoke again. "You want I should go up there? I could take my truck...should make it."

"No, I'll go. I'm done here. No reason for both of us to be out in this soup."

"Okay, be careful though. Don't get your ass hurt up there. The damn handheld radio might not work up on the peak. You'll probably have to get back to me on the truck radio."

Cell phones were useless at the ranch because the nearest towers were in the valley beyond Camden, so they relied on the use of the Personal Radio Service with the small handheld transceivers. The truck radio operated on the Private Land Mobile radio band and had significantly more power than the hand held units.

"I'll be okay, Ralph. I'll talk to you when I can. I don't know how long it will take to find the plane, so don't worry. I'll call when I find something."

"Okay. I'll keep both radios on. Be careful."

Tom thought about his friend. He knew that Jeff was very attached to his sister. Tom had never met her, but recalled that Jeff had gone to see her at a performance in Billings a few months earlier and raved about her singing and persona.

I gotta make an effort. Shit, I have to try and find that plane, he said to himself. *I owe Jeff that much at least. Gotta try.* He shook his head. *Christ, no one survives a crash in the mountains,* he thought. *God, this is gonna be bad – poor Jeff.*

Before breaking off radio contact, Ralph gave Tom the GPS coordinates the sheriff had relayed.

"Bandit, this doesn't sound good. We better get up there as soon as we can." Bandit lifted an ear, but didn't seem to be impressed.

"Poor Jeff... his sister." Tom shook his head slowly. "Bandit, no one can be alive, not up there."

Tom pushed the truck ahead, anxious to make his way to Timberline Cabin. He would look for the downed airplane on foot from there. He wondered just how accurate his small GPS locator was. He had never tested it before, in fact had never seriously used it. He thought there might be smoke or broken trees to help lead him to the wreck.

"Bandit, you suppose there could be any survivors? God, how long could they last in this weather?"

Tom thought again about his friend, probably not likely to see his sister again. Bandit seemed unperturbed, his gaze not missing much as the truck pushed ahead on the narrow and rocky road.

Tom thought back to the beginnings of their friendship. He and Jeff had been friends for several years. Their relationship had started when they met at the funeral of Tom's mother and was cemented later at the funeral of his father. Jeff had told him that it was Tom's father who had helped him get started at Preston's Lumber and Equipment. Jeff had admitted that he was imprisoned for assault and battery after he had come to the rescue of his sister outside a Chicago nightclub. He had severely beaten her attacker, sending him to the hospital. However, the drunken attacker had been politically well connected resulting in a three year imprisonment. Afterward, while working in Camden, Jeff pulled Tom's father, Herb, and his mother, Ann, from a serious car wreck. Although his mother died at the scene, Tom's father lived two more years at the ranch. But the loss of his wife left him broken and his health deteriorated rapidly. In gratitude for his help, Herb got Jeff a job at Preston's lumber yard in Elk Creek. Tom pleasantly recalled how Jeff had spent many a weekend on a job of road grading and culvert construction for him at the ranch almost two years ago. Subsequently, the construction of the guest cabins had been arranged through Jeff and his connections with the Prestons. Jeff Roberts had recently become Yard Manager at Preston's. Tom smiled when he thought of Jeff as the lead singer in the "Rustics" country quartet that played in Larry's Bar and Grill, for he, too, sang there occasionally.

15

THE CABIN DOOR OPENED with metal-scraping noises. A bloody-faced man stood at the doorway. His suit jacket was open, his white shirt bloody. Suddenly, he lost his footing and fell to the ground while grabbing uselessly at the door jamb for support. He lay in the snow for nearly a minute and then stood up with a cry of pain.

"What the hell happened?" he gasped. "Oh God, I hurt...I fuckin' hurt bad."

He turned to look at the aircraft. When he heard popping noises he labored to his feet and looked fearfully toward the smoking engine. He tried to still the shaking in his legs, but couldn't. He cried out in pain when he involuntarily took a deep breath.

He looked at the broken trees and deep snow. "Oh, Christ. Where am I? Got to get outa here."

He reached into the cabin door and pulled an aluminum briefcase from the fuselage, then fell to his knees, struggling from the attempt just to draw a breath. His bloody hands trembled as he fastened a fist around the handle of the briefcase. He again stood up and, briefcase in hand, stumbled away from the wreckage. "Downhill. Gotta head downhill."

16

It was a slow drive over the long abandoned and overgrown logging road to the remote Timberline Cabin. Tom stopped the truck, and quickly drank the remaining coffee from the thermos leaving some in the cup for Bandit. The small flashlight and GPS locator fit easily into Tom's pocket. He clipped a small hatchet near a belt loop, put on warm work gloves, and started off, Bandit stayed close on his heels.

The initial reading on the Global Positioning System (GPS) locator prompted Tom to hike farther east through the forest below the ridge crest. The trees were stunted and, a few hundred feet higher on the ridge, would disappear completely. Several inches of snow covered the ground, more in the open spots. The snow was increasing in intensity and the wind near the ridge made the cold distracting. Although the thermometer in the truck indicated 17 degrees, the wind chill was well below zero. Tom walked for almost an hour looking for the crash site. He thought the GPS locator had an accuracy of about a 100-foot circle. He was surprised and annoyed that he couldn't find the airplane right away. Tom was tired and numb with cold. His exasperation at not being able to find the wreckage was wearing on him.

"Bandit, where is that goddamn plane? I'm freezing my ass off here."

Bandit had been making circles through the forest, returning to Tom occasionally.

Tom heard excited barking not too far ahead of him. "Bandit. Where are you?"

"Bandit!" Again, there were some excited barks. Tom pushed ahead another hundred feet and broke into the area of destruction where the wreckage lay. Bandit came up to Tom, tail wagging.

"Good boy, you did real good. Holy shit …look at it."

Tom stood and stared at the sight. An involuntary shudder wracked his body. *Dear God,* he thought. *This has got to be a tomb.* A swath of broken trees indicated the path of the doomed flight. The blue and gold ProAir logo showed prominently on the raised tail section. The nose section was crumbled, completely obliterating the cockpit. He caught a glimpse of the starboard wing through the broken trees, 200 feet down the slope. He looked at the airplane fuselage, laying about 20 degrees to its starboard side, the deformed port wing in the air. Smoke still rose from the port engine and Tom scratched his head, wondering what sort of miracle had prevented an inferno.

A glance at his watch told him that sunset would be in half an hour…if only there were some sun. He was uncomfortably cold. He reached down to pet Bandit who sat by his side staring at the wreckage.

"Bandit…it's getting late…we better hurry and take a look …it's just too damn cold."

Tom approached the aircraft biting his lower lip, afraid to look inside, afraid of what he would see. He glanced nervously at the smoking engine and wondered how safe it would be to go into the cabin.

"I don't think we're going to find anyone alive in this mess," he mumbled to the dog.

The cabin door was open. There were blood smears on the door and the doorframe. Bandit smelled at the disturbed snow and irregularly spaced footprints that were quickly being covered by blowing snow.

"Hey Bandit, someone *is* alive! Amazing…and walked away?"

Tom followed the nearly covered footprints into the dense woods.

"Hello! Hello! Is anyone out there? Hello! Hello!" There was no response, but he wasn't surprised. Sounds wouldn't travel far in the heavy snowfall and dense evergreen forest.

When Bandit started off into the forest, Tom called him back.

"Bandit, come back here. I don't want to have to search for you, too."

He wanted to see if anyone else was alive in the airplane before he went looking for the person who wandered off. Besides, it wouldn't be long before it was dark, and the temperature would drop further. He had to hurry.

"Come on, Bandit...there *might* be someone alive in there."

Bandit made an effort to follow Tom into the cabin but Tom held him back. He just wanted to take a quick look. He wondered if Jeff's sister was among the passengers. Maybe she had missed the flight -- he hoped.

"Sit...stay." Bandit did as he was told.

He could feel his heart pounding as he stepped inside the cabin. He was jolted by the smell of human excrement. He placed his gloved hand over his nose and mouth. He steadied himself on the slanted flooring and scanned the cabin. A woman was in the back seat. An overhead rack had fallen bringing part of the ceiling with it and pinning her down. He spotted the red fire extinguisher lying at her feet; saw the section of bulkhead torn out.

"Jesus, the damn thing hit her," he exclaimed aloud as he looked at the side of her head and the blood-matted hair.

He touched her neck and smiled as he felt some warmth, and a faint pulse. His heart leapt. *She's alive. Can I keep her that way?* He moved quickly to check on the other passengers. Most of the seats had collapsed forward and the storage racks had fallen, the passengers squeezed between them. He checked each of the passengers, men in their 30 to 50s. All were cool to the touch. One man had part of a broken seatback tray embedded in his abdomen; blood pooled on the floor below him. The pilot and co-pilot were a bloodied mess, bodies smashed into the instrument panel and control yoke. He felt himself getting sick, and had to look away. The stench of death was overwhelming his senses. He rushed back to the door, jumped down to the ground, and retched. He washed his face and mouth with snow. He spoke quietly to Bandit, reassuring him, telling him to stay. Then he turned back to re-enter the cabin.

Tom knew he had to get control. He placed his shaking fingers on the woman's neck and forced them to be still. Her weak pulse was steady.

"Karen...Karen!" No response.

"Karen, don't die on me, damn it...stay with me." She was still. He heard faint breathing when he placed his ear to her mouth.

Tom tried to gather his thoughts. Though cold, he was perspiring heavily. His stomach was unsettled. He looked at the female passenger, *surely Karen Roberts,* he thought, alive but unconscious, sitting in the back seat with the seat belt still firmly around her. A collapsed bulwark and storage rack pinned her in place and seemed to be the reason for her apparent bloody head injury. Tom dismissed the idea of looking for the person who walked off into the snow. There was no way to know how long he had been gone or where he had headed. *Anyhow, the person was probably dead already*, he thought. Furthermore, it was snowing steadily and it was near dark, and he had to get Karen...he felt certain it was Karen...out of the airplane or she'd freeze to death. He jumped to the ground, again putting snow on his face and taking deep breaths of clean air. Tears welled up at the corners of his eyes. He thought of the many lives that would be impacted this night. He thought of Jeff, knew that he would have to do everything he could to help Karen. "I can't just let her die," he said to no one in particular. He knew he had to keep a clear head despite the feeling of nausea and panic in his stomach. He tried to reach Ralph with the personal radio he always carried, but was unable to get a response to his calls.

"Bandit, I gotta think. I gotta get her out of here...she'll freeze."

Tom went back into the aircraft cabin. He looked at her, almost certain that she was Jeff's sister.

"Come on kid, I've got to get you out of here. You'll freeze to death otherwise."

"Damn, I gotta move you. What choice is there? None at all. I just hope to Hell I don't make things worse... even though they can't get a whole lot worse. Besides that, I have absolutely no idea about the extent of your injuries."

He looked carefully at her head and explored with his fingers. He found only the one injury, but it looked ugly. He was sure the fire extinguisher, ripped loose at the crash and propelled by inertia, struck the side of her head. The scalp had been peeled back to what looked to be her skull. Her auburn hair was matted with dried blood and stuck to most of the wound. Blood had soaked into her blouse, now stained brown. *God, how much blood did she lose?*

"Christ, that is a nasty looking wound…damn." He took a deep breath and bit his lower lip.

"Karen, Karen! Hey, wake up kid!" She did not stir. "Come on girl, we got to move you."

"Hey Bandit, what're we going to do? Christ, I can't leave her here to freeze. Suppose I do something bad… internally." Bandit, sitting outside the cabin door watching him, cocked his ears.

There was no doubt in Tom's mind that the overnight temperature would drop significantly and there was no way he could keep her warm, or even keep her from freezing, inside the plane. Likely, with the storm still raging and the big wreck on the highway, it wouldn't be until sometime the next morning - at least - when rescue could be dispatched to the mountain.

"Well, I'm going to have to do it…move you to the cabin… at least I can try to keep you warm there." He talked more for his own comfort than any expectation that Karen would respond.

"Sorry kid, but I have to do some checking."

He carefully felt her limbs for broken bones but there didn't seem to be any, as least as far as he, a non-doctor, could tell. He opened her jacket, and gingerly felt her ribs and abdomen. He didn't notice anything to alarm him. Her breathing was very shallow and this worried him. He re-zipped her jacket.

A plan was beginning to form in his mind about how he could move Karen the nearly two miles to the cabin. He would have to extricate her from the seat and the storage rack that had her pinned down. Then he would have to immobilize her. He looked for any materials he could use to make some sort of sled, but nothing seemed plausible. He examined the storage rack and torn ceiling that pressed her into her seat and decided he could raise the storage bin safely in order to remove her.

"Don't go anywhere…I'll be right back."

He dropped to the ground and looked around for a downed tree limb that would bear the pressure he would have to exert on it. The snow cover made the search difficult, but he finally located a branch he felt might be suitable. He trimmed the many little branches with his small hatchet and hefted it into the cabin. Tom positioned the branch so he could raise the storage rack and ceiling section about six inches. The weight of the shelving was enough to keep the branch from moving with just enough room to reach Karen and slide her out with a minimum amount of twist to her body

"God, I hope I'm not making things worse…I'm sorry," he said to her as he wrestled with the twisted metal.

With the debris raised slightly above her, he carefully slid both arms under Karen to pull her toward him. Slowly he placed the inert body on the floor of the airplane. He crawled forward in search of a blanket and found one with little blood on it, on a deceased passenger. *You won't be needing this*, he thought, and pulled it from the seat and covered her. He looked at Karen and at the doorway. There'd be no other way but to pull her along the floor. He grabbed her under her armpits and slowly edged her toward the door. *How could she be so heavy?* Sweat burned into his eyes He wiped his hand across his brow. He focused on getting her to the doorway with the gnawing feeling that he was probably causing more damage. Finally he got her to the doorway. Bandit looked up at him and whined.

Tom left her at the doorway and dropped to the ground. He could construct a makeshift sled, he thought, a travois made from tree poles and materials from the airplane. He recalled how Native Americans had used this approach in the past century when they were traveling. However, instead of having a horse pull the travois, he would have to do the pulling himself. He found some strong, straight branches, which he trimmed with his hatchet and the sheath knife he had on his belt. He recalled seeing some mesh netting on the back bulwark of the airplane, not sure what its purpose was, but something he could use. He also found several Bungee cords used to secure the crew's luggage. Tom cut lengths of the netting to make a cord that he then used to assemble the travois. He worked quickly as darkness threatened, pausing often to warm his numb fingers inside his jacket.

Tom slid Karen the last inches to the door by pulling on her clothes. *Sorry, kid, but I gotta do this. Hope I don't hurt you any more,* he thought. Outside, he reached in and carefully picked her up and placed her onto the travois. Bandit sniffed and walked about anxiously. He came up to her, smelled her again and again and whined a few times. Tom spoke reassuringly to Bandit.

"It's okay, Bandit. That's Karen. Karen, meet Bandit," but Bandit kept pacing nervously, first walking away and then returning frequently and sniffing.

"Bandit…calm down…sit." The dog sat down but his eyes stayed on the woman.

Tom gathered the few blankets he could find in the aircraft cabin and used them to cushion and wrap Karen as he secured her to the makeshift travois with the Bungee cords. He loosely covered her face with a blanket to protect her from both the cold and the branches. He shook his head. *Not secure enough,* he thought. He climbed back into the cabin and pulled the belts from the waists of the three dead passengers and used them to secure Karen around her arms and legs. Out of the corner of his eye, Tom noticed a purse on the floor next to the feet of one of the dead passengers. On impulse, he picked it up and opened it, found the wallet, and checked the driver's license. He squeezed his eyes for a minute as he looked at the picture and the name: Karen Roberts. He tucked the purse with her on the travois. He was now certain this was Jeff's sister. Somehow he had to keep her alive.

17

NIGHT HAD COME TO THE FOREST. Tom tested his flashlight and set out in the direction he had come. Everything looked different in the low light and the additional snow.

"Let's go, Bandit...go home. Home Bandit!" The way home went by the cabin. *I gotta make it*, he thought.

Bandit charged ahead. He lunged through the snow, leaving a clear trail for Tom to follow. Tom carefully and slowly pulled the travois. He had the mesh netting cords around each shoulder. With each step into the deep snow, the travois moved, but not without a struggle. The jacket, although warm, did little to cushion him from the bite of the cords, the constant chafing and the strain on his shoulders. After a while the pain became a serious distraction. He didn't want to stop, he had to keep going, couldn't give in to it. He stopped frequently to check on his patient. He could barely detect her shallow breathing. He felt her pulse; it was steady although slow. Tom had lost touch with his religion long ago, but he silently prayed for Karen's recovery, and for strength to get her to the safety of the cabin. He unzipped his jacket to rub his shoulders, but soon zipped it back up. He had to keep going.

"I can't bear to lose you now, Karen...hang on kid." He spoke aloud.

Several times he stopped, unsure of his direction, and called to Bandit, who answered with several barks and came back to him, breaking the snow crust and indicating a path.

"I hope you know where you're going." In response, Bandit pushed ahead and was soon lost in the dark again.

Tom followed Bandit's trail. The trek to Timberline Cabin took them nearly two hours. Tom arrived numb with cold, sore, and exhausted. He unbundled Karen and carried her inside to one of the bunk beds. He loosened her clothing, and removed her shoes, wrapped her in the blankets from the airplane and covered her with the blankets from the other bunks. He lit the kerosene lantern and started a fire in the stove and then went outside to operate the radio in the truck. Bandit sat by Karen's bunk. He just stared at her. Once in a while he would whine and lay down on the floor next to her.

"Ralph, Tom here. You copy?"

Ralph answered immediately. "Christ, Tom, I'm glad to hear from you. We've been worried here. Where are you?"

"I'm at the cabin. I found the plane a while ago. The woman, and it is Karen, is alive. Unconscious...with a really bad head wound...she's here in the cabin. I also found three male passengers, all dead. I think there was someone else, but he...or she...is missing...wandered off I guess. Won't last in this storm. The pilots ...God, Ralph, the pilots are almost unrecognizable...crushed into the instruments. It is a sickening sight. I never saw anything like it."

"How is Karen? Will she be okay? I have to tell Jeff. What'll I tell him? I gotta tell him something." Ralph answered quickly.

"I don't know...I just don't know. She's unconscious. She has a serious head wound. She was pinned in her seat by everything that wasn't bolted down and some things that were. Fire extinguisher smashed into her...it's a bad wound...not bleeding anymore. I don't know what the hell to do; I'm just keeping her warm."

"You've done great. Really great. Stay at the cabin, keep her warm and still. Don't move her any more, she might have other injuries. Wait for the sheriff in the morning."

"Can't the sheriff send anyone...I mean, over the road?"

"There's no one to send. They're still at that big highway wreck. He'll have the helicopter over you as soon as the storm quits, by midmorning at the latest. If not, they'll try the National Forest road, but I'm sure it's drifted over. I'll call the sheriff right now. I'll also call Jeff...he's half crazy with worry and grief...I'll talk to him."

"Thanks. I'm scared. I don't know what else to do for her. I don't want her to die."

Ralph answered, "Hey, you're doing all you can...all that makes sense for now. Don't move her. Just wait for the sheriff in the morning. Okay?"

"Yes...thanks, I'll stay here. I'll call you in the morning, early."

"I'll leave the radios on. And I'll call Jeff."

"Okay, I'm clear."

Tom turned off the radio and went back to the cabin. He alternated between pacing the floor and checking Karen's heart rate and breathing. He heated snowmelt water in a pan on the stove and then tried to clean her head wound. The affected area was matted down with blood and hair. The injury looked serious, the skin pulled back from her skull. Tom rummaged through the storage bins and found some first-aid gauze, sterile pads and a tube of antiseptic ointment. He unwrapped a sterile pad, applied ointment to it, and wrapped the gauze around her head to hold the pad against the injury - not at all sure that it would do any good, or even if it was the right thing to do. He worried about Jeff and wondered how his friend would react to hearing that his sister was alive but seriously injured. Tom looked at her, her face calm, and saw her beauty for the first time. She must have been pretty before the crash, before this ugly wound. But then chided himself, "You'll be a beauty again." He silently prayed for her and tried not to think of her dying. Bandit stayed by her side, watching, sniffing, and occasionally licking her face, waiting for a response and then lying down by her bunk.

"I don't know, Bandit. It doesn't look too good. What can I do?"

Bandit looked up, then as Tom lapsed into silence, put his head between his paws.

Tom had paced the floor for what he felt was hours, but was no more than five minutes when, suddenly, Karen bolted upright, eyes open. She cried out in a chilling scream. Bandit jumped up and barked several times. Tom felt his heart race and he rushed to her side, but she fell back moaning, then became quiet again. Tom pressed his fingers to her neck. Her pulse was weak, but faster than it had been. He pulled the chair close to the bed. Gradually his own heart rate returned to normal, but he felt helpless as he sat staring at her.

"Karen, Karen...can you hear me?" he pleaded. No response.

"Bandit, tell me what to do. I can't let her die." Bandit cocked his head.

Tom, unable to sit still, rummaged in the cabinet and found several cans of beef stew. He opened two of them, poured the contents into a pan and placed it on the potbelly stove. In a few minutes he poured some of the steaming stew into a plate to cool just a bit for Bandit.

"Not exactly prime rib, is it Bandit?" After a few exploratory licks, Bandit busied himself until the plate was clean.

Tom ate the rest of it right from the pan; then he scoured the empty pan with snow and put more snow in the pan to melt for water. He made a cup of instant coffee from an old jar he also found in the cupboard. The wood bin was almost empty, so he went out to the lean-to behind the cabin and brought in some dry wood. The strain on his shoulders brought piercing agony, but he gritted his teeth. He built up the fire in the stove, hoping it would last until morning. Tom felt drowsy and very tired from the exertion of pulling the travois and from the pain in his shoulders.

Weariness overpowered him. He looked at his watch and shook his head at how late it was. He lay down on the other bunk.

"I'm beat, Bandit. I'm sore and tired." Bandit looked at Tom, but didn't leave his post by Karen's side.

In the dim light of the lamp, Tom reflected on the previous several hours. Images of the horror spun through his mind. *Who was the missing passenger*, he wondered? *Was the person dead already? Why had the person wandered off? Had it been despair, a befuddled mind, or something else?* He felt sadness, sure the storm would claim another victim, if it hadn't already.

He started to doze, but awoke with a start. Had she made a noise? He couldn't be sure; all was quiet. Bandit looked at him, ears erect. He got up from the bed, checked her pulse, felt her temperature; *a little too warm,* he thought. There was no bleeding from the crude bandage that he had applied and she seemed to be resting quietly. He worried about her temperature. *I'll need to check her again soon,* he thought. He lay back down with his clothes and boots on. The kerosene lamp burned into the night and he dropped into a fitful sleep.

18

It was just before dawn when Tom awoke. His first thought was to check on Karen and he went to her side with some trepidation. Her pulse was still slow and weak.

"At least she is still alive, Bandit." Bandit explored her face with his nose.

Her skin felt warmer than it had in the evening, and that worried him. "I'm afraid she's got a fever. Not too bad yet, I don't think." Bandit ignored his master and sat down by the bed.

Tom shivered with cold and went to the stove to add wood to the fire which had burned down to embers. He opened the door to the cabin slightly and looked out. The snow had stopped with about two feet on the ground. Bandit darted through the door, but a few minutes later scratched to come back inside.

Tom made a quick trip outside the cabin. Dawn was just filtering through the snow-laden trees and he gazed at the beauty and the stillness appreciatively. But, it was too cold to dwell on it long and he hurried back inside. Tom heated water and made some instant coffee from the nearly empty jar. He looked at Karen. Should he be trying to give her water? Suppose she couldn't swallow it? He decided not to do anything; he feared making things worse. Bandit was again lying by her bunk but his eyes followed Tom as he paced the floor. Tom looked at his watch; it was nearing 6 a.m. Would there be anyone at the sheriff's office at this hour? He went out to the truck and fingered the radio.

"Ralph...Tom here."

"Ralph...you copy?" No response.

"Ralph...wake up. Where is that damn rescue party?" Irritation was evident in his voice.

"Tom, I'm here. I've just been on the phone with the sheriff's office in Camden. The forest road has some big drifts towards Camden. The helicopter is the best bet now. It will be taking off as soon as the clouds lift off the peak...maybe couple hours...the sun is coming up here." He hesitated, "How is she?"

"I don't know. She feels warmer than she did last night. I don't like it, scares me a little. She screamed last night, just for a couple of seconds...and then she was quiet again. It scared the shit out of me. Damn, I wish I knew what to do."

"You've done everything you could. She's warm and quiet... Hey, she didn't freeze to death in that plane. Someone will be there soon. You've done okay, Tom. We can only pray for her now."

"How is Jeff? Did you talk to him?"

"He was a wreck last night. Wanted to come up here. Talked him out of it. I'm trying to sound hopeful for him. She's gonna pull through. All we can do is hope there's no irreparable damage and her fever doesn't go up anymore. EMTs will be there soon with the helicopter."

"I'm going back inside Ralph. It's too cold to sit here in the damn truck. The dashboard says 5 degrees. I'll talk to you later." Tom turned off the radio and left the truck. All was quiet when he went into the cabin. Bandit lifted an eyebrow, but didn't move from his spot next to Karen.

Tom looked at his watch. He paced back and forth, checking on Karen, fixing the fire, and making more of what remained of the instant coffee. He glanced at his watch again - seven minutes had passed. He opened another can of stew, heated it and shared it with Bandit. He went to the door often to look at the weather. There was no light from the window, since it was still shuttered for the winter. It was after 9 a.m. when he saw the sunlight burn through the remaining clouds. He went to the truck again and called Ralph, who informed him that the helicopter was taking off at any moment and would land in the clearing just south of him. It was almost 10 a.m. before he heard the helicopter circle overhead and then land in the nearby clearing.

19

IT TOOK ONLY A FEW MINUTES for three men from the sheriff's helicopter to arrive at the cabin bringing first aid gear and a rescue basket. Tom was at the door. He held Bandit by the collar.

"Christ, I'm glad you guys are here."

"Tom? Yeah, sorry it couldn't have been earlier. It's been a hell of a night. I'm Steve, he's Bill."

They moved quickly to the bed where Karen lay, pulled off the blankets and unwrapped the bandage from her head.

"I didn't know what else to do, it looked so bad."

"It's okay, we'll clean it up. You did fine." They started an IV in her arm. The two EMTs proceeded rapidly to cleanse the injury and apply a dressing. They then applied a protective hard shell on her head and neck. They checked for other injuries before placing her on a backboard and wrapping her in an aluminized thermal blanket. They attached monitors and secured them to the backboard as well. Karen was then lifted into the rescue basket. Eight minutes from when they arrived, they were leaving with Karen.

"We'll have her in Camden in less than fifteen minutes. Good thing you were here last night. Damn good thing for her."

"God, I just hope she makes it," Tom replied.

Tom watched as they trudged through the snow to the waiting helicopter. In a few minutes he heard the helicopter wind up its rotor and lift off to the hospital in Camden. Tom sat down, petted Bandit, and exhaled loudly. He looked at his shaking hands.

"Bandit, I am tired. I must have done a job on my shoulders last night; damn, they hurt." Bandit looked up at him as he continued. "Wonder what's going to happen to her? Poor Jeff...I've got to talk to him."

He thought of the men still in the airplane, of their families and friends, of the tragedy, of the ironies in life. He stood up and shook his head. *Can't think about that now*, he thought.

"Damn it, Bandit, let's get the hell out of here." Bandit stood up and looked toward the door.

Tom tossed what was left of the water into the stove to put out the fire. He closed the door securely. "This place could use some repairs," he mumbled. "I'll worry about straightening out the place later."

The truck engine cranked over slowly in the cold air and then started. Tom picked up the microphone. "Ralph...Tom here...copy?"

In a few seconds, he received a response. "Go ahead."

"The sheriff's helicopter just left. I'm heading back."

"You okay? She stable now?"

"Yeah, the EMT guys said she seemed stable. They started an IV and cleaned up her wound. They were out of here in less than ten minutes. I'm tired, really tired and I hurt my shoulders last night ...pretty damn sore."

"You did everything you could. She's still alive."

"Yeah, but the poor bastards in that plane. I'll never get that sight out of my mind."

"It'll take a while. Come on back. Drive careful, 'cause that road is shit. We'll be here, okay?"

"Yeah, I'm leaving now. Damn, it's cold up here. See you in a while."

"Okay. Take it easy. Ralph out."

Tom headed the truck back along the old logging road toward the ranch. It was slow going on those parts of the road obscured with drifted snow to a depth of several feet. It took him an hour and a half to get back to the barn, a trip which normally took him twenty minutes. He stopped the truck and sat quietly for a moment. Bandit looked at him, eager to get out.

"I sure wish I could forget that sight, those poor people." Bandit turned his head toward Tom momentarily. "There are only memories now."

"Hey Bandit, you've taken a liking to Karen, haven't you?" Bandit turned his head and looked toward the sound of his name. "She's hurt bad. Unconscious all this time...I don't like it. Got to see Jeff. He's got to hear it from me. Ralph and Susan first, though." Bandit shuffled himself on the seat and turned his attention back to the window. Tom shuddered at the thought of the devastation.

20

TOM OPENED THE DOOR AND got out of the truck, Bandit leapt to the ground. It was early afternoon; the sky was bright blue although over a foot of snow covered the ranch grounds. Tom stood for a moment, admiring the snowy landscape. The quiet had a calming effect on his spirit. The temperature had risen to 20 degrees and it felt comfortable in the sunlight. Tom left his truck by the barn and he and Bandit walked the short distance to the Stehling's cabin. Ralph had already made his rounds with the snow blower and walking was easy. Through the backdoor window, Tom saw Ralph, Susan and his daughter, Liz, at the kitchen table talking. He knocked and Liz jumped up to let him in.

"Tom!"

He smiled and hugged her. "Hi, Liz. Good to see you're home. School done already?"

"Yeah, for the summer. Dad arranged it so I could leave a couple of weeks early."

"What grade are you in now?"

"I'll be starting my senior year in the fall," she beamed proudly. At just seventeen, she was a year ahead of most students.

"Wow, I'm impressed. Hanover is probably the best private school in Montana."

"It ought to be, for what it costs," commented Ralph while he rolled his eyes toward his daughter.

"Oh, Dad. Wait 'till you start paying for college," she smirked.

Ralph nodded, "You'll have to start applying soon."

"I know. There are two in Montana I would like to visit."

"Okay, okay. Just let me know when."

"Coffee, Tom?" she asked.

"You bet, thanks," he answered with a smile and a nod.

She turned to the kitchen counter, poured a cup and brought it to the table as Tom plopped into the chair. Susan gave Tom a concerned look. "You look like hell." She thought of him more as a son than as her employer, and she wondered what he had experienced on the mountain.

Ralph spoke first. "Tell us what happened up there. Haven't heard from the sheriff yet."

Susan got up to make a fresh pot of coffee. She squeezed Tom's shoulder and Tom winced in pain. Susan jumped back, shocked. They all looked at him in surprise.

Susan gasped, "What's wrong? What did you do to yourself?"

"Hurt my shoulder last night, rope burn or something. It'll be okay after a while."

"Hogwash." Susan shook her head vigorously. "Take that shirt off...I want to look at that shoulder of yours."

"Okay." Tom knew better than to try and argue with her, so he started to undo his shirt. Susan helped him take it off. They pulled his T-shirt off over his head.

"Boy, that's raw. In fact, both shoulders are raw," she exclaimed. "Liz, please get me the stuff from the bathroom."

Ralph stood up and looked at Tom's shoulder. He shook his head, "Wow, you did a job on it. Just sit for a few minutes. Suze will fix you up."

Liz brought the first-aid box and helped Susan clean the wounds. They slathered ointment and placed thick bandages securely on the raw areas using a profusion of tape. They then helped Tom put on his shirts.

"Thanks, girls. I appreciate that."

"I've got a plate of snacks to go with the coffee," Susan said as she busied herself at the refrigerator. Liz bent over and kissed his cheek.

"What...?"

"Nothin'...just felt like it." She smiled at him.

Susan brought a plate of snacks to the table and refilled everyone's coffee cup while Liz retrieved some dinner scraps from the refrigerator and went out to feed Bandit. "I'll be right back. I don't want to miss any of the story."

She returned quickly.

Tom sipped his coffee for a minute without saying anything. Then he asked Ralph, "How is Jeff? Talk to him?"

"I called him as soon as I heard from you. He's obviously upset. He talked to County Hospital…she was admitted and stabilized, but they had no real diagnosis. He wanted to go see her, but when he called, the doctor said she wasn't responsive yet and that later might be better." Ralph rubbed his chin and then continued. "He's afraid she might die. I understand they were really close. And then there's his mother, she hasn't got long. It's tough on him."

"I'll go see him shortly. Maybe you can call him when I leave, tell him I'm on my way. I want to talk to him in person, not on the phone."

"Sure… I understand," replied Ralph, nodding.

Tom talked while he sipped his coffee, telling them what he had seen at the airplane, of getting Karen out of the wreck and back to the cabin, keeping her quiet and warm overnight, and then of the sheriff's EMT helicopter coming for her. Ralph and Susan didn't ask any questions; they just let him tell his story at his own pace.

When Tom was finished, Ralph spoke. "You did all you could."

"I just hope she pulls through," replied Tom quietly.

"It has to be tough on Jeff," Susan replied.

"I'm gonna leave for town and see Jeff," Tom said. "Susan, I can take your grocery list with me. I'll drop it off in town and pick up the stuff tomorrow. I'll probably go with Jeff to Camden tonight. I think I should."

"Yes, go with him. I think he needs someone right now. He'll appreciate it," said Susan as she folded the shopping list and handed it to him.

Tom finished his coffee and got up to leave. Ralph accompanied him outside to his truck.

"You look like you're trying to take the blame. Hell, you did all you could. You're not a damn doctor. You kept her from freezing to death. You did good."

"I don't want her to die."

"None of us *want* her to die, Tom. Just keep believing she'll pull through. They'll fix her up. You'll see. Go see Jeff, talk to him. He's a wreck...talk to him...be strong for him."

"Thanks. I will."

Ralph squeezed Tom's arm reassuringly. Tom thanked him again and opened the door to his truck. Bandit leapt into the seat. Tom got in, petted him, and they started out for Elk Creek.

21

Tom admired the job Ralph had done, plowing the ranch road during the predawn hours. *He couldn't have had much sleep*, Tom thought. He knew Ralph had stayed near the radio and telephone while he had been on the mountain. The road skirted the hills at the base of the ridge, crossed Elk Creek over the new culvert, and went through the snow-covered meadows before reaching County Road.

Crossing the culvert, Tom smiled and turned to Bandit. "It'll take a hell of a flood, Bandit, to take this bridge out." Bandit twitched an ear towards him. "Jeff's crew did a great job."

Tom looked back toward the mountains behind the ranch. "Well, peak runoff has yet to occur, maybe in a couple of weeks. It'll be warming up soon. We'll take a look at it then, okay? That'll be the real test." Bandit looked over at him momentarily, yawned, and then turned back to the window.

At the ranch gate, Tom turned left onto County Road and drove the few miles to the small town of Elk Creek.

The EMT facility was in the back of the Elk Creek Volunteer Fire Station, a small cramped building at the edge of town which housed both a fire engine and an ambulance. Tom saw Jeff's old car parked in front and he stopped his truck next to it. He wondered if Jeff had spent the whole night here waiting for news of his sister.

Allen Richards, a deputy sheriff, had a tiny office and a small lock-up cage in the back of the building. He spent much of his time, however, at the county seat in Camden as well as in the nearby town of Randolph where more law enforcement incidents seemed to occur.

Allen, smiling, got up from behind his cluttered desk as Tom entered the office. They shook hands. Jeff was just hanging up the telephone as Tom walked in.

"Thanks, Tom. I don't know what would have happened if you hadn't found her." Tears started in the corners of Jeff's eyes. He looked drawn and haggard. Tom put an arm around his shoulders.

"It'll be okay, you'll see. I'm just glad that I was close enough to get up there as soon as I did."

Jeff tried to thank him again and again. Tom directed him to a chair and pressed him gently into it. Allen Richards spoke in his usual quiet manner. "Karen is resting quietly now...not in the ER any longer. I think that's a good sign."

Tom raised his eyebrows. "That *is* good."

The sheriff's deputy nodded and continued. "Yeah, they did all kinds of tests. She does have a serious concussion. MRI shows swelling of the brain, especially around the impact area...skull crack there. They managed to bring her fever down to just a bit over normal. She arrived at the hospital with a temperature of 104 degrees."

Jeff sat in the chair with his head bowed in his hands. Tom tried to sound hopeful. "Hey Jeff, she'll be okay... take a little while ...hang in there." But he didn't feel any of the confidence he was trying to exude. He recalled her face lying in the cabin, lovely even in the terrible shock and trauma. He prayed silently for her recovery.

Allen spoke again. "Tom, the sheriff's team from Camden and the NTSB guys need to go over the logging roads to the crash site to retrieve bodies and investigate the crash. Would you sign this release to give them permission? It will cut down on the paperwork and such...speed things along."

"No problem," and Tom scribbled his name.

Allen went on, "The team expects to be there by late afternoon. They'll camp at the site so they can get their investigation done as quickly as possible."

"Yeah, not a problem. Give Ralph a call. Let him know they're coming," Tom continued, "Hey, you know, that cabin up there...they can stay in the cabin. No need to freeze their asses off outside."

"That would be great," beamed Allen. "I'll be sure to tell them. They'll be happy about that. I'll call Ralph and tell him what's going on."

Jeff got out of the chair and picked up his hat. "I'm going to Camden, got to see her."

"Sure Jeff, you go ahead," said Allen.

"Okay if I go with you?" asked Tom, "It'd be nice to see how she's doing."

"I'd appreciate the company." Jeff turned toward the door, embarrassed by the tears in his eyes.

Tom again shook hands with Allen. They walked several blocks toward the other end of the small town, to Preston's Lumber and Equipment, where Jeff worked.

"I can hardly believe this happened to her…my sister, my baby sister," his voice trembled.

"She's in the hospital. They're taking care of her." Tom tried to keep a hopeful tone to his voice.

"She might not come out of it. … They don't really know." Jeff wiped his eyes.

"I wouldn't say that. She's not in the ER any longer - got her stabilized and resting in a regular room. That's a real positive sign."

"I'm sorry. I am very grateful that you went up there and found her."

"I know. Come on, she has a good chance. County Hospital has all the latest equipment and they're affiliated with Helena General. She's going to get the best there is." Tom tried to sound hopeful, but he, too, feared for Karen. He would have to be strong for Jeff.

"I called my parents in Chicago earlier. They're coming into Camden airport this afternoon. They managed to get seats on some regional airline.

22

When they arrived at the lumberyard, Jeff disappeared into the offices and came back out a few minutes later.

"Everything okay?"

"Yeah, I talked to the old man. He said to take whatever time I needed."

"That was good of him."

"Yeah, the old man is okay. I like working for him."

"Ready to go?"

"Yeah. Let's go. I'm really anxious to see her. It's tough, haven't seen her in a long time."

"I know. Say, Jeff, do you mind taking your car? I want to leave my truck at the garage for service; it's overdue."

"Sure, I'll drive. You go ahead and take care of it. I'll spend a few minutes here and then be down to pick you up."

As Tom walked back the four blocks to where he had parked the truck, he stopped for a few minutes at Mason's General Store and left Susan's list of supplies asking that they be ready for him on the following afternoon. Brenda and Bill asked about the airplane crash and Tom gave them a brief summary, anxious to get started for Camden.

Tom hurried the rest of the way to his truck and drove it the short distance to Al's Automotive at the edge of town. As he walked into the garage, he saw Al Shaw and his daughter under the hood of a car. Chris, recently turned twenty, ran the towing service and helped her father in the service bay. Tom called to them. They immediately stopped what they were doing and wiped their hands with shop rags they then stuffed into their overalls pockets, as they walked to Tom. Al and Tom shook hands.

"Hello, Tom. It's been a while. Heard you had some excitement out your way." His expression told Tom that he wanted to hear a lot more. News spreads quickly in the small town.

"Yeah, had that plane crash up on the peak."

Chris put an arm around Tom's waist and smiled warmly. "We heard a little from Allen. You found a survivor. She's in the Camden Hospital. I couldn't believe that it was Jeff's sister." Chris looked up at him expectantly, "What happened up there?"

"It was a real bad scene. She was hurt pretty bad, head injury. Jeff and I are going up to the hospital now. He's coming by to pick me up any minute."

"Come by when you get back," suggested Al. "I'd like to hear what happened up there."

"I'll stop by." He nodded toward the truck, "Can you do the usual stuff?"

"Sure. We'll get to it this afternoon."

"Chris, may I leave Bandit with you? I don't want to take him to Camden. I guess I should have left him home, wasn't thinking."

"Love to have him. I'll get him." She hurried over to the truck and let Bandit out of the cab. He ran around her, tail wagging furiously. She hugged and petted him.

She looked up at Tom. "Sorry you can't stay a while. I haven't had a chance to pick on you in weeks." She smiled teasingly.

"Yeah. Get over it," he grinned at her. "Anyhow, I'll be back tomorrow afternoon."

Just then, Jeff pulled up and Tom waved, excused himself and joined Jeff for the ride to Camden.

The afternoon slipped by as Tom and Jeff drove east. Jeff talked about life at home in Chicago with his sister and parents. He admitted that his stint in prison had taken its toll on his mother and father, but now they were reconciled to what had happened and happy that Jeff was building a good life in Elk Creek. Tom had heard about the trouble that put Jeff in prison, but he let Jeff tell it again, hoping that talking would help him cope with what was happening.

"Yeah, Karen came to visit me every weekend she could. Depended on where she was performing. It made all the difference."

"How about your parents? They came too, didn't they?"

"Once in a while. They came on holidays; you know, Easter, Christmas, birthday and some others. It took my father a long time to get past it. I think the embarrassment of having a son in prison overshadowed everything else for him."

"And your mom?"

"I think she understood what happened, that I had to do it. Anyhow, she came to accept it."

"The jerk you pasted had connections."

"Yeah, he did. You know...he was drunk and wouldn't let Karen alone. She didn't want anything to do with him and she left the place. He followed her outside and attacked her by her car ...hitting her, tearing her clothes. The drunken bastard was hard to subdue. I had to really hit him. Maybe I went a little crazy. They had to pull me off him. Damn cops came and, of course, arrested me."

"You got three years."

"The asshole public defender was worse than useless."

"Damn, that was tough. I recall you said your parents didn't help you much when you got out."

"You kidding? My dad was still stewing over it. No, Karen helped me. She gave me a few thousand bucks...all she had saved up, so I could go somewhere else and work and live. I've paid her back in the past year."

"When was the last time you saw her?"

"A year ago. I went to see her sing at the Silver Stirrup in Billings. She has a fabulous voice."

"She still lives near your parents?"

"Yeah, she has an apartment about a mile away... close enough to drop in to see Mom every few days. No one really knows how long she has. Doctors told her a year, but who really knows though."

"I'm sorry...tough on your father too, huh?"

"Yeah. I think he's scared, but he won't talk about it. Say, you know, I almost forgot. Karen had left a message on my answering machine."

"Really? What?"

"She said she had just completed her singing job in Banff, and was flying on a ProAir charter flight out of Calgary to do a gig at the Reno Gold Dust Casino. She said the engagement in Reno would give her some really good exposure, help her get to Nashville. Apparently, the casino arranged Karen's flight at the last minute. She was just leaving for the airport when she called me. When I called Reno about her flight arrival, they told me there had been no official change in schedule, but the flight had been delayed." Jeff's lips were trembling. "What the hell did that mean? Must be a polite way of not telling me the plane crashed."

"Don't think about the flight. Think about Karen getting cared for at the hospital. She needs you to hold it together. And your parents, too…they'll need your support."

"I know. I'll be okay." Jeff nodded several times.

23

"Jeff, pull over there into the Pine Haven Motel. Might as well stay here and go back home tomorrow."

"Okay, yeah, good idea." He crossed the road into the motel parking lot.

"I'll register. You pick up some shaving and toothbrush stuff," said Tom as he stepped out of the car. "I'll even spring for supper."

"Be right back," Jeff mumbled and pulled away.

After a hot shower and a shave, Jeff and Tom set out for County Hospital. A large sign, *Receptionist,* was immediately in front of them as they came through the front doors. Tom looked casually at the back of a man standing at the desk in khaki trousers and an all-weather blue bomber-style jacket. The man stepped aside as Tom and Jeff reached the desk. While Jeff asked about his sister, Tom glanced at the man a few feet away. Something about the man gave Tom pause. Was he trying too hard to appear disinterested in him and Jeff, he wondered? He was close enough to hear Jeff's conversation.

Jeff tugged at Tom's sleeve, nodding toward the main hallway. Tom tried again to reassure Jeff as they walked down the hallway towards Karen's room. Jeff and Karen's parents were talking to a doctor in the hallway. Edna Roberts dabbed at the tears in her eyes and smiled at Jeff as he approached. John looked up at Jeff, a smile starting to form at the corners of his mouth.

"Hi, Mom. I'm glad you're here." He kissed and hugged her.

"We only arrived a half hour ago," she replied as she again dabbed her eyes.

Jeff turned to his father, nodded and shook his hand. "Nice to see you, Dad."

"It's good to see you, too. You're looking pretty well."

Jeff looked anxiously from his mother and father to the doctor. "How is Karen? What's happening?"

The doctor moved closer, glancing from one to the other. "As I was saying, the swelling of the brain is the main issue. We're taking all prudent measures to reduce the swelling and of course, the pressure. She's being constantly monitored."

Edna stifled a sob. Jeff put a reassuring hand on her shoulder and the doctor continued. "Karen's temperature is still elevated, but I think that is not too much of a problem; it's to be expected with this serious an injury. It has come down considerably since she arrived."

"What else did you find?" asked John, biting his lower lip.

"We did a full set of CT scans and an MRI, but there isn't any sign of other injuries. I'm having some experts at Helena General review the scans for a second opinion. There are no broken bones - a miracle indeed."

"Thank you, doctor," said Jeff. The doctor nodded and walked off, checking his clipboard.

Jeff looked at Tom, who was pretending to be busy reading the notices on the bulletin board.

"Mom, Dad, I would like you to meet my friend, Tom. Tom, please join us."

"Tom? Hi, I'm Edna and this is John. You know our Karen?"

Tom shook hands with them and then turned to Jeff who explained, "Tom Bauer is the one who got Karen out of the plane. He saved her."

Edna grabbed Tom's hand in both of hers and looked up into his face. "You're the man that…that found our girl?" she asked with glistening eyes. Tom nodded, feeling uncomfortable.

"Oh, John," she looked at her husband, "This is Tom, he…"

John gripped Tom's arm and faced him. "We owe you … so grateful." His lip quivered. Edna held onto his arm.

"I was glad to have been up that way...able to help." He shifted his gaze to the window by Karen's room.

"I'll be in with Karen," said Jeff moving to Karen's doorway.

Jeff pushed open the door and took a seat beside her bed. Tears came to his eyes when he saw her head wrapped and various instruments connected to her, and an IV feeding into her hand. A sob broke the stillness.

In the hallway Edna tried to get Tom to talk about the night on the mountain. "Jeff told us about how you had gotten our Karen out of the plane and into a shelter. We'll always be grateful."

John pursed his lips. "If she makes it, it was all because of you, of what you did. We are indeed grateful."

"She'll make it. You'll see. The doctors haven't given you any reason why she won't recover." Tom tried to sound hopeful.

"Oh God, I hope so." Edna bit her lip. Tears continued to well up.

John put his arm around her.

"Tom, go in, see her...it'll be okay," suggested Edna as Tom shifted his weight from foot to foot.

He nodded, smiled at them, and went to the door, slowly pushed it open and stepped inside. Jeff was sitting by the bed, his hand cradling Karen's, not disturbing the IV needle. He turned to

look up at Tom with tear stained face. Tom blinked back his own tears.

He stepped closer and looked at Karen, her head wrapped in bandages, tubes running into her nose, electrodes attached to her scalp. *Despite all that, she looks at peace*, he thought. He squeezed Jeff's arm, then turned and stepped into the hallway with his parents.

After a while they all gathered outside the room. Tom suggested they have supper together.

"I saw a Chili's up the street. Would that be okay for everyone?" asked Edna. Everyone nodded in agreement.

"Sounds okay to me, they have some variety on their menu," Tom replied.

As they left through the main entrance, Tom looked around in the lobby and outside, but did not see the man he had noticed earlier.

24

THE CONVERSATION AT SUPPER was about Karen and her life, but then Edna wanted to know more about what Jeff had been doing for the year, since they had last seen him.

"You're living in that upstairs apartment still?" Edna asked.

"Sure, it's a comfortable place and convenient. I sing a few nights a week downstairs in the lounge."

"What do you eat; you don't cook for yourself, do you?"

"Oh, Mom. I usually eat supper in the lounge. I fix my own breakfast though."

"I thought you'd have a girlfriend by now, maybe even fix meals for you." She looked at him with a smile. "No girlfriend yet?"

"Well, no. Nothing serious. I'm pretty busy at Preston's and at night in the lounge. I get out a few times during the month."

Tom cleared his throat and looked at Edna and then at John. "Jeff is doing really great at Preston's. They love him there. He also does pretty well at the lounge, especially on weekends."

John looked at Tom and changed the subject back to Karen. "What happened up on that mountain? What can you tell us?"

Edna looked at Tom, eyebrows raised.

"Bandit, my dog, and I got to the crash site around two hours after the plane went down. It was a miracle that there was no fire. The front of the plane was smashed, and one wing had come off. Luckily Karen was seated in the back, but the sudden force of the crash collapsed some of the overhead structure and many of the seats had ripped loose from the floor. Part of the ceiling had fallen on Karen, giving her the head injury and trapping her in her seat."

Tom saw John's lips trembling. "No one else was alive?" he asked, almost in a whisper.

Tom shook his head. "No one else in the plane was alive. I think however that someone did escape and walked off to die somewhere else. No one found him."

Edna urged Tom to continue. "Please, go on. Tell us about it."

"Well, I had to get the ceiling structure propped up so I could slide Karen out of her seat. Then I made a sled of sorts so I could drag her to a cabin a couple of miles away where I started a fire in the stove to keep her from freezing. It was a snowy night and cold."

Tom had paused for a moment and Edna urged him on. "Did she wake up?"

"Not really. She screamed and bolted up in her bed once, but then she was quiet again. I had called the ranch on the truck radio and the sheriff's rescue helicopter came as soon as they could in the morning, as soon as the mountain peak cleared. They brought

Karen right to the hospital." Tom looked from Edna to John, but neither one said anything. Edna started to cry.

25

After supper, Jeff and Tom drove Jeff's parents to the Camden Hotel before returning to their motel room. Jeff and Tom joined Edna and John at breakfast the following morning.

"You look tired, John," commented Tom as he slid into the booth next to him.

"Yeah, I can't ever get a good night's sleep in a strange bed," he offered.

Edna appeared calmer than she had the previous day. She talked about the childhood that Karen and Jeff had had and then she asked Tom about his life. He told them anecdotes of his childhood while living with his parents and then, looking at his watch, suggested that it was time to visit the hospital.

They stopped in front of the nursing station near Karen's room and Jeff stepped up to the counter to inquire. "Has there been any change?"

"The nurse smiled thinly. "No, but we are monitoring her continuously. The doctor looked in on her earlier."

Jeff looked at his parents; they nodded. "Thank you. Is it okay if we stop in and see her?" he asked the nurse as he started down the hallway.

She smiled and nodded and then added, "Oh, by the way, a man came by earlier this morning wanting to see if he could talk to Karen. I told him that she was not conscious, and that only family was allowed to visit her at this time."

Jeff, surprised, turned back to the nurse. "Who? Not a doctor?"

"No, I never saw him here before. I asked if he wanted to leave a message for the family. But he said no, and walked back toward the entrance."

"Do you think he was some investigator?" asked Jeff, a puzzled look on his face.

The nurse wrinkled her face. "Actually, he looked a little sleazy."

Tom nodded, "We'd appreciate it if you could get his name if he comes around again."

She nodded, "I'll try."

They all went into Karen's room together. Jeff held her hand for a moment. Edna began to weep and John and Jeff eased her out into the hallway. Tom, standing alone, whispered, "God, let her live."

26

Jeff and Tom drove back quietly to Elk Creek in the late afternoon. Finally Jeff spoke.

"It was nice to see my mom and dad. It's been a while."

"I'm sorry about your mom."

"I heard about it from Karen just a few weeks ago."

"Yeah, you told me it was inoperable. Any chance the uterine cancer will go into remission?"

"Karen didn't think so. Mom gets regular chemo treatments though. She has an appointment later next week. The medication she has for the pain helps a lot, at least for now." He paused. "Karen said the prognosis was for maybe another year, but that's all."

"Sorry."

"I'm afraid. Losing my mother...now Karen." His voice broke; he fell silent.

"Hey! Karen's going to make it. Don't you give up on her, Jeff." Tom smiled, trying to keep his voice upbeat.

There were a couple minutes of silence and then Jeff asked, "What do you make of that strange visitor for Karen? Kinda spooky."

"Yeah. By the way, there was this guy at the receptionist yesterday that made me uncomfortable. See him?"

Jeff shook his head. "Don't remember. Wasn't the same guy my parents saw?"

"No. This guy wasn't a greaseball."

"Maybe some sort of insurance investigator?" asked Jeff.

"Could be."

27

WHEN THEY ARRIVED BACK in town, Jeff drove directly to Al's Automotive. Tom got out of the car and Jeff drove back to the lumberyard. Chris and Bandit came out of the garage to meet him.

He smiled warmly at Chris and bent down to pet Bandit.

"Tom, how is she? And how is Jeff?" she asked.

Standing up again, he smudged one of several grease spots on her face with his thumb. *God, she's cute*, he thought. A smile broke at the corner of his mouth. She looked at him curiously.

Tom spoke, "Karen is resting, but not awake. She has a serious concussion, brain swelling. I just hope she makes it. Jeff is so-so, better now I think. I met his parents. They're nice folks. His mom is very ill, cancer. It is so damn sad for them, all this happening." Tom averted his eyes from hers, looking toward the ground.

She put an arm around him and hugged him. "You did what you could."

He smiled at her. "Yeah, I guess so."

"Come in the office, sit a spell," suggested Al as he made a tentative move in that direction.

"Can you stay a while?" asked Chris. "You can even have some of my coffee…couldn't be more than six, seven hours old," she said with a wry grin.

"Sure, I'll stay a while." He rolled his eyes toward the ceiling.

"Oh, all right. I'll make a fresh pot." She grinned and hurried off into the garage with Bandit on her heels. "Come on, Bandit. I'll find something for you."

Tom went to the office and sat down with Al. Soon Chris brought in a fresh pot of coffee and poured each a cup.

Tom began to tell the story of the night up on the ridge, the wreckage, and about Karen. Chris and Al listened, often asking questions. Chris went out to the fuel pumps occasionally to service a customer, but rushed back to hear more of the story.

It was getting dark when Tom turned to Chris. "Want to go to Larry's with me? It's getting on towards supper time."

"I'd love to," she beamed.

She jumped up, put her arms around him, and kissed him fully on the mouth. His swing just missed her buttocks as she scampered away. She hurried up the stairs to the apartment to clean up and put on clean clothes.

"She's a piece of work," Al commented.

"Say, would you like to come to Larry's with us, get some supper and a couple of beers?"

"Thanks but I have stuff to do here. I'm way behind on getting my quarterly financials over to my accountant."

"You're more than welcome to join us."

"Appreciate it. I'll take a rain check, though."

"Is Chris seeing anyone these days?"

Al scowled before he answered. "Not really. She socializes with some young ladies who live in Camden. There is, though, that young man from Larry's, Jim, I think his name is. I keep hoping she'll find someone her own age she could continue this business with when I'm gone. She knows just about everything I do, and she's been to school for the new-fangled electronic stuff." Al sighed, looked away, and reached for his coffee cup.

"I know she loves being in the garage and working with you more than anything. She's a sensible young lady. I don't think you have much to worry about. She'll find someone when it's right for her."

"She's a real joy for me. She likes you a lot, though. Frankly, it makes me nervous at times."

Tom looked kindly at Al. "She's given me a lot of support and encouragement and I appreciate her companionship and her unselfish friendship. We're like brother and sister.

Al, there isn't anything else."

Al smiled thinly. "I know. That's what I worry about."

"She's lucky to have a dad like you."

Tom and Al turned their heads toward the stairs as Chris scampered down smiling happily. She wore clean jeans and a blouse, with her strawberry hair around her shoulders, and just a hint of makeup. Tom looked at her appreciatively.

"Chris, you sure look pretty without all that car grease on your face."

"I'm glad you noticed, cowboy."

"I hope you behave, Chris," cautioned Al with a sly grin. "You know these older guys can't stand much excitement." He nodded in Tom's direction.

"Oh Dad, don't embarrass me." She ran over to him and kissed him and then she was out the door with Tom.

28

CHRIS AND TOM WALKED THE short distance to Larry's Bar and Grill. Larry served food only at night, by gentleman's agreement between Larry and Ken's Diner, since Ken closed in mid afternoon. Tom glanced at the menu on the blackboard over the bar. He shook his head and thought, *Boy, he hasn't changed that menu in years.* It still featured steak, hamburger, pizza, salad and various side dishes. Tom selected one of Ronnie's tables and pulled out a chair for Chris. He sat kitty-corner at the table so they'd be able to hear each other over the din of the crowd. Larry had three waiters on the floor on the busy Thursday through Sunday evenings, but Ronnie was Tom's favorite.

Chris and Tom often came in together, and no one raised an eyebrow. Sometimes Al would accompany them. Tom casually glanced at the bar and saw Jim, the bartender, looking at them, but he quickly dropped his gaze. Tom wondered if Jim had been out with Chris recently.

Ronnie smiled at Chris and Tom as she came over to their table. "Hi there, kids." She opened as she messed up Tom's hair. She never missed a chance to tease him.

"Hi Ronnie," greeted Chris. "I have him tonight."

"Oh damn, just my luck."

Tom looked up at her, "Hi, gorgeous. Can you rustle us up a couple of burgers...you know, medium rare with everything?"

"You bet, couple of beers?"

"Oh yeah...to start with," Chris said with a smile. She squeezed Tom's arm. "Thanks for bringing me here."

"You're okay for a grease monkey," he said with a grin.

"I kinda like you too, cowboy." She smiled as she reached over and took a poke at his ribs.

Ronnie brought their beers in frosty mugs, and set them down on the table. "Here you go folks. I'll check on your food," and she walked off toward the kitchen.

"I think she likes you," Chris suggested teasingly.

Tom smiled but then turned more serious. "Ronnie's a good person. She works hard here and also at the grocery store in Randolph. She hasn't had an easy life. She's finally divorced from that asshole of a husband."

"Didn't I hear that he beat her pretty bad once?" asked Chris.

"Yeah, he came around here more than once, making trouble. A few months ago Larry and I took him out back... had a little chat with him. He hasn't been back since, and he's signed off on the papers, too."

"Wow! You and Larry?" she exclaimed with a look of surprise. "I didn't know that. Talked to the guy, huh? Yeah, I bet..."

"She didn't need his drunken trouble. He was a mean one," he replied with a pensive look.

"You and Larry...I'm impressed."

"It needed doing. He hurt her a lot. I hope he leaves her alone now."

Ronnie reappeared with their hamburgers, plates heaped with the house-special home fries that were done to a golden-brown perfection.

"Anything else, big boy? I get off at 11." Ronnie grinned at him.

"Oh, we're okay for a while, gorgeous. Go torment someone else," he smiled.

"Oh, I'll be back," and she drifted away.

Chris and Tom bit into their burgers. They kidded each other about their eating habits, about the ketchup they used, and anything else they could think of.

Tom, thinking about what her dad mentioned, asked, "Have you been out with Jim again, or was it just that one time?"

She glanced at the bar. "Uh huh, we were in Camden a couple of weeks ago, took in a movie, got something to eat afterward. He seems like a nice enough guy."

"Do you like him?"

"Well...I'd go out with him again. I just don't want anything too serious." She looked down at her plate and didn't meet his glance.

"You set the pace, Chris."

She looked over at him, and then kissed him on the cheek. "I know...but thank you."

Larry, the middle-aged owner and cook was a friend to Tom and Chris, often sitting with them when he had the time. Tom saw him making his way to their table bringing a paper bag of leftovers for Bandit.

"Hi Chris. How'd you get Tom to take you out for supper?" Larry raised an eyebrow.

"It was easier than I thought. He asked *me*," she grinned.

"No kidding? What a guy!" He placed the bag of leftovers on the table. "Here's something for Bandit, mostly steak bones."

"Thanks, Larry. I'm sure he'll enjoy them. I'll see if he wants to send you a thank you."

"Say, Tom," Larry lowered his voice, "You went with Jeff to the hospital. How is his sister?"

Tom shook his head. "Not too good. She has a serious head injury. No one knows when she'll come out of it. We're all hopeful, though."

"How do you think Jeff is handling all this? His sister and mom. Christ. He said that he wanted to sing tonight...I don't know."

"It'll be good for him. Get his mind off his troubles."

"You think so?"

"Yeah, he needs to have something to occupy him."

"Sure, yeah. Damn, what a tragedy for his family." Larry shook his head, his countenance sagging somewhat. "If I can do anything, you'll let me know?"

"No one knows when she'll come out of it. Try to keep him hopeful when you can."

Larry nodded and headed back to the kitchen, ordering them a round of beers as he passed Ronnie. "Put it on my tab," he said to her.

"Not too many around like Larry," said Chris, her eyes following him across the room.

"If Larry is your friend, you can count on him and he looks after the folks that work for him."

"Yeah, Jim said the same thing. Has Larry ever been married?"

"Once, some time ago. He doesn't talk about it." Tom spoke hesitantly, looking down at his plate. He felt her touch his hand. He looked at her.

Chris smiled thinly. "I'm sorry, Tom. I don't need to know. He's a good friend."

Tom nodded. "They don't make them like him anymore." He withdrew his hand and reached for his mug.

"My dad told me that Larry got started here with help from your father. How did they meet?"

"Well, Larry had been a bartender and a restaurant manager at different places out west. After his divorce, he came to Camden and was working as a bartender. When my father came into his bar, they got to talking and Larry helped him make some good connections for buying and selling cattle and some equipment. They got to be good friends. When Larry told my father about his dream to open his own place, my father told him about this place. At the time it was closed and he picked it up for short money. My father gave him a loan to refit the place. He's made a real success of it."

"Wow, I'm glad for Larry. I don't remember your parents though. I was still in high school. Your dad sounds like he was a nice man."

Tom's face saddened. "Yeah, he was. I just never got to appreciate him, too busy thinking about myself those days." Tom fell silent and played with his mug.

"You look sad. You okay?"

"I wasn't there for them." He idly scraped frost off of his mug.

"Your parents would be proud of what you're doing with the ranch, keeping it all together, the Stehlings still living there, and your helping the Sullivans."

"Yeah, it would be nice if they knew." Tom stared off into space.

"Maybe they do."

He turned and smiled at her. "Thanks."

The Rustics came on stage dressed in their signature western outfits, carrying their acoustic instruments. Randy had the bass fiddle, Bill carried a mandolin and banjo, and Steve had his violin. Jeff, the lead singer, came down from his upstairs apartment carrying his guitar. The Rustics, a local quartet, performed at Larry's mainly for their own fun, but received a percentage of the bar take for the nights they worked. The Rustics played mostly classic country and bluegrass tunes.

They had started playing a bluegrass instrumental when Ronnie appeared with a second round of beer, "It's on Larry," she said, placed them on the table and picked up the empties.

Tom grinned at her. "Thank you. Thank Larry, too."

"You're welcome. Hey, are you going to sing something for us today?" She ran her hand through his hair, smiling warmly at him.

"I just want to relax, okay?" His voice echoed the tiredness he felt. "Chris and I just came in for a quiet bite. It's been a tough couple of days."

"Okay, I won't say anything. Can I get you anything else?"

"We're okay, thanks." She moved away threading her way around the other tables.

Larry's was filled to capacity and the band played non-stop. Jeff approached the microphone with his guitar. He started into one of his old ballads, and the audience clapped their approval.

Chris looked at Tom. "He's got a great voice."

"He's single and only a few years older than you." Tom smiled at her.

"I know, but he hasn't asked me out. I don't think he likes me all that much." She looked at him inquisitively.

"Well, he only recently got himself squared away financially from the trouble he had some years ago. He was probably embarrassed at being broke. He's mentioned you a few times."

"He has? Are you teasing me, you scoundrel?" She smiled and began to blush.

"I'm not teasing. You could do a lot worse than Jeff."

"He's a good guy. I just didn't think he was interested." Her eyes went to the bandstand. "I really like this band."

"Yeah, I remember when I first came in here," Tom said wistfully. "Jeff let me try out with them that afternoon. I liked those guys right away."

She smiled. "I think they liked you, too."

He laughed. "You know, I hadn't sung in front of anyone for years before then."

"You've got a gift though," Chris said seriously. "I'm surprised someone hasn't signed you up by now."

Tom shook his head. "No, that's not me."

She squeezed his arm, "I know."

"I always liked their acoustic instruments. I hate drums in country and bluegrass, and electronic stuff. It just doesn't sound like the old time originals, and it's usually too loud."

"Mmm." She changed the subject. "I think Jeff is headed this way."

Jeff had left the stage as the band started another instrumental. Tom watched him cross the small dance floor and thread his way around the tables.

"I love it, Jeff," smiled Chris.

"Thank you. It sure is nice to have good friends like you guys. Say, I wonder if I could borrow Tom here for a song?" Jeff beamed at them, glancing several times at Chris.

"Oh, I don't know Jeff. I just came in to unwind, get something to eat. We're happy just listening to you and the band."

"Bullshit! Get up here. Everyone wants to hear you." Jeff looked hopefully at Tom, as his face softened.

Chris looked at Tom. "It'll be okay," she whispered. Her eyes held his. He smiled and got up. Tom followed Jeff to the stage. He decided on an old Hank Williams tune, "*Half as Much*," knowing that he could really get into that song.

Jeff introduced Tom and the crowd welcomed him with a round of applause. He whispered to the musicians and they were ready. Tom's voice carried well over the noise. The din of conversation and laughter suddenly waned, and as the song ended the crowd roared their approval with clapping, yells and whistles.

The band broke into an instrumental bluegrass number as Tom left the stage. When Tom approached the table, he saw that

Chris was wiping tears from her face. She smiled warmly as he took his corner seat next to her.

"That was wonderful."

"Thanks. I wasn't sure I was ready for it."

"You were. I knew you were."

Larry suddenly appeared at the table. The smile had disappeared from his face. "Tom, forgot to tell you. There was a stranger in earlier today. There wasn't but one other customer in the place. This guy stood at the end of the bar by the door, ordered a beer and then started asking questions about the airplane crash, the ranch, about you."

"Huh? What kind of questions? Who was he?" Tom looked curiously at Larry.

"Some sleazy looking dude, shiny looking suit, expensive, medium height. Built like a brick. I didn't like the way he came on ...forceful jerk. Talked funny, too."

"What'd he ask? What did he want?" Tom looked at Larry, saw his serious countenance, and wondered what it could be about.

"I asked who he was. He didn't give me a name, just said that he was from an insurance company. I didn't believe him for a second. He wanted to know if the plane crash was in the National Forest or on your ranch. He knew your name, probably from the newspaper in Camden. I didn't like his attitude – nor his shiny suit. Pissed me off."

"What else did he say? What was it he wanted?" asked Tom a little exasperated.

"That's it. He tossed down his beer and left."

"Larry, you think it was feds or state?"

Larry shook his head.

"Could be an insurance investigator. That wouldn't be unusual for something like this."

"No, not this sleazeball. He looked like one of those movie mobsters. Next time he shows, I'll try to get something out of him."

29

A LITTLE WHILE LATER, TOM WALKED Chris back to her home. She shared the upstairs apartment over the garage with her father. At the backdoor entrance, she turned to him, put her arms around his neck, and kissed him. He held her, and then she gently pushed away.

"You better go," she whispered, "before I do something I... I'd like to do." She kissed him again lightly. Tom let his hand run over her shoulder and her arm. She quickly hugged him and broke away.

"Thank you, Tom. I really enjoyed tonight," she smiled warmly at him as she was turning to the stairs.

"Goodnight Chris." He waved and walked away between the buildings and back to the street. He turned his thoughts back to the hospital.

30

Tom started back toward Larry's and where he had parked his truck. The street was quiet. All the storefronts were dark. The only two street lamps in town were old incandescent types that gave off a soft circle of light. He thought of Karen lying unconscious in her room, and of her distraught parents and brother. He recalled her face and auburn hair, a certain beauty despite the bandages and the tubes and wires strewn around her. He hoped she would recover.

He was a dozen car-lengths away from his truck when he heard Bandit barking ferociously. Tom saw a brief movement ahead of him, just at the edge of the street light. He saw someone coming around the back of his truck and he yelled.

"Hey! What are you doing?"

As Tom started forward at a run, the person at the back of the truck suddenly darted between two buildings. When Tom reached the alleyway, he approached it cautiously. The narrow alley was dark. He couldn't see any movement against the faint light at the other end. A vehicle started up and he knew the person was gone. Bandit was still barking.

When Tom went back to the truck, he saw a Slim Jim lying on the ground. He realized that someone had been trying to get in. Bandit was snarling. Tom opened the door with his key and reassured Bandit, calming him.

"Thanks, Bandit. Good boy." Bandit remained attentive, peering out of the window toward the alley.

"That guy wake you up, boy? Bet he went home to change his drawers, didn't know you were asleep in there."

He grabbed the end of the Slim Jim with his handkerchief. He did not want to ruin any fingerprints, although he doubted there were any. He didn't recall ever hearing of a burglary or a car break-in in Elk Creek in all the time he had lived there. He thought again about the person who was inquiring about him and the wreckage on the mountain. *No, they wouldn't likely leave any prints*, he thought. He placed the Slim Jim behind the seat.

"I'll drop this off with Allen tomorrow." Bandit licked his face.

"What the hell was this guy doing?" he wondered aloud. Bandit looked at him. Tom petted him, talked to him, and let him out. He took the bag of kitchen scraps out of his jacket pocket and put them in the bowl he kept under the seat. It didn't take Bandit long to dispose of the tasty treats and begin on the bones.

31

SCHAEFER'S ROOMING HOUSE was located on the street behind Larry's Bar and Grill. Tom drove the truck the short distance and stopped in the parking lot.

"We'll stay here tonight, Bandit. I want to get an early start tomorrow, and I'm sure we'd lose half a day if we went back home tonight. There's always something there that needs attention. You get to talking and soon half the day is gone. Anyway, I need to see how Mrs. Schaefer is doing. Tomorrow I have to sit down with Jeff and get the construction projects going. It'll be a full day."

Tom and Bandit got out of the truck. Bandit stiffened, his nose sniffed the air.

"You've been here before. Don't act so suspicious." Bandit stood still, the hair on his back bristling. He stared into the shadows alongside the rooming house.

Tom looked in the direction Bandit was staring, but he couldn't see anything in the deep shadows. He started walking toward the building. Suddenly tail lights flashed beyond the building and a car sped away. It turned onto the street behind the rooming house, under the corner street lamp which let Tom see that it was a blue Ford.

"You knew who that was, didn't you Bandit? Good nose! I'll be damned." Bandit looked up, his interest in the whole affair waning now that the car had disappeared.

He entered the rooming house with Bandit at his side, and met Joanne Schaefer in the foyer.

"Hi, stranger. It's been awhile. Come on in." Joanne smiled and they shook hands. Tom followed her into the kitchen. He marveled that in her early fifties she was still an attractive woman.

"Nice seeing you again. Sorry it's been so long. I thought I'd stay tonight, get an early start."

"Sure, the little bedroom off the hall is empty, why don't you crash in there?"

"I don't suppose you'll let me pay for it?"

"Not damned likely. Your dad made this all possible. I ain't charging you to stay here, so forget it." Joanne smiled broadly. They spent some time at the kitchen table over a cup of coffee.

"How long has it been since David's accident, four years now?" asked Tom. Her husband had died when the Highway Department tractor he was operating rolled over into a ditch.

"Yes, hard to believe. If it hadn't been for your dad, I don't think I could have gotten this place started. He was such a good friend to Dave."

"Well, you paid that off already. You're doing good here."

She smiled contentedly. "Well, between the state settlement, Social Security and the rooming house income, I get by."

"Plenty of vehicles parked out there."

"I've had pretty good occupancy. A few long-term folks here, but most are highway workers, lumber people, and utility company workers. They stay a few days at a time. There was this fellow in earlier. He paid for a room for a few days, but went out and hasn't been back. I mean it's getting late and I sure don't want to wait up for him."

"I saw a car leaving as I pulled up. What's his name?"

"I'll go look. He gave me a credit card." Joanne left the table and went to the front of the house. Tom suspected that this person was likely the same guy Larry had seen.

"Here...here it is." Joanne came back into the kitchen with a credit card receipt and the registration card, which she handed to Tom.

"Jake G. Rafferty. Nationwide. Chicago. Ford. Could be the car I just saw out there. And what the heck is Nationwide? Insurance company?"

Joanne shrugged. "It's pretty late. Where would he go?"

"Don't worry about him. Lock up the place. If he comes back later, I'll let him in."

"Oh, would you? Thank you so much. It would be nice not to have to traipse to the door in my bathrobe." She took a few steps then turned back. "Almost forgot. Early this afternoon, this guy comes in. I was watering my plants by the window. He asks if he could look at the registration book. 'It's on the counter,' I say." She shrugged, "He left before I could ask him anything."

"What'd he look like?"

"Clean cut, medium height, salt and pepper." She bit her lip, "Blue jacket, khakis."

"Didn't say anything?"

"Didn't have to." She raised her eye brows. "I know a cop when I see one."

"Okay. Well, I'm beat." Tom headed back to his room. "See you in the morning."

"Good night. I'll have coffee on by 6 o'clock."

He smiled. Tom went down the hall and Bandit got up and followed, giving up his spot by the kitchen stove. Tom lay on his bed thinking about the sleazy stranger in town asking questions. He wondered if it had something to do with the plane wreck. *Who was that guy at the hospital*, he wondered? He dozed off. Bandit curled up on the floor at the foot of the bed.

32

Tom left Bandit in the truck and entered Ken's Diner, picked up a copy of the morning newspaper, and sat in a window booth where he could check on Bandit occasionally.

"Tom, what are you having this morning?" Ken's cheerful voice came to him through the service window to the kitchen.

"Let me have a couple over easy with some well done bacon," Tom responded.

"How about some toast and juice?"

"Sounds good to me."

"Get yourself some coffee. I don't have any help until 8 o'clock."

"Okay. Take your time, I'll be reading the paper." Tom got up and poured himself a mug of coffee, picked up the creamer from the refrigerator, and sat back in the booth.

Tom took a few sips of coffee while he scanned the first few pages of the Camden Gazette for any mention of the airplane crash. *Three days and already the news disappeared from the paper.* Disappointed, he turned to the editorial section. He folded the paper to get a better look at the Letters to the Editor.

Ken came through the swinging doors from the kitchen with Tom's breakfast. "Here you go. I'll get you some juice."

He went behind the counter, brought out two glasses and filled them at the refrigerator and was back at Tom's table. "Tomato and orange juice, one each, as you like it."

Tom looked up and smiled. "Thanks Ken. This'll probably hold me."

Ken sat down to talk. "Anything interesting in there today?" he asked nodding at the newspaper.

Tom scowled. "All of today's letters are about the distress of the small ranchers in today's economy and dealing with land use policies and development. It's really depressing. Listen to this shit."

Ken flipped his ever-present towel over his shoulder and leaned forward.

"This fellow writes that sustained-yield forestry methods had been abandoned by the timber industry in 1983. Instead, clear-cutting had been employed to maximize immediate corporate profit. The biggest impact was in the western part of Montana resulting in immense tracts of clear-cut. He goes on to say that this has been the cause of deterioration in water quality, reduction in animal habitat, and the poor aesthetics that greets the resident and tourist alike."

"I thought the timber folks have been changing their methods of late," said Ken.

"Yeah, a bit. Public pressure and shareholders have been forcing some companies to do a better job. But they have the politicians in their pockets."

Ken nodded in agreement.

"Oh, here is another interesting letter." Tom looked down at the newspaper. "This is from a Native American up near Libby. He says that silt from clear-cut areas as well as pollution from abandoned mines is still causing serious deterioration of fish spawning grounds."

"Oh hell, can't even eat the damn fish anyway because of the mercury and other crap in the water." Ken looked disgusted.

"Here's another. This guy talks about small ranchers. He says making ends meet is nearly impossible, and developers are devouring the ranches closer to the bigger towns of Helena, Billings, Missoula and Kalispell. He goes on, but you get the idea."

Ken looked at Tom. "Changes are coming. We can't stop it."

Tom scowled. "I want to keep Bauer Ridge intact. Matter of fact, Sullivan and I have an agreement whereby both places can't be developed or broken up and we each have right of first refusal."

Ken smiled, "Good. That's good. I'm glad to hear it."

The bell at the door tinkled as a couple of men came in and ambled to counter seats. Ken got up and went to serve them. Tom gazed out of the window and smiled to himself as he remembered the gentlemen's agreement his father had made with the Sullivans for the protection of both their lands. He thought of the discussion he had with the Sullivans. In the mid-1900s, the U.S. Forestry Service had made many attempts to purchase the timbered portions of both the Timberline Ranch and the Sullivan Ranch. Tom's parents as well as the Sullivans had rebuffed these less-than-friendly overtures by the government. Instead, they had agreed that neither property would be sold to the government, to land speculators, or to developers.

After a while Ken returned to Tom's table, refilled Tom's coffee cup, and stood chatting for a few minutes trying to pump him about any more news on the crash. With nothing new to add, Tom mentioned the stranger, the so-called investigator, asking questions about the ranch.

Ken stood up straight. "Really? You know, there were a couple of strange dudes in here yesterday. They had a blue rental car parked out front. They came in for lunch, pretty hungry they were, spent twenty bucks. Anyway, they talked a lot between themselves, but every time I got near their table, they stopped. They were dressed pretty well. One was big, a heavy guy. The other was taller, but rather skinny. They were here almost an hour and then they took off. You think they might be the ones you mentioned?"

"Could be. I think they're interested in the plane wreck and maybe with me too, since I was at the wreck."

"Mmm. I'll keep my eyes open." Ken said in a serious tone.

"Thanks. If anything comes up, let Allen know."

Ken nodded and went back behind the counter as Tom got up to leave.

33

At Mason's General Store, Tom paid for the supplies he had ordered, and loaded them in the back of the truck. His next stop was Preston's Lumber and Equipment. He entered and waited for Jeff to get free.

"I stopped in to fill out the work orders for the summer projects at the ranch. How's everybody doing?"

"My parents are staying for a few more days. They want to be there when Karen wakes up. I hope she does…she's got to." His voice cracked.

"She will…it takes time for the swelling to go down. The brain is just protecting itself. She'll come out of it soon. The tests are still okay, aren't they?"

"Yeah, tests are good, actually. The docs are pleased. There's just a little fever. They'll probably do another MRI tomorrow and check the swelling."

"How's your mom?"

He shook his head and hesitated. "She's not well…tires so easily…sleeps often. This ordeal with Karen has taken a lot out of her. She rescheduled her treatments, but has to get in there soon. No one gives her more than a year. Dad hides it pretty well, but it's getting to him, too."

Tom shook his head, "I'm sorry. It's really tough for both of them and you, too."

Jeff looked up suddenly. "By the way, a couple of the boys here told me a slick-dressed stranger came into the yard yesterday while we were in Camden. He asked about the downed airplane and Timberline Ranch. He wanted to know what access there was to the crash site."

"Really? Did you tell Allen?"

"No, forgot actually until just now. The boys didn't tell this guy anything useful. I mean, they didn't know anything, and besides, they aren't inclined to talk to strangers anyway."

"This is getting a little spooky. Last night there was a guy out by my truck. He was going to break in with one of those Slim Jim things. Bandit must have been asleep when he sneaked up to the door. I guess Bandit nearly gave him a heart attack though. He took off down between the buildings."

"Holy shit."

"Damn, with that guy out by my truck, guys asking questions here and at Larry's, there's something weird about all this. Ask your guys to keep an eye out for license plates. Might be useful. I'll stop by Allen's office on the way home. I'll see what he thinks. Maybe he knows something."

Jeff bit his lip. "Do you think Karen is in any danger? I mean, if these guys want something to do with the airplane, maybe they think Karen knows something about whatever the hell they're looking for," he said while fiddling with his hands.

"I don't know; maybe. They probably won't get aggressive in the hospital, but let Larry know to keep an eye on who's in the lounge."

"Yeah. I'll talk to Larry later. Incidentally, I gotta thank you for going to the hospital with me."

"Not a problem. That's what friends are for. Besides, I wanted to see her, too. Here, let me sign these work orders. I gotta run."

The deputy sheriff's SUV was parked in front of the fire station and Tom made a U-turn to park next to him. He found Allen in his office having his coffee and donut.

"What a life. Hope I'm not interrupting," said Tom.

Trying not to speak with his mouth full, Allen merely shook his head. After he swallowed, he said, "You are. This," waving the donut, "is one of the basic food groups." He opened his mouth and most of the donut disappeared.

"Well, you are getting all your cholesterol and calories all at one time. Has to be a real time saver." Tom smiled.

"Oh good grief! I have to hear it at home and now from you, too. What the hell did I do to deserve this visit?" Allen scowled.

"Oh, just wanted to tell you that some jerk tried to break into my truck last night. That was before he woke Bandit up. I think he probably rushed home to change his drawers, but he dropped this Slim Jim in his haste. Do you think you can lift a print?" He handed the plastic bag to Allen.

Allen shrugged. "Guy was probably smart enough to wear gloves." He put the plastic bag on the corner of his desk. "Where'd this happen? Here in town?" Allen wiped sugar from his face with a napkin.

"Yeah, near Shaw's garage. It was close to 10 p.m. I heard Bandit barking and then I saw a guy by the truck. I hollered at him and he took off between the buildings. When I got up there, I heard a car start up at the end of the alley."

"I don't think we'll find anything on this." Allen pointed to the Slim Jim. "No self-respecting thief is gonna leave his prints. But, what the hell. I'll give it to the lab guys when I go up to Camden tomorrow. It'll give them something to do."

"I don't think it was just a thief," said Tom. "We haven't had one of those here in all the time I remember. No, I think this has to do with the strangers coming in and asking questions and looking for information about the plane wreck."

"You could be right. The sheriff called earlier. Wayne said an FBI guy was in town from Chicago. I forget his name now. Wonder what brings the FBI into this. Maybe there's some sort of criminal connection. Strange..." Allen wiped his mouth again. "Anyway, Wayne hasn't told me much yet. I'll check with him tomorrow. In the meantime, don't be surprised if he bumps into you."

"I think some feds are already in the area, maybe even an insurance guy. Be nice if all these idiots knew the meaning of the word, *coordinate*."

"Well, you'll be seeing this guy soon."

"Wonderful. Just what I need in my life." Tom looked a bit exasperated.

"Hey, cheer up. I stopped a guy yesterday here in town. He was driving a rental car, and so I made some excuse to pull him over."

"Yeah? Who was he?"

"I didn't ask him to get out of the car; that would have been pushing my luck, so I don't have a real good description. Dark hair, maybe 40 years old, and heavy. He had an Illinois driver's license and told me he was staying at the Downtown Motel in Camden. Later, I checked it out and called in the credit card that he used. The bank told me that it was issued to a Chicago nightclub."

"That's it?"

"Well, yeah. He hadn't done anything. I wished him a good afternoon and he went on his way."

"I don't like any of this." Tom had a worried frown on his brow.

34

IN A FEW MINUTES TOM AND Bandit were on their way back to the ranch. As he approached the ranch gate, Tom saw an unfamiliar blue car parked at the entrance. "Uh oh. Bandit, you better stay alert. I might need you." Bandit was already staring at the unfamiliar car.

Alert to possible danger, Tom stopped well behind the blue car. He got out of the truck, commanding Bandit to stay with him as he walked slowly to his rural mailbox. He collected his mail, and slowly walked back to the truck while looking over the car and the driver who was now getting out.

"He might be trouble. Stay alert, Bandit." Bandit stayed close to his leg, his eyes on the stranger. He gave a low growl as the man turned to walk toward them.

Tom put the mail on the truck seat and turned to face the stranger. He saw a trim man in his early fifties, dressed in a well fitting gray suit. A hint of recognition crossed Tom's mind, thinking of the man at the hospital.

He met Tom's inquiring look directly, a thin smile starting on his face. "Nice dog," he said as he nervously looked at Bandit who was still growling.

"Bandit, no...sit." Bandit did as he was told, but his eyes never left the stranger.

"Can I help you with something?" asked Tom.

"Well, yeah, maybe." The stranger reached into his vest pocket. "I'm Special Agent Oberman, I'm with the FBI, organized crime unit out of the Chicago office."

The man produced a leather folder, flipped it open and quickly put it back in his pocket. "Not so fast," said Tom. "May I see that again?"

The man scowled, flipped it open, and held it for Tom to inspect.

Tom nodded and smiled thinly. "I'm Tom Bauer. I live here, up this road. What's the FBI doing in these parts?"

"I just flew in to look into the airplane crash, ProAir 109, up on the mountain."

"Really? The sheriff's crew and the NTSB guys have been all over it already."

"I know. I'm looking into it also." The agent looked at Tom evenly with only a hint of a smile.

"What can *I* do for you?" asked Tom, petting Bandit.

"What can you tell me about that airplane? We know... you were there...according to the news account and the sheriff's report."

"Well, Yeah. I was there. I saw the dead crew. I saw three dead male passengers and one female, badly injured. I think one other passenger may have wandered off."

Tom bit his lower lip for the moment until Oberman responded. "Why's that? How did you know there was a fifth person? Where do you think he went?" His voice was even and he looked directly at Tom.

"I never saw him. All I saw were footprints in the snow and blood on the doorway. I figure he wandered off and died somewhere. I'm guessing there's no way he could survive the cold that night."

"Which way did he go? Could you tell? Did you follow his tracks?"

"Frankly, it was snowing and damned cold. It was getting dark. I didn't go look for him. The woman was alive. I thought it was more important to look after *her*." Tom's voice showed his annoyance at having to defend himself.

"Okay. Just trying to get a picture," Oberman said, his face showing no emotion.

Tom continued. "The sheriff's team came for the survivor, a woman named Karen Roberts, the following morning and took her to the hospital in Camden. But you already know that."

Oberman nodded with a slight smile.

Tom continued. "The sheriff's recovery team and the NTSB were supposed to have gone up that evening and come back yesterday. I've been here in town overnight. Did you talk to *them* yet?" Tom angled for some information and was glad to take the spotlight off himself.

"We're looking into it. Did you see any unusual packages in the airplane - boxes, briefcases, anything out of the ordinary?"

"I wasn't really looking for anything. There *were* some cardboard boxes at the back of the plane, held in with some netting. Didn't notice anything else. I just wanted to get the woman out of the plane. Anyway, the sheriff's crew and NTSB guys probably picked up anything that wasn't screwed to the floor." Tom shrugged.

"Okay, I appreciate your cooperation. Do you mind if I poke around the old logging roads?"

"Sure, not a problem. I'll tell my foreman that you'll be around. By the way, there are only two ways up into the area where the airplane crashed. This ranch road leads up past my place and up onto the ridge. There are some old logging roads in the area. There is also a locked Forest Service gate if you come in from the north. That road eventually goes into Camden. But that's it; there is no other way in by road."

"Thank you."

"Say, when you're wandering around on the ridge, you might bump into my dog, Bandit. He won't hurt you unless you threaten him. Just stand still and let him come up to you and smell you. Don't touch him until his tail starts wagging. He's a bit of a wild dog, part wolf."

"Okay. I hope I don't run into him."

"Don't worry, he'll remember your scent." Tom was petting Bandit and rubbing his ears.

"I'll be going. Again, I appreciate…"

Tom interrupted him. "One thing, Agent… Oberman, is it? That car…you might want to exchange it for something with more ground clearance. When I said there were old logging roads, I mean old. They're overgrown and rocky, and haven't been used much in twenty years or more."

"Good point. Thanks for the advice."

Tom nodded, "No problem."

"We'll be looking into all aspects of the crash, including anything out of the ordinary. I appreciate your cooperation and letting me on your property."

"I want to help where I can."

"Well, I wanted to introduce myself and so I waited here for you. I saw your truck in town. The sheriff described you to me."

Tom moved to go back to his truck. "I'm glad I got to meet you. How do I contact you if I think of anything else?"

"You can get in touch through Deputy Richards."

They shook hands and got into their vehicles. Oberman headed toward town. Tom turned onto his road and went slowly the six miles to the ranch buildings. He went over all he could remember of the crash site, but he couldn't think of anything else he could have told him.

"I think he'll be okay, Bandit. He seems professional. We'll see." Bandit flicked his tail a couple of times, looking out the window towards home.

35

THE FOLLOWING MORNING, Tom joined the Stehlings at breakfast before heading out to inspect the fence along the ridge. The days had turned warm after the storm and the snow was melting quickly. The sun streaked into the window, lighting up the breakfast table. Steam rose from the stack of pancakes and the coffee cups.

Ralph handed the coffeepot to Tom. "So how did it go in town the last couple of days?"

Tom looked up. "Jeff and I went to see his sister at the hospital. I got to meet their parents. They're nice people. It is all so sad, though. The doctors are hopeful that Karen will recover, but her mother is getting chemo treatments in Chicago and they don't give her long. It's a really tough time for that family."

Susan looked up and asked, "What are the doctors saying about Karen?"

"They are non-committal. All the tests show improvement, they say, but she hasn't come out of it yet. I guess there's no telling about that." Tom dropped his eyes, shaking his head slowly.

"How is Jeff handling all this?" Susan asked softly.

"I think he will be okay. It was tough for a while. I'll make sure to talk to him every couple of days."

Liz caught Tom's eye, and tried to tease him. "Did you stay out of trouble in town?"

Tom smiled at her and raised his eyebrows. "Well, I did go with Chris to Larry's for supper."

Susan said, "I like her. She's always gracious and helpful when I go to the garage."

Liz looked at Tom, still with her wry smile. "Did you sing at Larry's, or just hold hands and bump knees."

Tom laughed. "Yes, Jeff got me up there for a song."

"You walked her home?" Liz asked.

"Yes."

"And?"

"And nothing. Gimme a break."

"Liz, give it a rest," admonished Susan.

Liz stared at Tom with the same teasing grin.

"Any other excitement, Tom?" asked Ralph.

"Well yeah. There was a guy wanted to break into my truck until he woke Bandit. He broke some kind of speed record running out of there. I couldn't catch him."

"Really? He wanted to steal your truck? That's never happened around here," commented Ralph with a look of surprise. Then he shrugged, "It *is* but a year old."

"I don't know if that was it, or he was looking for something. Anyhow, I ran into another guy, said his name was Oberman, down by the ranch gate. Said he was an FBI agent. He's looking for the fourth guy from the plane wreck...the guy that was lost."

Everyone looked expectantly at Tom. Tom looked across the table and glanced at each of them. A serious tone came into his voice. "I think there are some bad guys out there, looking for something from the plane wreck. They're asking a lot of questions. It's tough to know just who the bad guys are and who the good guys are. We need to be careful around here. Keep your eyes open. Let me know of anything unusual. If I'm not here, call Allen Richards right away. Don't take any chances."

Susan was concerned. "You think we'll have trouble... they'll come here?"

"I don't know. Allen hopes to get a handle on this. But in the meantime, we need to be alert."

He saw a troubled look on Liz's face. "Liz, be careful when you're hiking or on horseback. Let someone know where you go. It might be better if you stay close to home for a while." Liz nodded.

Ralph asked, "Are you going to go out on the ridge fence, or are you going to stick around here with these goings-on?"

Tom shook his head. "I'm going. Time is running out. Have to get it done and see what repairs are needed."

Ralph nodded a couple of times. "Now that you mention it, the Sullivans will be turning out their cattle by mid May."

"Yep, and the Forest Service guys were kind of cranky last fall about cows getting into their area. I better see what we have to do to get the fence in shape. "Anyway, I thought if I got going by noon, I should be able to check most of it."

"You thinking about going all the way to the peak? Might be a stretch to get back before dark," cautioned Ralph. "Some of those slopes are still snow covered."

Tom nodded. "I wanted to go over a few things before I set out," Tom said as he picked up his coffee mug. They all waited for him to continue. Tom looked at Susan and Ralph, "How about staffing for the summer? How're we fixed?"

Susan responded, "Liz will help me with the housekeeping. Just need to keep the lodge clean, gets a lot of traffic. That should hold us this season, since we won't have any guests until next spring. But she has to be back in school the first week of September."

Liz scowled and nodded.

"We'll need some permanent staff next season," said Tom. "Be good to start looking now for some wranglers who can do fence work and shoeing. I'm looking to hire someone good this year."

"Ralph and I will keep our eyes open, ask around," said Susan.

"Okay," Tom nodded and turned to Ralph. "How are you set for all the things we have to do this summer? You have summer help lined up?"

"Not yet, but I got a line on a couple of seniors who would like a summer job. They're not afraid of hard work. I got a call from their adviser at Camden High the other day."

"Good," Tom agreed, "Have them come out and see if they're really a fit."

"Great, I'll do that." Ralph smiled, "It'll be nice to get some help with the heavy lifting. I guess one of the first things is to get that old tanker-pump truck ready for fire season. It needs fixing and filling since we drained it last fall. The Forest Service guys will be coming by to look at it one of these days."

Tom nodded. "Mmm. Put the kids on getting that ready before anything else."

Tom turned to Susan. "I've been looking at the plans and furniture items that you picked for the cabins and lodge. I really like your approach, the rustic western style. I think our guests will appreciate the look. They get enough modern stuff where they normally live and work. We should give them a place of peace and quiet, comfortable and elegant, but in keeping with the old west. I like the way you went about it."

Ralph grinned, nodding his head toward Susan. "It's Suz with the good taste. But I like it, too."

"Liz helped, too. We spent many an evening selecting items and drawing floor plans. We did watch the cost, though. I think we're all right there." Susan smiled at Liz.

"Thanks. I have to review the budgets; can't put it off much longer." Tom wrinkled his face. It wasn't his favorite task. He didn't like anything that kept him indoors, even if it was just cleaning out the barn.

Liz turned to Tom. "What about your office? I mean, it looks like a warehouse, stuff everywhere. It really needs help."

Tom winked at her, knowing she couldn't pass up an opportunity to kid him about his chaotic office. In fact, the office equipment and several furniture items were still in boxes.

"I know. I got to get in there soon and figure out what to do with all the stuff. There are a lot of manuals to read. I'll start with the computer, get it up and running. Are you up for helping me with some of it?"

"Sure, just say when. It's stuff I use at school. Well, most of it anyway."

"Okay smarty…I'll be calling you," said Tom.

Ralph spoke again. "Tom, should we go ahead and order all the furniture, bedding, towels and that kind of stuff? It's what we listed on the plan you have."

"Makes sense to me. It'll take time to get it all here. We need to have everything completed before the snow flies."

"We can get it all done with time to spare," Ralph assured him. "Oh, I need to call the County. Damn inspector hasn't showed up for the septic system, and it's been finished for a week."

"Yeah. Keep after them." Tom wrinkled his face in frustration.

As Tom turned toward the door, the telephone rang in the kitchen. Susan handed Tom the telephone. "It's Jeff."

"Jeff, how are you?"

"Hi Tom. I'm okay. Listen, my parents called last night from Camden. They said they saw a stranger at the hospital. This guy looked in on Karen, and then as my parents approached her room, he asked whether she had spoken. My father shook his head and the guy just turned and walked away. Damn weird, I'd say."

"Did you tell Allen?"

"Yeah, I called him. I don't like this at all. What the hell is going on?"

"Well, I met a guy yesterday at the ranch gate. He's here looking into the missing guy, the fourth passenger. I don't know any more yet. How is Karen?"

"Her MRI is looking pretty good…swelling is way down. God, I hope she wakes up soon."

"She will. Jeff. She will."

"I'm afraid."

"I know."

"My parents are flying home today. Mom has her cancer treatments scheduled in Chicago tomorrow."

"I hope it all goes well."

"She'll be sick from it for a few days."

"Stay strong. She'll get through it and Karen is going to make it." Tom tried to keep his own apprehension out of his voice. "If I hear anything from the sheriff, I'll let you know."

36

SHORTLY AFTER LUNCH, TOM saddled Dakota, fed him grain and watered him. He tied the horse to the corral fence and went toward Ralph, who was coming out of the lodge.

"Ralph, I'm saddled up. Decided the heck with the office work. It can wait."

Ralph grinned. "So what're you gonna do?"

"I'm going to head up to the ridge and then ride the fence line, see what kind of shape it's in. The snow is melting fast; it'll be almost 50 degrees this afternoon I bet."

"The Forest Service will really be pissed if Sullivan's cattle get into their area and eat the new seedlings they planted last year."

"Damn, don't even think that. I'll check along there, the gate too. I'll see if we need a crew out there. Can you make a list of available guys?"

"Sure thing."

"Okay, I'm off."

"Got your radio?"

"Sure do." He patted his jacket pocket. "I'll be along later, not sure when."

"Okay, we'll have the radio on in the kitchen."

37

Tom's favorite horse, Dakota, a 4-year old roan gelding, waited at the corral. He was always troublesome to bridle, but after a few tries, he accepted the bit in his mouth, working it with his tongue until it felt comfortable. Tom tightened the cinch, walked the horse a bit and tightened the cinch again.

"Dakota, are you glad to get out of the corral?" Tom ran his hands over the horse's neck and chest while talking to him. "Yep, a little exercise will do you some good."

The horse, he thought, was a majestic animal, sensitive, smart, wanting to please, and only asked for respect and kindness. Mounting up, Tom again felt the exhilaration of being on a horse and on the move. It was a feeling that he had come to look forward to since coming back to the ranch. Ready to head out, Tom whistled for Bandit, who, with a couple of barks, ran up.

Tom used a well-worn game trail that headed up the notch behind the lodge and offered a reasonable grade. Patches of snow clung to the shady spots, but he saw green shoots poking through. *Spring is on its way*, he thought. He saw elk and deer trails that led from the easy graze and water in the meadows to their highland rest spots. Every evening, deer and elk gathered in the meadows, readily visible from the lodge. Tom and Dakota climbed steadily, crossing numerous small brooks and edging past dense stands of aspen. Bandit was out of sight most of the time, exploring the forest for interesting scents. Tom let Dakota have his head to pick the best footing along the rocky trails. Relaxed in the saddle, Tom let his mind wander, thinking of Jeff and his family. He hoped that Karen would pull through and not suffer lasting effects. He took a deep breath, exhilarated by the clean air and the smell of the forest, particularly in the shaded glens where the moisture stayed in the air with the aroma of trees, moss covered rocks and early plants.

After an hour, he rested Dakota for a few minutes in a sunny spot and let him drink from a small brook of snowmelt. Tom looked up at the towering ponderosa, thankful that the loggers of old had not selected these majestic trees for the lumber mill.

"Take a breather, big boy." He petted the horse. "This is a nice spot. Hey Bandit, where are you?" Bandit came out of the woods, tongue hanging out, gasping for breath. His coat was wet and clumped with bits of brush.

"Where've you been, boy? Rolling around in the brook? Don't shake it off on me." Without hesitation, Bandit gave a violent shake showering Tom and Dakota. "Great. Thanks a lot." Tom wiped his face with the back of his hand. Bandit lay down in the sun, looking up at Tom. "Don't smile at me like that."

Early flowers poked up through the forest mantle. Before getting back on Dakota, Tom glanced up at the ridge in the direction he was heading. In the shadows, he could see pockets of snow he wanted to avoid. It took another hour of steady climbing to reach the fence along the ridge line. The old barbed wire fence stretched from the Sullivan property to the west, up and along Bauer Ridge and eastward around the slope of Mathews Peak to the steep precipice on the east face. An immense pile of rocky debris at the foot of the peak gave mute testament to the geological violence that had cleaved the mountain. The fence in the upper elevations of Bauer Ridge was an old 3-wire structure, the original strands dating back to the early 1920s. Tom turned eastward and followed the wire, slowly making his way through stands of Douglas fir and alpine larch while keeping within sight of the fence. He made notes of the exact locations of fence damage using his pocket GPS locator. He thought that the fence crew should bring a chain saw with them to remove the large fallen branches and tipped-over dead trees that had caused a lot of damage. It seemed to Tom that most of the old wooden fence posts were still serviceable but some had been broken. "Wonder why there are so many broken posts?" he mumbled. "Could be elk, I guess. Hmm." He mused that new wire and posts would need to be installed, even if only to placate the National Forest people, who had cautioned him more than once about letting cattle range into the forest.

38

JAKE EASED HIS BIG FRAME out of the Jeep, grabbed the bolt cutters, and went to the gate at the cattle guard. He snickered when he saw the *Private Property, Keep Out* sign attached with wire. *That Bauer guy and me will have to have an understanding one of these days,* he thought. He snapped the shanks on the two padlocks but left them in the latch. He leaned his arms on the gate, looked in the direction where the plane crash had occurred and thought about what he had to do. He knew that Sam and he would have to do a well-planned search if they had any hope of finding the missing briefcase in this wilderness. They would have to wait, however, until the snow covering the shale slide area melted a bit. He would have to get the boss on the phone and explain it to him, but he knew that Frank Capri would not have much patience. On the other hand, he had told them to keep a low profile. "You can't have it both ways, Frankie boy," he mumbled to himself. He had bought a topographical map on the way out of town; *We'll study it tonight*, he thought. That the injured courier had walked off with the briefcase was possible, he knew. But, it also occurred to him that Bauer, first man on the scene after the crash, had already found it and hidden it somewhere. He recalled his telephone conversation the previous night. Frank wanted the briefcase returned intact and quickly, but had also warned Jake to be sure it did not blow up in their faces. Jake had sensed that if anything were to go wrong, he and Sam would be on their own. "Yeah, Frankie boy, I get the picture," he said aloud.

It was already ten years since he had left the Special Forces. He knew he wasn't in fighting shape any longer. Actually, he had to admit that life as a bouncer and all-around enforcer hadn't done much for his physique. His boss had given him Sam, a skinny guy fresh out of the joint for armed robbery, to help him retrieve the missing property. Sam seemed okay and it was a bonus that he could ride a horse. He had dropped Sam off at the Baldwin Ranch on the way to the National Forest. The ranch hadn't looked like much but had a sign advertising horses for rent. Jake wondered where Sam was now. It had been an hour and a half since they had parted. *He's got to be up in this area somewhere,* he thought. *Well, I'll drive through the gate and make my way to the wreck. I'll come up with a search plan, maybe see Sam out there.* He leaned on the gate for a few more minutes and then turned to remove the locks from the gate. His eyes caught a glimpse of a horse and rider on top of a small hill, a couple of hundred yards off to the west. *Shit! Who the hell is that? Can't be Sam in that direction.* Jake slowly moved away from the gate until the trees shielded him from the rider's view. He then scurried to the Jeep, and backed up the narrow road the way he had come until he could turn around. Then he drove quickly over a rise that shielded him from the gate and kept going. *I'll wait for Sam at the ranch,* he thought.

39

IT WAS WELL INTO THE AFTERNOON when Tom topped a knoll just before having to make his way through a thicket of fir to the National Forest gate. At the knoll, Dakota picked up his ears and looked toward the gate, just visible through a break in the trees. Bandit stopped, his hair bristling. He barked several times. Tom pulled Dakota to a stop.

"What is it boy? Bandit, stay!" Bandit stood motionless. "Do you guys hear something?"

It was then that he heard the faint sound of a vehicle engine. He heard it again; then it disappeared.

"I can't see anything down there, Dakota. I guess you guys heard it though, sounded like a car engine. We better check it out." He put Dakota into a trot; Bandit took the cue and raced ahead.

Tom dismounted at the gate. The National Forest road, a relic of the logging days, wasn't used much anymore. It saw an occasional work crew and a few hunters in the fall. Farther north, there was a connecting road that eventually led to Camden and another that went on to the Idaho border. The shared gate had both National Forest and Timberline locks with each party having a set of corresponding keys; *a silly arrangement* thought Tom, but that was how the local NFS office wanted to do it. He glanced at the locks and then went closer to look again. A bolt cutter had cut the shanks of both. Oddly, the locks had been left in the gate latch. There were tire tracks, but only on the National Forest side of the fence.

"Bandit, these tracks were made today. I wonder, did we just now scare them off? Well, you and Dakota heard them; good thing, I probably would have missed it." Bandit looked up at the mention of his name, but quickly went back to sniffing the breezes. Tom looked back along the fence line and realized that he could have been spotted as he topped the knoll.

"I'll bet they were just here. No doubt, they spotted us and left in a hurry. What the hell are they up to?"

Tom walked toward the gate, but Bandit held back, away from the cattle guard grating. The gate didn't look damaged, but he made a note to have the Forest Service replace their lock. He wished then that he had brought his camera. The tire prints were very clear in the moist earth.

"I'll have to call Allen and tell him what we found." He looked again at the broken locks. "Damn! Why all the interest in the plane wreck? And why are they trying to see Karen?" Bandit stood quietly as Tom ran his fingers through the dog's thick fur and muttered. "I wonder...did she witness something? I don't like this...someone wants to get to the plane wreck...but for what?" He recalled that the authorities had hinted of a package on the plane, but what? He didn't recall seeing anything out of the ordinary and besides, the sheriff's crew had retrieved everything from the plane. He wondered if the fourth guy had taken something with him.

Tom got back on Dakota and they continued along the fence line east toward Mathews Peak. There was more snow; several inches covered the ground. He passed nearby Timberline Cabin and thoughts of the night with Karen came back to him. He felt a sudden sadness, and wondered if he would ever see her awake and recovered. He continued toward the sheer precipice at Mathews Peak, which formed a natural barrier. It was slow going. Low branches, underbrush, and saplings frequently blocked the way. He made notes to have the fence crew clear a swath along the fence. *They will definitely need a chain saw*, he thought. There were many places where the wire had been broken or where a fence post had fallen over. These were all noted along with the GPS locator reading. The fence continued eastward on the slopes of Mathews Peak, separating the National Forest from adjoining private land sections.

"I'll have to get started on this fence soon. Damn, there's a good three weeks work here for a couple of guys." Dakota turned his ears when Tom spoke. "Then there's the section over toward Sullivan's. I really need to get started on it."

Tom turned back when he reached the sharp face of Mathews Peak. He made his way back along the fence until he again came near Timberline Cabin. He pulled on the reins. "Whoa, big boy. Hang on a second."

He gazed into the woods towards the airplane wreck. Then looked at his watch, frowned, and kicked his heels into Dakota. "Come on guys. Let's take a quick look."

40

THE SHADOWS WERE LENGTHENING when Tom arrived at Tim-berline Cabin. He pressed down on the latch. It opened when he put his shoulder to the door.

"Good thing the latch held, huh Bandit?"

Bandit busied himself sniffing at the base of the door.

"A bear gets in here; we'd never recognize the place."

Tom pushed the door open, relieved to see the sparse furniture upright and the cabinets undisturbed. He was startled by flashbacks of the night with Karen. He suddenly missed her. It seemed to him that whoever had been at the National Forest gate had not gotten this far. The tire tracks hadn't crossed the cattle guard and the cabin seemed undisturbed. Still, he wondered if they were somewhere in the area. Tom was satisfied that no one had been there after a quick check of the stove ashes and the cabinet contents. Then making sure the door was closed securely, he mounted Dakota, riding the short distance to the wreck site where he dismounted, secured the horse's lead rope to a tree and loosened the cinch.

The sheriff's yellow tape was still draped through the trees marking the investigation site around the downed aircraft. More yellow tape surrounded the wing, barely visible some distance away through the broken trees. Tom hesitated.

"They still have this marked off," he mumbled. "I wonder why? Guess I better stay out of there." Bandit didn't have any reservations and investigated the area around the wreck, walking back and forth with his nose to the ground.

Tom thought about the missing man and the footprints in the snow. He recalled that the footprints had quickly become obscured by the snowfall, but appeared to be heading down-slope and toward the shale-slide area. Tom walked to where he thought the footprints led.

Bandit followed close beside Tom and looked up at him frequently as if not at all sure what was expected of him. After a few hundred yards, they were at the shale slide area, still covered with a few inches of snow. The forest came right up to the loose shale on all sides. Tom looked over the site carefully but saw nothing out of the ordinary.

"How far could he have gone? He had to have been seriously injured," he said aloud. "You don't suppose, Bandit, he was unlucky enough to try to walk on the shale? Surely he's a goner. No one will find him until summer, and then the critters won't have left much."

Bandit stayed close to Tom, as they began an awkward descent. Tom stopped and looked again around the forested perimeter, but saw no clues. He made his way carefully just inside the forest edge.

"Easy does it, Bandit. We don't want to hurt ourselves here."

He moved from tree to tree to maintain his balance as he stepped carefully down to the bottom of the slope.

"Okay, Bandit, we made it. Getting back up is gonna take some work."

Bandit had been following along, but he now took off with his nose to the ground and disappeared into the trees at the bottom of the shale slide. Within a minute Tom heard a couple of barks, then a couple more. He knew that Bandit had found something.

He called to Bandit, "Stay!" He picked his way cautiously to where the dog had disappeared into the trees. As Tom came into view, Bandit stood up and whined. A partly snow-covered body lay next to Bandit, face down, arms and legs twisted oddly underneath him.

"Good boy, Bandit. Stay." Tom looked at the body. *"He probably didn't suffer long,"* he thought. "Poor bastard," he muttered.

Tom sat on his heels, petted Bandit, and looked at the body. The crows had been busy on the face but decay had not gotten much of a start in the cold weather. He felt uncomfortable touching him, but rifled through the man's pockets and inspected his wallet. The driver's license was from Illinois with a Chicago address. Joseph P. Solerno was listed as 43 years old. Tom saw what looked like an expensive gold necklace and an odd ring with diamonds. It did not look like a wedding ring. Tom replaced the man's wallet, stood up, and looked at the body at his feet. He knew he had to alert Allen.

Scanning the area, he spotted a patch of shiny metal, sparkling in a beam of sunlight about twenty feet farther. It had come to rest against a tree when Salerno had lost his grip on it. Going to it, he brushed away the snow and exposed an aluminum briefcase.

"Wow! The poor bastard dragged this thing with him!" he said aloud. Bandit came over to Tom and poked his nose at the briefcase.

The case was badly dented. Tom pried at the cover with a stick. The stick broke several times before the cover eventually popped open. He stared in amazement as he gazed at more money in $100 dollar bills than he had ever seen in one place.

"Bandit! Holy shit, look at this!" Bandit sniffed the money.

The bills were bundled and banded and Tom made a quick estimate. "There's got to be a million here, maybe more!"

He lowered the cover but was unable to get the latches to work. "Oh, damn. How am I going to get this out of here?" he asked aloud. Bandit looked at him but then walked off to test the ground around the body with his nose. "I guess now we know why there are strangers asking questions and why the gate locks have been cut. Oberman was right...the fourth guy is key to all this. I've got to get hold of Allen."

Tom made several attempts to close and secure the briefcase cover but was unsuccessful. He knew he wouldn't be able to climb up the treacherous slope and carry the case, because he would need both hands to make the climb. Futilely, he tried to cover the case with snow, but then thought better of it. "Oh hell, this won't fool anyone. I just have to get Allen."

He felt the hair on his arms begin to stand up. He wondered whether anyone was watching him at the moment He decided that he had to get in contact with Allen quickly. If anyone *was* watching, the money and whatever other evidence which may be here would be gone that day. He thought again of trying to disguise the body and briefcase, but thought better of it, thinking that Allen might want to examine it himself. Tom tried to contact Ralph on his portable radio but there was no reply. *I'll try again*, he thought, *from the top of the ridge*. He looked around and noticed that he was shielded except for a direct view from the top of the shale slide. He felt hopeful that no one had seen him.

"Come on Bandit, let's get back up the hill. We can't do anything for this poor guy. We'll leave everything here."

They started climbing the slope the way they had come. Part way up Tom stopped to get his wind and looked about casually. On an exposed ridge several hundred yards east, he saw what appeared to be a horse and rider in an open area. He had almost missed them. He pulled out the binoculars from under his jacket, but at that distance he could not make out any significant details. He had no doubt now that he was being observed, but by whom? He had never seen anyone on horseback in these mountains before. Could it be a sheriff's deputy? Was it someone looking for the money he had just found? If it was, the rider could easily figure out where he had just been and retrieve the money. He knew that it was essential that he get in contact with Allen and have him get there quickly. When he started to climb again, he couldn't see the rider any longer. On reaching the top of the slide area, he looked back, but the ridge was hidden from view.

41

SAM, A TALL THIN MAN, PUT away the binoculars, and reached into his vest pocket for a small spiral-bound notebook and pen. He flipped through the pages to a clean sheet and began to sketch the area where he had seen the man and dog go into the trees. He looked around and noted distinguishing features, a tight stand of ponderosa and two large boulders, things he'd be able to find again. He reined the horse and found a sheltered spot inside the tree line where he could watch the hill unobserved. He knew he had been seen, but was now hidden; he thought that he would avoid getting the guy too nervous.

What the hell did he find down there? Shit, I can't go back without something for old Jake. Goddamn candy-ass won't even get on a horse. He thought about Jake's temper and decided to stay a while longer.

42

TOM AGAIN TRIED HIS SMALL radio. He was happy when Ralph answered. The signal was weak and noisy, but intelligible.

"Tom...yeah, I copy you...not well, but go ahead."

"Hey, you'll never guess! I found the missing passenger from the wreck. Dead of course."

"No shit? Where was he?" asked Ralph. Tom could hear the slap on the table.

"At the bottom of the shale slide. Know where I mean?"

"Yeah, I know where that is. What in hell were *you* doing down there?"

"When I got back to the old cabin, I remembered the footprints in the snow from when I first got to the airplane and found the evidence that a fourth guy was missing. Anyway, I just figured it would be natural for an injured and maybe half-crazed person to head downhill if he wanted to get to civilization - just a hunch. So I went toward the slide area, the nearest downhill slope. I hiked to the bottom and Bandit found him."

"That's what, 300-400 yards from the wreckage?" asked Ralph.

"Yeah, I'd say so. Maybe closer to 400, the shale slope is probably 100 yards."

"Amazing. Critters been gnawing on him?"

"Not bad actually. The crows have been at work on his head. Eyes gone. Ain't pretty. But it's been very cold up there and snowy and I think he's probably still frozen solid. It doesn't look like the bigger animals have found him."

"Yeah, but it's warming up. He won't keep long," added Ralph. "By the way, Allen and Agent Oberman just came in looking for you. I'll put Allen on."

"Okay, I'll talk to you later about what I found along the fence line."

"It'll keep. Here's Allen."

"Tom? Do you hear me?"

"Yeah, I hear you okay. It's noisy but I hear you. I think you'll be interested in what I found up here...the fourth guy."

"That's what I gathered just listening to Ralph. I thought you were going up along the fence."

Tom heard a hint of suspicion in his voice. "I did, but on the way back, I remembered the footprints in the snow when I first got to the airplane. I wanted to follow a hunch and went looking at the bottom of the slide area, about 300-400 yards from the crash site. I probably wouldn't have found him except for Bandit."

"What's he look like? I mean, what shape is he in?" asked Allen.

"Still frozen solid. The crows have been at him, but now that it is warming up...well, he won't keep long."

"I'll get hold of the sheriff and he can put a recovery team together tonight and bring him out first thing in the morning."

"By the way, the padlocks on the Forest Service gate have been cut. I saw tire prints at the gate...looked fresh."

"Mmm. I'll pass that along."

"Also, I saw a rider on a ridge east of me. He saw me for sure. He couldn't see what I saw from his angle...but he knows I was there."

"Okay. He isn't one of ours. Did you disturb anything?" Allen asked casually.

"Nothing too serious, but there is something I want to tell you ...but not on an unsecured radio. Actually, you both need to see this." Tom didn't want any news of the briefcase full of money to be overheard by someone with a similar radio. He'd let Allen and Frank figure out how to deal with it.

"Okay Tom, we're coming up. I've got my 4-wheel drive. I'll start out right away. You need to stay there and make yourself conspicuous. We don't want anyone at that site. Copy that?"

"Roger. I'll stay here. Make sure no one disturbs it. Talk to you when you get here."

Tom went back to where Dakota stood quietly and untied his halter rope. He led him up to where he wanted to sit overlooking the slide area and tied the horse again. He untied the canteen and took the snacks out of the saddlebag, going to a rock ledge that allowed him to observe the place where the body and the briefcase had gone into the woods. He was sure that anyone coming toward the area would see him and hesitate, hopefully long enough for Allen to get there. Bandit lay down but kept his eye on the snacks Tom was opening.

43

SAM, PARTIALLY HIDDEN BEHIND some brush, focused the binoculars on the man and dog sitting at the top of the hill.

Damn, he's been sitting up there for an hour. What the hell is he doing? Just sitting and munching on fuckin' candy bars. Goddamn dog looks like a mean bastard. I wonder if it's the one scared the shit out of Jake the other night.

Then he saw the horse partly hidden in the trees. *Well now, must be that Bauer guy from the ranch that Jake is after.*

Suddenly his attention was riveted. The man and dog had turned to look at someone coming through the trees. He refocused the binoculars.

Shit! Goddamn sheriff deputy. He wondered if he should make a hasty retreat or stay. The shadows were lengthening and he knew that he had at least an hour's ride to get back to Randolph. He didn't want to lose his way in the dark.

Damn, I better stay just a little longer. These guys must have found something.

He sat down behind the scrub brush, resting his chin on his knees.

44

IT HAD BEEN AN HOUR BEFORE Allen arrived. Tom saw the FBI agent get out of the vehicle.

"Shit, this could complicate things," he mumbled.

Bandit had heard the vehicle minutes before and was nervously looking in their direction as they walked through the trees, amidst the late afternoon shadows. Tom held Bandit's collar as he growled at the visitors.

He looked at the FBI agent. "Just pet him, he'll be okay."

The agent hesitantly reached to pet Bandit and the dog quieted.

"You know Agent Oberman, right?" said Allen.

"We've met," replied Tom.

They shook hands and Tom explained again why he thought about looking in that particular area and exactly what he had found. He pointed out where they could find the body and the briefcase.

"There...at the bottom of the slide. Just go into the trees, maybe thirty feet or so. The briefcase is just past the body, straight back maybe another twenty feet. You won't miss it."

Oberman looked at Allen and asked, "Didn't you guys do a search pattern around the wreck?"

Tom bristled at hearing the criticism toward Allen. He stifled the remark he was about to make as Allen responded.

"Well, yeah. We didn't go down the shale slope though." He saw the quizzing look on Oberman's face. "Well, hell. You could probably walk right by him and not see him, especially in the snow. We didn't have any dogs."

The agent looked exasperated.

Allen turned to Tom and again asked, "Did you disturb anything?"

Tom was somewhat defensive. "Shit, yeah. I opened the goddamn briefcase. Didn't disturb anything inside. Just guessed that there was at least a mil in there."

"Okay, okay...don't get cranky on me. I got to know these things," Allen said smiling.

"I couldn't get it closed again; locks are busted." Tom looked a bit sheepish.

Allen shook his head. "Frank, how about you and I hike down there. We'll take a look, take some pictures. We have to retrieve that briefcase right now, can't leave it." Allen said firmly.

Oberman nodded in agreement. "Good idea. We'll store it in Camden. We can use a bank vault for now. I'm worried though, if there is someone watching us. I don't want them to know we have the briefcase. It's our only leverage."

Allen, his face wrinkled in thought, replied. "Right, we'll camouflage it when we bring it out. I have a backpack in the vehicle. I also have a tarpaulin. We could go down there and make the briefcase seem part of the backpack with the tarp. I mean, what the hell. Whoever is watching is far away and, even with glasses, we should be able to fool him."

"Get the stuff. I think we can do it. If we climb out a little farther into the tree line, whoever is watching won't see much, and the shadows are deepening." Allen went off to his vehicle.

Allen put the backpack on his shoulder saying, "The sheriff will send a forensics team here in the morning and retrieve the body."

Oberman seemed anxious to get the briefcase into safekeeping. "It'll be great if we can get the briefcase into town without anyone knowing. It's probably the only real piece of evidence we have about this ProAir business."

"What ProAir business?" asked Tom.

"It's a mob pipeline, we think," replied the agent in a matter-of-fact manner.

"The FBI's working with the Mounties on a narcotics and money pipeline using ProAir. It's all mob money," revealed Allen. "But we didn't tell you any of that."

Tom smiled and looked at Oberman, who nodded in resignation and said, "We've been working on it for some time. This is the closest we've come to actual evidence. The agent turned back toward Allen, "Let's get going. The temperature is dropping and it'll be dark soon. Got a flashlight?"

"Yep, here in my pack."

"Hey, guys. Do you want me to stay and help?" asked Tom.

Oberman looked exasperated. "Thanks, but we got a handle on it. Come on Allen, I want to get that briefcase out of there while I can still see."

Allen, his face wrinkled in annoyance, turned to Tom. "Just one thing. In the back of my vehicle I have two coils of nylon rope, first responder stuff. If you could tie one end around a tree here and bring the other end as far down hill as it will go. I'd appreciate it. I think coming back up may be a struggle, particularly in the dark."

"Sure. How long is it?"

"It's 200 feet, both together."

"Good luck down there. Don't get hurt. Sure you don't want me to stick around?"

"No, we'll be okay. Do the rope and then head home. We'll catch up to you there."

Tom went to the sheriff's vehicle and found two 100-foot coils of rope with snap connectors. He hefted a heavy coil onto each shoulder and headed to the slope. He attached the first rope to a stout tree and went carefully down the hill. At the end of the rope, he attached the second 100 feet and took it farther down the hill. There he secured the end to a tree, and looked to where the two men had gone. He couldn't see them and didn't hear anything. He hoped that they were all right. Bandit had stayed with him and they both headed back up the hill. Tom made use of the rope and found that it eased the climb significantly.

"Yeah, this was a good idea," he mumbled and walked to where Dakota was waiting. "Let's go home, Bandit. They'll catch up to us."

45

HE STARED THROUGH THE binoculars. The man and the dog had disappeared, but now the deputy sheriff and another guy were headed down the hill.

What the hell is going on over there?

He saw that the deputy sheriff had a backpack. *What's that for?*

He watched them disappear into the trees at the bottom of the slide area. Then he saw the man with the dog stringing a rope through the trees. *What the ...?*

He looked at his watch. *It's getting late, too dark to see much.* He nervously recalled that he'd have an hour's ride back to the ranch where he had rented the horse.

Several minutes later he saw them again, climbing up the hill in the deep shadows of the trees. He looked at them through the binoculars, but couldn't see anything unusual. They didn't seem to be carrying anything, just the backpack. He got up, untied the reins, and got on his horse. "Shit, I got to get a move on. Come on boy, move on out." He broke into a trot.

46

TOM FED DAKOTA THE GRAIN in the saddlebag and gave Bandit a dog biscuit. He drank from his canteen and let Bandit have some as well, dribbling it slowly from the spout. His mind was filled with thoughts of what he had discovered, and thoughts of the danger posed by the mob people trying to retrieve the money.

"Bandit, I hope those guys don't hurt themselves. FBI man was a little touchy, wasn't he? I guess he's used to running the show. He'll get over it. Come on, let's go home."

Tom tightened Dakotas cinch and untied the lead rope. Bandit ran ahead along the old logging road. Tom urged Dakota into a trot.

47

It was dark when Tom unsaddled Dakota in the barn. He led him outside and turned him loose into the corral with Sioux. Hearing the crunch of gravel, he turned to see Ralph approaching.

"Hey, Ralph."

"So you got distracted up there, huh?" Ralph shook his head in mock bewilderment.

"Well, yeah. I got to thinking of the footprints in the snow and the missing passenger. I had to check out my hunch."

"But why down the shale slide…bummer of a place." Ralph scratched his head.

"My guess…just a guess…was that he didn't have it all together, probably hurt bad, and decided to head downhill, presumeably toward 'civilization.' The natural slope up there would send him right to the shale slide area…and if he didn't know about it and with snow covering it, well, that would do it."

"Pretty good thinking. Whoever it was probably *would* head downhill, seems only natural," commented Ralph.

"Anyhow, I wanted to take a quick look around, figured the bottom of the shale slide would be worth a look. I went down the edge, hanging onto the trees. There's plenty of loose rocks and shale well into the trees. When I got to the bottom, Bandit was ahead of me. sniffing around. He found the dead guy right away. Probably died of injuries from the crash, and I'm pretty sure the fall down the shale didn't help much. Or else…well, he froze to death that night."

"Poor bastard." Ralph shook his head.

"Yeah. A metal briefcase was nearby, up against a tree, covered with snow. There was just a corner exposed, where the sun hit it. I couldn't believe my eyes when I opened it. Had to be over a million."

"No shit," exclaimed Ralph, "a mil?"

"Could have been more. Anyway, I left it the way I found it. I knew that Allen would want to see it right away. Ralph, you got to keep quiet about the briefcase. It could be dangerous for anyone to know about it."

Ralph nodded and smiled. "Damn. You get all the good stuff around here. So someone was watching from over on the hill to the east?"

"As I was climbing back up, there he was, sitting on a brown or black horse. Just sitting there, looking at me. I put binoculars on him but…at that distance."

"That's got to be what? Maybe 300 yards?" Ralph scratched his shadow of whiskers in contemplation.

"Yeah, that's what I figure. It looked like an all brown horse with a rider, but that's all I could be certain of."

"One of the bad guys?"

"Well, probably. Allen says they don't have any mounted patrols out around here. And I've never seen the Forest Service on horseback in these parts. I'm thinking it's one of the guys that've been buzzing around town. That's why I wanted Allen to come up there fast. The guy could easily have rode to where I was and found the briefcase if I had left the area."

"You should have seen their faces when you told them about the dead guy. I thought they were going to pee their pants, right there in my kitchen."

They both enjoyed a laugh. They spent a few more minutes talking about the fence crew they needed. Tom reached into his vest pocket and pulled out the notes that he had made of the needed fence repairs.

"This is what I found out to the peak. When you get some guys up there, have them ride the stretch back towards Sullivan's. It needs to be checked out."

"I'll call around town and get a crew together. Three might be better than two for this job."

"Yeah, I think you're right. If you can find three, that's okay. They'll need a chainsaw, too."

They walked slowly toward the lodge discussing the condition of the fence and the work required. At the lodge Tom plopped into a chair while Ralph went toward the office.

"I'll give Jeff a call," said Ralph.

"Okay. Say hello for me." Tom put his head back and closed his eyes.

48

A **COUPLE OF HOURS LATER,** Allen and Agent Oberman returned with the briefcase. They stopped at the lodge and reported that they had not seen anyone while they were there, but that they had disguised the briefcase as they brought it up from the base of the slide area. Allen thanked Tom for playing out the rope. Frank hoped that anyone watching was far enough away to be fooled by the tarpaulin "backpack."

49

THE SHERIFF'S FORENSIC TEAM arrived early the next morning in two utility vehicles, while the Federal agent arrived in his rented car. Tom noticed that the Fed had exchanged the previous economy sedan for an all-wheel drive vehicle that had more ground clearance than the previous car.

"Nice wheels, Agent Oberman."

"Yeah, thanks. Took your advice."

Allen turned to Tom. "Frank and I have been talking some about setting up a sting operation to smoke out these guys, maybe get us a big fish."

Frank continued. "The briefcase is our trump card to draw out the guys involved in this ProAir thing. The Mounties and FBI would like to know what's going on and who's running the show."

Tom nodded. "Okay. Sure. I already told Ralph to keep this to himself. He will. You can bet your ass I'm not going to be talking to anyone."

"What about Ralph's wife and daughter?" Allen looked at Tom.

"I'll tell Ralph and Susan to keep all of this to themselves and not to mention it to Liz. They'll be okay."

Frank responded, "Good. The briefcase is in a bank vault."

Allen spoke up, turning to Tom. "The sheriff doesn't have any idea who the horseman could have been. He called around. Most likely someone rented a horse at one of those rinky-dink ranches around Randolph. It's too early in the season for a tourist."

50

It was well into the next afternoon when the sheriff's team and Frank returned from recovering the body. The sheriff's crew drove through Tom's ranch and kept right on going to the morgue in Camden. Frank stopped and came up to Tom, who was raking the barn floor.

"Hi, Tom. My, you do good work."

"Thanks, need to keep after it every day." Tom stood leaning on the rake handle.

"Thanks for the help up there. I appreciate your calling us right away. I was just talking with Allen. We're definitely going to put something together with the money as bait. It's all we got."

"Well, if there is anything else I can do, let me know. I'm just hoping that these guys will leave us alone out here."

51

TOM WAS RELIEVED WHEN Ralph told him the next morning that a call to the County had finally brought the inspector to the ranch with approval of the septic system. He had promised to come again in a couple of weeks to inspect the kitchen. The lodge and cabin furniture that Ralph and Susan had ordered was expected in a few weeks as well. Things were coming together and he felt encouraged about being able to open for guests in the spring.

I better sit down and go over the budget, he thought as he entered the lodge. He had avoided the tedious paperwork for some time, but knew that he had to get it completed to make sure that the various accounts balanced. He trudged down the hall, away from the kitchen.

Liz was working with the vacuum cleaner in the lodge when Tom entered and went to his office. She turned off the vacuum, went down the hall and stood at the office doorway, hands on her hips, shaking her head at the chaotic state of affairs. He looked up from his cluttered desk and grinned.

"Yeah, yeah...I know."

"With this disaster area, maybe you can qualify for federal aid? Whataya think, huh?"

He picked up a piece of paper, wadded it, and threw it at her. "Great idea," he replied, looking sheepishly at his messy desk.

She laughed. "What are you working on?" she asked, coming into the office. "Need any help?"

"I'm trying to see if I'm anywhere near budget on these projects. I'm almost afraid to look." He had pencil in hand and was drawing grid lines on a piece of paper. Liz looked over his shoulder.

"Good grief, Tom. You've got the computer here, with all the software you need. I remember my dad ordering it for you. Here ...here it is...in this office software package. It's called a spreadsheet." She held up the box.

"I haven't had time to read all these manuals. I haven't even loaded it in the computer yet," said Tom weakly. "Besides, I've always been comfortable with my paper and pencil."

"Oh, hell. Get up," exclaimed Liz in exasperation. "Let me at it for a few minutes. Go do something. Get coffee. Anything. I'll have this software loaded in no time. It's easy to use. Go on," she chided, pushing him away.

"Okay, brat. I'll be back in a few minutes. Get some coffee. Want any?"

"No...no thanks. Maybe a Coke. Give me a few minutes. You won't be sorry. I promise."

52

Tom went into his cabin. He threw out the dregs of the morning coffee and made a fresh pot. When the coffee maker made a growl and a hiss, he knew it was done and he poured a big cup, grabbed a Coke from the fridge, and headed back to the lodge.

At the steps to the lodge porch, he stopped and placed the cup on top of a railing post. He was none too anxious to face Liz and the computer. He had never been comfortable with computers, used them only when he had to. He casually looked around and inhaled deeply of the aroma of pine. All was still except for the never-ending chatter of birds and chipmunks. His eyes drifted across the treetops and along the steep slopes of Bauer Ridge rising behind the ranch buildings. Suddenly a flash of light reflected momentarily from the cliffside a few hundred feet above him. He stared at the spot but the flash of light did not reappear. He had not been mistaken, he assured himself. *It was a reflection*, he thought, *but of what?*

Son of a bitch! Someone is up there, he thought. *It may be binoculars catching the late morning sun.* He peered intently for several more minutes, but could see no other flash of light and no movement. He knew that he had not been mistaken; he was convinced that someone was up there, spying on them.

53

JAKE TURNED HIS BIG FRAME toward his accomplice. "Shit! I think he knows we're up here."

Sam looked at him. "How you know? He can't see this far."

"Well, he turned and looked right at me, I could see him through the glasses. Oh shit, that's it! The damn binoculars!"

"What the hell you talking about?"

"I bet he saw the sun shine off the lenses."

"Well, so what? Maybe it'll make the bastard worry a little. We're going to have to make a move pretty soon, ain't we?"

"Yeah, the boss wants his money."

"They got the courier's body outa there. What's his name, Joe Solerno? I wonder if they found the case?" asked Sam.

"Nah. You didn't see anything. I'll bet that prick hid it somewhere. I bet he's angling for a big finder's fee."

"What we gonna do? How we gonna get him to give it up?" asked Sam. "Break his legs?"

"No. We gotta make sure who has it before we make a move."

Sam shook his head. "Break his legs, he'll tell us."

"Forget it. Boss wants a low profile."

Sam scowled, "He wants the damn money."

"Yep," said Jake. "The snow will be all gone in another week. We can make a thorough search between the plane and where they got the body, every square foot."

"Shit." Sam shook his head.

"We *are* going to do it," said Jake. "But I keep wondering if Bauer moved it and hid it somewhere else."

"Yeah, well, there's *one* way to find out if he has it," said Sam with a note of resignation. He patted the pistol in his shoulder holster.

54

WHEN TOM ENTERED HIS OFFICE, Liz looked up and beamed. He decided not to mention what he had seen. No need to frighten her, at least not yet.

"Okay, I've got the office software installed. Come here. Look at the spreadsheet program. It should make what you want to do rather easy."

He went to the desk, set his coffee cup down, and peered at the screen. Liz pointed out the office program icons, indicating the one for spreadsheet. Keying on the icon, she had the program running on the screen in a few seconds.

"Okay, let's start with what you have here on this paper. We'll set up the columns and rows like you started to do. We'll make it so the cost accounts summarize at the bottom. We'll put the budget amounts in the next column... like this. Now all of the spaces are mathematically related. See? Right-click on the mouse and you see the formula assigned to that space, or you can put one in there. We can enter any mathematical function you want in each space."

Tom scrunched his eyes in resignation. "Thanks, I think. I'll practice on this worksheet and read up in the book. I'm sure I'll have more questions. The pencil seems a lot less complicated, though."

"You can make a separate worksheet for each project as well...as much detail as you want. Try it and let me know. I can come back and help you after supper if you would like. Oh, by the way, make damn sure that you save everything you do. See it here, the 'Save' tag?"

"Got it."

"I've got to finish up here before supper or mom will be after me."

"Thanks…really. I'll let you know how I make out."

She gave him a quick kiss on the cheek and hurried out of the room.

55

Tom got up from the desk and picked up a pair of binoculars from on top of a pile of magazines and went to the window. Focusing, he looked for the overlook spot on the ridge above the buildings. When he found it he refocused for clarity but didn't see anything unusual. He felt sure they were being watched and that their movements could be monitored from several vantage points. He would have to caution Ralph.

He picked up the telephone and punched in the number for the deputy sheriff. Allen picked it up on the second ring. "Sheriff's Office, Deputy Richards."

"Hey Allen, Tom Bauer. Something strange just occurred."

"At the ranch?"

"Yeah. I was outside, standing by the steps to the lodge. I saw this flash of light, some kind of reflection, from up on the slopes, few hundred feet above me, probably at the overlook off the old logging road. I'm sure there was someone there watching me. I'm a bit nervous. I don't like this one bit. What are they going to do next? They mean to get their money back and they might think I have it, that I took it out of the plane. I don't like this."

"Whoa! Slow down, Tom. There's no point in my going up there now. They're long gone, especially if they saw you staring in that direction. Their bosses can't be too thrilled about them not finding the money."

"I'm worried about Ralph and his family. Susan and Liz are often here by themselves. I don't like it one bit."

"Listen, changing the subject a bit; I stopped a car yesterday. It turned out to be a greaseball from Chicago staying in Camden. It wasn't the same guy I ran into before, not that heavy guy. This one said that he was driving around getting the lay of the land. When I pressed him he said he was a 'consultant' for their company, that some of their property went missing in the crash, or some such story. So I pressed him some more and he tells me the company name is...get this...Blue Note Investments. They list an address that I later find out belongs to a nightclub...The Blue Note...cute, isn't it?"

"Yeah, real cute." Tom wrinkled his face. "This is getting a little too spooky for me. I don't want anything to happen to Ralph and his family or to Karen and Jeff."

"I know you're worried. Our FBI friend and I will be watching them. We'll be in touch and I'll keep you in the loop."

"Okay, thanks." Tom hung up, but he didn't feel any better. He spent the next few hours working on his spreadsheet program until Liz came by.

"Tom, supper's on in a few minutes. How are you making out?"

"Well...it would help if I knew what I was doing." He grinned at her and got up from the desk. "Actually, I am getting the hang of it. Let's go eat."

"See? There is hope for you." Liz smiled broadly. "Not much, maybe. But some."

56

Tom telephoned Jeff again, trying to keep his spirits up. He heard the sadness in Jeff's voice and knew he was having difficulty coping with both his sister's coma and his mother's illness. Tom couldn't think of anything to say to cheer his friend up.

Tom realized that he, too, was thinking often about Karen, and shook his head, as he turned to Bandit, "I hardly know her, never talked with her. What the hell is wrong with me, Bandit? I'm old enough to be her father."

Bandit looked up at him then laid his head on Tom's foot.

"You're right, Bandit. I got to stop thinking about her. What is that old saying? 'There's no fool like an old fool?' Yeah, that's me."

57

NEAR MID-MORNING MONDAY, Tom was working at his computer, busy with spreadsheets struggling to establish a budget for his guest ranch. It had been a quiet morning, and he felt good after wading through the intricacies of doing a spreadsheet on the computer after years of paper and stubby pencil. His mind wandered to Karen. It had been almost two weeks since that the airplane had crashed. The telephone on his desk rang and then rang again. Tom pushed aside the papers and books and reached for the handset.

"Tom! She's awake! She's awake!"

"What? Karen is awake?" Tom's heart was pounding.

"Yeah, I can't believe it. Oh God, she's awake Tom!" His voice cracked.

"That is great news! Did you talk to her? What did the doctors say?"

"Doctor said that she came out of it last night. They ran all kinds of tests today. Doc said that she seems to be all right, no real memory loss. She can even stand and walk with a little help. Oh God! She's awake, Tom!"

"Jeff, did you actually talk to her?"

"Yes, yes. It was so wonderful. She couldn't say much. They medicated her, wanted her quiet."

"Did you call your parents?"

"Yes, I just did. They're flying into Camden later today. You know, the doctor said that Karen was really okay... that she might even be able to come home for the weekend, and then go back for more tests. When she is discharged, she can stay with me, close to the doctors, just rest and regain her strength."

"This is really great news Jeff."

"I'll keep you posted. I'll call you."

"Wonderful. Thanks for calling."

He said a silent prayer of thanks as he hung up the telephone. He ran to Ralph and Susan's house to tell them the news. Bandit joined him in the run sensing some excitement.

58

LATER THAT EVENING JEFF called again and said that he and his parents had decided that, if the doctors agreed, he would bring Karen to his apartment in Elk Creek at the end of the week, and Jeff would bring her back for tests and look after her until she fully recovered. His parents had reluctantly acknowledged that they would have a hard time taking care of Karen.

"You work all day, Jeff. How can you take care of her?" asked Tom.

"Oh, I already got a nurse coming over from Randolph. She'll be stopping here every day for a while."

"Great. You know we're available to help you and Karen. Just say the word."

"I appreciate that."

59

OVER THE WEEKEND, JAKE had drawn a search plan onto the topographical map. He explained to Sam how they would do another search around the crash site, this time using a grid pattern.

"We'll use this grid approach. Let's face it Sam, our first search was a bit haphazard."

"If you say so. The damn snow is still there, though."

"I'm sure the snow will be gone by mid-week. It's been fairly warm. When the snow is gone we can do a detailed search of the whole area. I bought these binoculars today; they're pretty powerful. We'll use it to check every damn square foot of the rocky slope. It sure beats trying to walk on it."

"Damn straight! One slip and you gonna break a leg or worse." Sam had his face distorted in exasperation. "What a way to make a living."

Jake then called his boss, Frankie, who, other than being irritable and impatient, had given approval to proceed with the plan.

Frankie interjected, "I have a 'consultant' looking around in Camden. He's a guy with previous 'government experience,' out there to assess the appropriateness of other options in this little operation of ours."

"Frankie, we can deal with it," said Jake sounding a little defeated.

"Look, I'm getting lots of pressure to get the money back. But there is a big risk here if we get careless. I just want to know what options we have, things that maybe we haven't thought of."

"Okay. You want us to look him up?"

"No. Sal will look *you* up if he needs anything. You two go and work the plan you got. Give me a call every evening; keep me up to date. Okay?"

"Sure, we'll do that, Frankie. Be talking to you." Jake turned to Sam when he hung up the telephone. "Son of a bitch," Jake spat.

"What...What?" exclaimed Sam.

"Goddamn Frankie, sent a soldier out here to spy around and look at other 'options.' Can you believe that guy? What's he think *we* are, a couple of goddamn morons?"

"Other options? Who's the guy?" Sam looked worried.

"His name is Sal. Frankie said this guy would look us up if necessary. You believe this shit?"

"We gonna do our search plan, or what?" Sam raised his arms in the air in exasperation.

"Yeah, he wants us to do the plan. I gotta call him every night; tell him what's going on."

"We don't want to do anything without checking with daddy."

"We'll work the plan, Sam. It's a good plan."

60

On Thursday evening, Tom heard the telephone ringing as soon as he opened the door to his cabin.

"Tom. It's Jeff. I'll be bringing Karen home tomorrow. I'm picking her up around noon, after I drop my parents off at the airport. God, I can hardly believe it."

"That's great. How is she?" Tom smiled into the telephone.

"She sleeps a lot. Needs a lot of rest and still has headaches, sometimes pretty severe. I was surprised her scalp looks as good as it does. Good thing she's a girl. Her hair covers the scar. She'll stay with me for a few weeks anyway. The docs want to see her a few more times."

"Your parents must be thrilled."

"They are, but we owe you so much. She wouldn't be here if you hadn't gone up to the wreck. Karen wants to see you, to thank you and Bandit. Can you come by tomorrow evening?"

"Jeff...well...sure...I'd love to. It'll be nice to see her and really meet her. She knows Bandit, huh?"

"She remembered a dog by her bed. I told her it was up at the cabin, that it was your dog."

"Sure, I'll bring Bandit. I'm glad she is doing so well."

"Yeah, I can hardly believe it." His voice cracked and he paused.

"Okay, I'll be there around eight, maybe a little later."

"I'll tell her. See you then."

Tom's heart was pounding as he hung up the telephone. He wanted to see her. He wondered, *who is this girl?* He picked up the telephone and punched the number for the Stehling cabin. When Susan answered, he told her the news. She said she would tell Ralph and Liz as soon as they came in from their chores.

61

THE SUN FELL BEHIND THE ridge as Jake and Sam finished the last search section below the slide area. They were tired and exasperated at having found no trace of the briefcase or any mounds of loose dirt.

"Shit, looks like a herd of elephants been through here - all these prints," muttered Sam.

"There isn't a thing here," said Jake, bent over with his hands on his knees, gasping for breath. "Bet that son-of-a-bitch Bauer has it," he muttered.

"We gotta get to him, can't wait any longer. Damn it Jake; tell Frankie we don't have no choice. We have to get that prick, maybe break some bones. We been here three fuckin' weeks."

"I know, I know. I'll talk to Frankie. Damn, I'm tired and hungry and I ache all over."

"Yeah, I ain't been this tired in a long time," said Sam, "and I can use a cold brewskie."

"Let's get back to the Jeep. We'll get supper at the Mexican joint near the motel."

"No argument from me." Sam folded the topographical map and handed it to Jake.

62

It was Friday evening. Tom took one last look in the mirror. He had on his newest jeans and western shirt and recently acquired Tony Lama boots. As he left the cabin, he whistled for Bandit, who came at a run. He let Bandit jump in the truck and then got in, started the engine, and headed down the ranch road. He felt his stomach turning and wiped sweat from his brow. "I've got to get over this nervousness. Bandit, I feel like a high school kid." Bandit's ear twitched but he kept his attention at the window. "I've got to admit, I've got some kind of attachment. I don't even know her; never even spoke to her, and I'm nearly twice her age." Bandit looked up, but turned back to the window when Tom fell silent.

63

"**Well Bandit, looks like** we have to park up by the General Store. The place must be packed, a great Friday night for Larry." It was almost 8:30 when he finally found a spot.

"Hmm, looks like everyone's in town tonight. I'll bring something out for you, but I'll be a while." Bandit yipped and then settled himself into the seat.

Tom lowered the windows enough for Bandit to poke his head out into the night air. The temperature was above freezing. *A nice evening*, he thought. The sounds of the band reached him well before he reached the door.

When he entered the lounge, Jeff was on stage singing with the Rustics. Tom waved to Jim, tending bar. Jim smiled and poured a draft beer for him. Ronnie came up behind him and wrapped her arms around his waist, pressing her firm breasts into his back, and whispered into his ear.

"Hey handsome, have you come in here to carry me off and ravage me?"

He turned toward her. "Why else would I be here?"

"I'm off at eleven, big boy." She smiles lecherously.

"Ronnie, you've been *off* for a long time." He patted her rump.

"You don't know what you're missing."

He turned and kissed her cheek.

"That wasn't what I had in mind," she said as she picked up her tray of drinks and sashayed off among her tables.

He looked around; there wasn't an empty table or barstool in the house. He thought, *This looks like a real red-meat crowd.*

Tom took a few sips from his beer. Jeff finished his song and left the stage, heading toward Tom smiling. They shook hands.

"Thanks again for being there. That beer is on me." Jeff motioned to the bartender.

"How's Karen? I hope she hasn't gone to sleep already."

"She's still awake, wants to see you. She's not very strong yet, tires easily, and sleeps often during the day. She's not asleep now though. If the racket down here doesn't keep her awake, waiting to see you will."

"When should I go up?" asked Tom.

"Right now if you want to, but first go get Bandit. She wants to see him." When Tom gave him a worried look, Jeff added, "Just put him on a leash...no one will care."

"Okay, but does she *remember* Bandit? I didn't think she remembered anything of that night."

"She must have had a few lucid moments up there. She *said* she remembers a dog. What can I tell you?" Jeff threw his hands in the air.

Tom smiled and nodded. "Be right back," he said. He took a gulp from his beer, left it on the counter, and turned to the door.

He returned a few minutes later with Bandit. Jeff, Tom and Bandit went through the crowd to the back, along the hallway, and past the kitchen. Bandit didn't react to the noisy crowd, and they ignored him. "Wait here. I'll make sure she's awake," said Jeff as he started up the stairs to his apartment. Within seconds, he signaled Tom to come up, and at a nod, Bandit bolted up the stairs. Tom felt a flutter in his stomach.

64

KAREN GOT UP FROM THE sofa as Tom reached the top of the stairs. *She looks even more beautiful than I remember*, he thought. She was dressed simply in blue jeans and a white blouse that did little to hide her figure. Her shoulder-length auburn hair shimmered in the lamplight. Jeff stood by her side, smiling. *Was that a wig*, he wondered? Some of her hair had been shaved off, where the bandage had been. Then his eyes met hers; his heart beat faster.

Tom greeted her rather sheepishly, his face reddening, "Hi, Karen."

Tears welled in Karen's eyes. "Hi." She paused, looking at the dog. "Is that Bandit?"

Tom released Bandit and he went directly to her, tail wagging. He whined a few times before sitting down in front of her. He looked up at her as an old acquaintance. Karen stooped to hug him and pet him. Bandit's tail thumped loudly on the floor. Karen, tearful, came up to Tom and hugged him and kissed his cheek.

"Thank you for all you did for me." She looked into his face, her eyes glistening. "I can never thank you enough."

"I'm just glad I was able to get there and help. I hope you're mending well."

"Oh, I am. I'll be good as new before long. Jeff is like a jailer, keeping an eye on me," and she looked toward her brother, smiling.

"We'll give her a week or two to rest up and get checked out again," Jeff offered.

"How is your injury? I mean, how is it healing? Will you be okay?" Tom had difficulty putting his thoughts together. He felt his heart pounding. His stomach felt odd.

Karen smiled, "I'll be okay. They did a good job at the hospital."

"You look lovely." His face flushed.

Karen smiled, "Thank you, but you might have been out on the range too long."

They all laughed. He surreptitiously glanced at her a few times, taking in her body from head to toe. *She is beautiful.* They made small talk for a few minutes and then Jeff mentioned that he had to return to the band. He turned to Tom.

"Would you mind terribly if I make you give the crowd a song? I didn't promise them anything, but I'm sure they'd like it."

"You sing in the band?" asked Karen, raising her eyebrows.

Tom tried to make light of it. "I sing with the Rustics sometimes, when I'm in town, and if the spirit moves me."

Jeff didn't let Tom hide behind his modesty. "Don't let him kid you, sis. He is the best I've heard in these parts. They love him downstairs."

Karen came up to him and hugged him again. "You better not keep your fans waiting," she teased, smiling into his eyes.

He followed Jeff to the stairs while Karen gave Bandit another hug. Tom felt strangely close to Karen. Unsettling emotions clouded his mind.

"Would it be alright if Bandit stayed, until you're ready to leave?" she asked.

"Well, okay. I'm sure he'd love it," he smiled and nodded. "Bandit...Stay." Bandit looked up at Karen and then at Tom, settling onto the rug, his head on his paws.

Jeff and Tom descended the stairs and into the lounge. Tom stood at the end of the bar and kidded with Ronnie while Jeff went onto the stage. At the end of the song Jeff introduced Tom and nodded at the band, and suggested that Tom sing the Hank Williams' number, *"Take These Chains From My Heart."*

The boisterous crowd applauded as Tom went onto the stage. The Levis, boots and a western plaid shirt Tom was wearing was in sharp contrast to the stylish western garb worn by the regular band members. Tom moved to the floor microphone and picked up the lyrics to the first stanza as the fiddle introduction ended.

"Take these chains from my heart..."

The din abated somewhat as the crowd listened to the timbre and emotion that Tom carried to the close of the first stanza. As the second verse began, a hush fell through the room.

Many looked toward the stage with glistening eyes as the stanza ended. They saw Tom step back from the microphone stand and the guitar move forward. The refrain began.

Karen quietly entered the lounge from the hallway. As the guitar played the refrain, she slowly climbed the steps to the stage. Jeff looked at her in a double take, surprised and concerned.

Tom was suddenly aware of her presence, of her moving toward him. As the refrain ended, he moved to the microphone. He felt her hand on his waist as she steadied herself next to him. Tom and Karen continued together into the third stanza.

The powerful delivery and a perfection of harmony held everyone spellbound; even the waitresses turned toward the stage. Tears wet Karen's face during the fourth stanza. The timbre in Tom's voice, the perfect harmony, and the strain of emotion on both of their faces did what no recording could have done in this crowd. As the last fiddle and guitar note faded away, it became quiet, before the audience erupted in a clamor of clapping, whistles and vocal ovations.

Jeff moved in to help Karen from the stage and they disappeared down the hallway to the apartment. Tom thanked the crowd and left the stage to take refuge at the end of the bar. His heart pounded.

Ronnie placed a beer in front of him. "Have a fresh one; I tossed your old one."

Tom let his breath out slowly. "Appreciate it."

"That was wonderful, both of you," she said into his ear over the din of the crowd.

He turned and smiled at her.

Larry had come out of the kitchen and had seen the performance. He now came over to Tom. "That was just great. Both of you."

"Happy to do it," replied Tom. "Karen surprised me, too. I never expected it. She was marvelous."

Larry nodded and went back to the kitchen. Jeff reappeared from the hallway and nudged Tom. He suggested that Tom go see Karen and get Bandit because she was exhausted and should go to sleep. He then mounted the stage and joined the band as they finished a bluegrass instrumental. Tom took a long swig from his beer and went down the hallway to the apartment stairwell.

65

TOM KNOCKED AT THE DOOR twice before he heard Karen reply, "Come on up, it's okay." Bandit, tail wagging, looked down at him as he climbed the stairs. A wet tongue lapped at his face when he reached the top and Tom hugged and petted his dog. Karen stood by the sofa, a smile on her face. Tom moved toward her, and Karen tearfully went into his arms. "I owe you my life." He held her as she cried softly. She looked up at him, "Was it horrible up there?"

He couldn't find words. He moved his head up and down several times.

She bit her lower lip, as she tried to stop from crying. Tears continued to well in her eyes. "Those people, their families, I don't remember hitting. I...I don't remember."

"No one saw it coming in that storm."

"I remember Bandit, though. I must have been awake for at least a few seconds. I remember he licked my face."

"Sounds like him. He's a kisser, as you could see."

She laughed, looked in Tom's eyes and smiled. She asked him to sit on the sofa. As they settled on the cushions, Bandit came up and nuzzled her. She petted him, bent over and kissed his head.

"You were wonderful on stage, Karen."

"I took my cue from you. You're the *real* artist."

"I just like to sing a few songs, never had any training."

"I had to come down and hear you. But then...I don't know, that song has always been special to me. I just wanted to join you."

"It was an honor."

"The honor was mine." She lay her head against his arm. He put his arm around her and held her. They didn't say anything for nearly two minutes before she began to tell him how she ended up on the ProAir flight.

"I got this last minute chance to appear in a casino in Reno. My agent and the casino arranged to get me on that charter flight. I guess the same company that owns the casino owns ProAir. I've only been singing in country music places around Chicago; haven't made it to any auditions in Nashville. I was hoping that the Reno appearance would help."

"They don't know what they're missing. You were wonderful downstairs."

"Thank you," she whispered.

The pleasant scent of her hair and trace of perfume wafted into his nose. He wanted to keep holding her.

"I better go. Jeff said that you had to get plenty of sleep. It's getting late."

He rose from the sofa. Her hand found his, and held him back for a moment. She got up. He touched her face, and then kissed her tenderly. Her response thrilled him.

"Get some rest. I'll see you again."

"Mmm. I'll look forward to it."

He pulled his eyes away from hers, heart racing. He signaled to Bandit and they started down the stairs.

Karen stood by the sofa and watched Tom and Bandit as they disappeared down the stairwell. She suddenly felt empty, as if a part of her was missing without them. Tears welled in her eyes again. The words of the song that they had sung came back to her.

Take these chains...set me free...

Could she ever be free? She thought of her parents, her career, and the friends she had back home. Wasn't that where she belonged? She thought of Tom, and how he had so effortlessly reached into her heart.

66

TOM DESCENDED THE STAIRS in a daze. He stopped at the bottom to gather his wits. He remembered to put the leash on Bandit before proceeding into the lounge. The crowd was boisterous and the place was filled to capacity. Ronnie stepped out from the kitchen door and handed him a bag of treats for Bandit. Tom thanked her and moved into the lounge.

He spotted Chris and her dad sitting at a table against the wall. He hadn't seen them there earlier. He walked over to them, Bandit close by.

"Didn't see you folks sitting here in the shadows." *Did she just brush away a tear?*

"We saw you…heard you, too. That was quite something." Chris looked up at him, a warm smile brightening her face. She reached over and began to pet Bandit.

"How is Karen doing?" asked Al before Tom could reply to Chris.

"She's pretty weak still, but coming along well." Tom looked at Chris. *Had she been crying?*

"Sit down a while, won't you?" asked Al.

"Thanks. I really want to head home. It's been kind of a long day."

"Stop by some time cowboy. You can have some of my day-old coffee." She grinned teasingly.

"I will, thanks…I think." He smiled and headed toward the door.

A stranger stood at the far end of the bar near the door. Jim, the bartender, recognized him as the same bulky man who had been there earlier in the week. He had traded his slick suit for Levi's and a canvas field jacket. Jim followed the stranger's gaze as he stared at Tom. Concerned, Jim reached under the bar and pushed the "panic" button just above the sink. Responding to the buzzer, Larry stepped out of the kitchen and into the hallway. Jim signaled with his eyes and a slight nod of the head toward the stranger. Larry nodded and walked forward to the stranger who by then had turned to face the bar.

"Hi there. I'm Larry. I own the place. I've seen you here before. Are you looking for someone?"

"Passing through, staying in Camden, stopped in for a cold one," he said without looking around.

"Here, have one on me." Larry gave him his most disarming smile, and signaled Jim for another beer.

The stranger turned to look at him, his expression unchanged. "Some good singing; who were they?" he asked, his eyes glancing back to the stage.

"They're local folk, you wouldn't know 'em."

The man accepted the beer, and chugged it down. He nodded to Larry and left the lounge.

Tom and Bandit moved through the crowd shaking hands with several patrons. As they approached the door, Larry reached over and grabbed his arm.

"Hold up a second." Tom stopped and looked curiously at Larry's serious face.

"What's up Lar'?"

"Jim rang me out back, indicated a stranger at the bar. When I tried to talk to him, he just up and left. If we hurry, we might catch him out there."

"Yeah, let's see," said Tom, and they both rushed out of the door with Bandit tugging at the leash. Outside, they looked left and right and just then saw taillights come on and a Ford sedan pull away from the curb. Bandit barked and then looked back at Tom, as if for further instructions.

"Shit...there he goes."

"Damn asshole."

"I'd like to get my hands on him...I'd like to know what's going on around here. What did the guy want?" Tom said in exasperation.

"I dunno, but I'll keep a better eye on who's in the place. We'll catch up to him at some point."

Tom walked toward his truck. Bandit smelled the food in the bag and kept nudging it with his nose. At the truck, Tom put the contents into Bandit's bowl. It didn't take long for Bandit to polish it off. Then he poured some water. While Bandit lapped the water, Tom tried to make sense of the mixed emotions he was feeling.

"She's something, isn't she Bandit?" Bandit looked up briefly. "You can't fool me, blind man could tell you like her." Bandit returned his attention to his now empty bowl.

"God... She is something," Tom muttered.

67

"**Frankie, listen…we did** a search of the area. It took three fuckin' days; we covered every goddamn square foot between the plane and past where the body was, and twenty yards to each side."

"All right, all right…Sal called earlier. He used his old connections in the *'bureau'* to check on what the sheriff and this FBI guy could have found. He tells me that everything brought back from the airplane is in a leased building at the Camden airport. Sal got in there the other night and looked at everything they had, all of the luggage and other stuff, but there was no sign of what we're looking for."

"Yeah, but what about with Solerno's body?" asked Jake.

"His contact said that only the body was retrieved. No other items. He feels there is more to the story though. That FBI dick isn't hanging around for nothing. Something else is going on, but Sal couldn't find out what. He did find out that the agent is from the Chicago OCS."

"OCS?"

"The Organized Crime Section. They may be trying to make a connection here with our particular interests. I'm going to have a talk with the big man. I got to make him understand why we have to go slow. This could get real complicated. At some point he may want to write this off."

"What the hell d'you want us to do?" Jake asked in frustration.

"Well, if this Bauer guy has the stuff hidden so he can retrieve it later, it's still up on that mountain. He probably buried it. I *know* you looked everywhere, but that's the most likely scenario. He wouldn't have brought it to the ranch; too much chance that someone would see him with it or find it. No, I think it is almost certain the Bauer guy has hid it. Before giving up, go out and buy a metal detector and go over that area again. I don't know if you'll find one in Camden. Go to Missoula, if you have to.

"Why are we pussyfooting around with this guy, Frankie, if you're so sure he has the stuff?"

"Until we are *absolutely* certain, we have to keep looking. If we act too soon, we just play into their hands. I don't know why that FBI guy is still there, but I don't like it. I'm talking to Carmine tonight; try to make him see this clearer."

"Okay. We'll get on it with one of those metal detector thingies."

"I'll get back to you." Frankie hung up.

68

JEFF CALLED **T**OM **THREE DAYS** later.

"How's Karen?"

"Good actually. She's been healing well. She doesn't have those nasty headaches like she did. At least not as often."

"That is good to hear. She's doing really well after less than a month. Have you been back to the hospital?"

"Yup. Doctors still want to keep a close eye on her. Her strength and stamina have come back real good. She walks around the town every day unaided, but needs a nap as soon as she gets back to my apartment."

"Fantastic. That's an amazing recovery."

"Do you suppose it would be alright to bring Karen out to the ranch for a visit on Saturday? She keeps telling me to ask you. She wants to see the place, and I think she has a soft spot for you, or maybe it's for Bandit."

"Saturday …sure. That would be great."

"Okay, I'll tell her. Look for us then and thanks."

Tom walked to the window and stared out into the forest. *Sure do miss her.* He thought again of the night at Larry's. Her beauty and bearing, her voice, her soft eyes, drifted through his mind. He chided himself that she was half his age. He tried again to convince himself he didn't want to form an attachment to her, or to anyone else. *But,* he wondered, *haven't I already done that?*

69

TOM SAW THE CLOUD OF DUST as Jeff approached up the ranch road. He leaned against the railing in front of the lodge and watched the car come into view. He had put on his newest Levi's and western shirt and had cleaned his new boots. He was glad she was visiting, but felt the butterflies in his stomach again.

Jeff stopped the car in front of the lodge. Bandit raced to the car barking an alarm. Jeff opened the door for his sister and she got out of the car, looked toward Tom and smiled. On seeing Karen, Bandit went up to her, happily barked and wagged his tail. She bent over and hugged him.

God, she is beautiful. She was dressed simply in blue jeans and white blouse; he looked at her and smiled.

Karen stood by the car for a minute, held in awe by the beauty and serenity of the surroundings. She looked around slowly inhaling the mountain air.

She turned to greet Tom as he approached. "Hi Tom."

"Welcome to Timberline." They hugged each other. He was keenly aware of his heart pounding; he could feel his face flush and felt the knot in his stomach. "I'm so glad that you could come."

"Oh, me too. This is so beautiful," she said. She smiled into his eyes.

"I hope you're both hungry. We're invited over to the Stehling's for lunch."

Karen hesitantly turned to Jeff.

"We'd love to," said Jeff and then looked at Karen. "The Stehling's live here on the ranch. Ralph is the foreman. I think I mentioned them to you."

"Yes, I recall that." She looked at Tom. "It's very nice of them to invite us."

"Come on, we'll chase down some hors d'oeuvres." Tom led the way to the Stehling cabin. Bandit raced ahead.

"This cabin is beautiful. Is it an original?" asked Karen.

"Yes, early 1900s, but with all the modern conveniences."

Susan and Ralph met them in the living room. Ralph grinned broadly, "Welcome, we're really happy you could come. Liz is in the kitchen."

Susan and Liz had been working all morning preparing a special meal for their guests. Liz was at the stove when Jeff introduced her to Karen. Liz looked over her shoulder at Tom, winked and rolled her eyes. Tom grinned, knowing her penchant for teasing him.

Tom and Karen went into the living room. Karen marveled, "The décor, it's beautiful. Is that rug Native American?"

"Everything is authentic. Most gathered over the years."

Ralph joined his guests in the living room. Susan brought in a plate of cubed cheese, sliced vegetables, and several dips. Small talk centered on Karen, although everyone avoided talking about the crash.

After a few minutes Susan called everyone to the dining room. Susan and Liz had prepared a pot-roast with roasted potatoes and carrots and a side dish of buttered peas. They both served the table while nibbling at the food when they got a chance. Tom marveled at Karen's broad smile and noticed her occasional glance at him. He smiled back inwardly. Tom felt Liz nudge him from behind whenever she saw Karen look over at him. Everyone helped themselves to seconds. Dessert was fresh baked apple pie, and ice cream. "You're gonna love this ice cream. I just made it this morning," said Ralph. "Help yourself."

70

Over coffee, Susan and Ralph tried to entice Karen to stay at the ranch for a week, in one of the guest cabins.

"It would be no problem at all. We'd love to have you. The first cabin is completed. It has everything. You'll be comfortable," said Susan, smiling broadly and looking at Ralph.

Ralph looked at Karen. "Please stay. You'll like the cabin. We'd love to have you."

Karen tipped her head up and looked at Jeff.

"It will do you good. A little peace and quiet. You can walk, and it's sure a hell of a lot better than sitting in my apartment," said Jeff as he looked over at Tom for support. Tom nodded in agreement, smiling.

"I can't. I...I haven't brought anything - just my purse," replied Karen, shaking her head. "This was supposed to be a day trip."

Liz jumped in excitedly. "Oh, I bet you're my size or pretty close. I've got all kinds of stuff you can wear that'll fit. Don't worry about it."

Liz saw Karen look at Jeff with concern. Jeff looked at her and nodded. "I can bring anything you need from town tomorrow."

"Come on, Karen. I'll show you what I have in my room," exclaimed Liz as she got up from the table. Karen excused herself and followed.

71

WHEN THEY WERE IN HER ROOM, Liz turned to Karen. "You look worried; it'll be okay. Really."

"I...I don't know."

"Is it Tom?" asked Liz.

Karen looked at her wide eyed, as her face flushed. "Liz, I... I'm a little afraid."

Liz opened her closet and motioned for Karen to look through her clothes. "Tom is okay. Next to my dad, well... he's a very special person."

"Oh, no, I didn't mean...I'm just scared."

Liz, undaunted, suggested, "Here, try these on. Then there are blouses on this side. I have loafers and boots under here. It's going to be okay."

Karen smiled, "Thank you."

72

As the afternoon shadows lengthened, Jeff headed back to town. He had promised to help the Prestons close the books that evening. Tom and Karen stood by the barn and waved as he disappeared down the dusty road.

"You and Jeff have been friends for a long time." Karen said.

Tom turned toward her. "I met him when my dad passed away. Actually, Ralph introduced us at the funeral. Jeff is a good man, a real friend."

"He's been a friend to me, too. Even more than a brother."

"Take a walk?" he asked. "I can show you the place."

"Love to. Can't wait to see it. It's all so beautiful."

He led her down the path past the lodge and to his own cabin. "This was my parent's home. I've modernized the interior some and rebuilt part of the stone foundation. Also, the metal roof is new, used to be wood shingles in pretty bad shape."

"I'd love to see inside."

"Sure."

On entering the main room, she stopped and said, "This is lovely. Look at that fireplace, and that old rocker. I'll bet I know where you are on a cold night."

"It is a good fireplace, draws well and throws a lot of heat. The furniture is old, my parent's stuff; but I like it."

"Oh, don't change it, it's wonderful. I love those wide-board floors - friends back east have them."

"Well, they're worn, need to be sanded and refinished."

"Maybe, but it will lose its character, the history of all who walked here."

Tom looked at her. "There are a lot of stories in this place." He lightly took her elbow to guide her into the rest of the cabin. She reached her hand into the small of his back and turned toward him.

"I am glad to be here," she said softly and hugged him softly.

"It is so nice to see you again," he said huskily.

They were soon back on the front porch and he pulled the door closed.

"Gosh, I wouldn't even leave the door unlocked to walk out to my car at home. This is refreshing," Karen commented.

"We're far from County Road and I've never seen any strangers around here except in hunting season." Tom smiled, "And then there's Bandit."

Karen laughed. "That'd be the high point of his day, seeing a stranger about."

When they got to the first guest cabin, Tom stopped. "This is the only one that's completely furnished. Liz will have it ready for you in a little while. Here, take a look."

They stepped up onto the small porch and Tom opened the door. Karen stepped inside.

"Wow. You have native rugs in every cabin?"

"We do. Ralph has friends in Arizona that make them for us."

"They're beautiful."

"If you need anything, ask Liz. She knows where everything is."

Karen nodded, still looking wide-eyed at the furnishings and decoration in the cabin. "I'm sure I'll be fine."

They continued along the path while Tom described his vision for the guest ranch. As they passed the last cabin, Karen stopped.

"It is so beautiful," and she took his arm. "Listen. You hear birds, chipmunks, buzzing of bees, even the breeze in the aspens. It's so serene." Her face glowed.

"You know, I'd forgotten how it was, until I came back," said Tom.

"I haven't ever felt this sense of peace and tranquility." She looked off into the trees. A woodpecker was investigating different spots on the trunk of a western larch.

Tom offered, "I love going out onto the ridge on horseback, just exploring and wandering around. I haven't had much time for that this season though, with so much going on."

"Yeah, you have so many projects going. Opening the guest ranch in the spring should be an exciting time." She looked at him as his eyes scanned the ridge. Then his attention was back to her.

"What were you thinking?" she asked.

"I thought I saw a movement, but I guess not." Tom thought back to the nervous feeling he had the previous week and the flash of light he had seen.

"Ralph and Susan and Liz...you're all one big family. That is really nice," she said.

Tom nodded, "Without the Stehlings, I might not even be here. They held this place together after my father passed on. They've been the main architects in furnishing the cabins, the lodge, and my office. I'd show you everything but my office is always a mess."

"It's a working office, bound to be a little messy."

"It sure is," he acknowledged.

"I got the feeling they think a lot of you, just from what I saw," she offered.

"We're friends and they're my advisors on just about everything. We are indeed a family."

"I liked them as soon as I met them. Liz sure checked me out ...in a friendly way. I see she likes to kid you a lot."

"She's a sweetheart. We're always razzing each other about something. She's a smart girl and very perceptive."

"I got that impression, too."

"The schools in Camden didn't challenge her, so Ralph and Susan sent her to a private school in Billings. It takes all they can muster to pay for it, but it should be worth it."

"Ralph and Susan, always work on ranches? They seem to know so much, just listening to them."

"A ranching background, mostly in Wyoming. They can both ride and move cows if need be. They're experienced in all aspects of ranch life. I'm the neophyte."

"I like Liz. She seems to have a heart of gold. We sat in her bedroom for a while. She showed me clothes I could wear and talked a lot, mostly about you." Karen looked at him and smiled.

"Liz is like the daughter I never had," replied Tom, his eyes looking away.

The radio at Tom's hip suddenly paged him. He pulled it off his belt. "Excuse me, Karen, I better take this."

"Oh sure." She stepped to one side.

Within seconds, Tom turned toward her. "I'm sorry. I have to go see the work crew in the kitchen - some problem with the new cooking equipment. Could take a little while. Make yourself at home. I'll catch up to you."

"I'll be fine. You go ahead." She smiled and nodded.

"Thanks," Tom looked exasperated. "It's always something." He left her and walked purposefully toward the lodge.

73

KAREN WATCHED TOM WALK away, looking him up and down as he made his way toward the lodge. In a moment, she was alone. She heard the flutter of aspen leaves as the breeze stirred the trees. She sighed. *When have I ever felt such peace*, she wondered? Bandit appeared and Karen petted him. His tail thumped on the ground raising puffs of dust. When she saw the two horses looking at her over the fence, Karen walked to the corral to greet them. Bandit followed, nuzzling her hand occasionally. The horses explored Karen's face and hair with their muzzles giving a soft snort, and pressed their head against her hand as she petted them. She started walking along the old road, then noticed the steep incline. Instead, she decided to sit on a tree stump in the sunshine. Bandit lay down at her side.

"This is so beautiful, Bandit." He looked up at her. She reached over and stroked his head.

"Oh Bandit. What's happening to me? I thought I knew what I wanted. But now?" Bandit looked up again at the sound of his name and then put his head between his paws. The chattering of chipmunks and the rattle of woodpeckers in the trees caught her attention. The breeze wafted the scent of the summer forest to her nose and she inhaled them deeply.

She got up suddenly, and walked toward the Stehling's cabin. Bandit ran ahead. Karen knocked lightly on the back door and Susan waved her in.

"You don't have to knock, just come right in." Susan smiled warmly.

Karen tried to hide her anxiety. "What are you making? Can I help?"

"Just putting on fresh coffee. What'd you do with Tom?" she asked.

"He was paged to the lodge a while ago. He didn't seem too happy about it."

"No, they only page him if there's a problem."

"I went out by the horses. Bandit kept me company."

"Worried about your parents, your mom?" asked Susan, glancing quickly at Karen.

She saw the sincerity on Susan's face, and her eyes glistened. "Yes, it's so hard, knowing my mom is dying. And my dad; he won't even talk about it." She wiped away a tear.

"I hope she'll pull through. Any chance at all?"

"The doctor said that it wasn't likely, but she should continue her chemo treatments. Miracles have been known to happen."

"Sit down. Coffee's almost ready. How is Jeff doing with this? I know he was beside himself when he heard that you were in that plane wreck."

Karen smiled. "Jeff's a good guy. We've always been able to talk. He's handling all this pretty well. I know Tom helped him a lot when I was in the hospital. We both owe him so much."

"He gets uncomfortable talking about that. He's vulnerable, too - a lot more than he wants folks to know." Susan reached for the coffeepot.

"I can't help liking him. I know he's so much older, it's just that..." Karen looked at Susan, eyes wide open.

"Tom's a good man." Susan poured coffee for them both and looked up again. "I think he is a little confused too, about you. Well, maybe not confused...maybe just resisting."

"I don't know what's happening to me." Tears welled in her eyes again. "At home I have my parents, my career, and my friends. It's been what I am and what I wanted. Now I'm afraid, not sure about things. I don't know what's happening." She looked down at her cup.

"You've had a lot happen to you. Give yourself a chance."

Her lips trembled. "I...I didn't want to be attracted to him. I have to go home."

"Of course you do. Your parents, your career...it's all back there, isn't it?" Susan looked at her, but the question hung in the air.

"Yes," Karen nodded reluctantly.

"Is there someone special back home?" Susan raised her eyes from her coffee cup.

"Not any more. Not for almost a year."

"Tom had a struggle some years ago, his divorce when he was back East. He doesn't often talk about it, but he does mention it occasionally. He's not bitter. I think he's just sad."

"Any children?" asked Karen.

"No. That was a real disappointment." Susan's face saddened.

"That's a shame...life is so strange sometimes." Karen stared at her empty coffee cup.

"Tom treats Liz as if she were his own daughter. I guess he misses not having one of his own. He is kind and gentle, but no pushover. She tested him a few times early on, as teenagers do, but now they're the best of friends."

Susan reached for the coffeepot and refilled Karen's cup.

Karen bit her lip and looked into her coffee. "I shouldn't be thinking about Tom. I have to get home. Besides, he's so much older. It's scary."

Susan played with her cup handle. "I'm sure Tom is scared, too. He hasn't said anything, but I'll bet he's scared of what he might be feeling."

"Do you think he...?" Karen looked up at Susan, uncertainty shadowing her face.

"I saw how he looked at you." Susan was smiling.

"Oh Susan...." She bit her lip.

"Just give yourself some space. This place is yours, let it envelop you, you'll figure out how you feel."

74

JAKE AND SAM SAT ON A LOG overlooking the shale slide. The late afternoon sun had just dropped over the crest of the ridge. They had spent the whole day retracing their steps of the previous week, this time scanning the ground with a metal detector. Jake carried the equipment and Sam occasionally dug into the ground with a spade. They had bought the metal detector and spade at an Army-Navy Surplus store, not far from their motel. After a half-hour of use, Jake had mastered the operation. Now, sitting on the log, Sam lit a cigarette and vented his frustration.

"It ain't here! It just ain't here! We woulda found the goddamn thing. It's so big, it would have knocked the detector outa your hand."

"This is depressing. You're right, though. There's no way we would have missed it. All we got is three rifle shells, a busted hunting knife, a rusted bucket, and an old belt buckle. Frankie is gonna love this." Jake shook his head and looked at Sam in exasperation.

"Maybe he hid it up by the plane, or maybe around that old cabin somewhere. I guess we could come out tomorrow and check it out. I mean, we got the damn equipment."

"Yeah. That's a good idea," said Jake. "We'll come out tomorrow, unless old Frankie boy calls tonight with some other bright idea."

"Swell. How about we head back. Maybe we can get us a good Mexican supper on Frankie's credit card." Sam grinned and put out his cigarette.

75

Tom looked at Karen across the Sunday breakfast table. "Do you want to take a look inside the lodge? There's a lot going on there."

Liz gave Karen a wry grin. "Just don't go in his office. It's a hazardous area."

Karen glanced at Tom, who rolled his eyes in mock exasperation.

"I haven't unpacked a lot of stuff, but I'm working on it," he said.

Tom stood up and Karen got up from her chair. "We'll be in the lodge for a while. See you later, brat." He grinned at Liz.

"Wear your hard hat, Karen!" she yelled as they left by the back door.

Tom looked at Karen, grinning. "She's a piece of work."

"Yeah, but you two are special. I can tell."

"She is a terrific kid."

"I like her. Liked her right away."

Tom opened the front door and let Karen into the main room of the lodge. "Oh wow, is this ever beautiful," exclaimed Karen, her eyes wide, taking in everything at a glance.

"Most of this I can thank the Stehlings for. Especially stuff like the stonework in the fireplace."

"It's lovely, and look at those beams."

"The whole place is solid cedar logs, like the cabins. We got some craftsmen in from Idaho that do nothing else but log houses. We had them all put up in one season."

Karen stood in the middle of the room admiring the fireplace, then the beam ceiling.

"Susan and Ralph are still working on the furnishings and decorations. We'll have it all done by autumn."

"You think that you can open for guests next spring?" asked Karen.

"That's the plan. I sure hope to. Here, let's start at the kitchen end." Tom led her out of the main room and into the entry to the big kitchen. Several men were working there; plumbing and electrical material lay on the floor.

"Wow, all stainless. This is a huge kitchen." Karen was wide-eyed.

"Let's stay out of their way," and he guided her with a touch to her arm back into the hallway and past the big dining area. He pointed out the bedrooms and baths, and at the end of the hallway, the business office.

"Ready?" he grinned at her, his hand on the doorknob.

"Sure." She pushed on the door as he turned the knob.

"Whoa," she exclaimed. There was new equipment and supplies still in boxes stacked on the floor, the desk covered in paperwork and books piled in various places.

"Liz tried to warn you." Tom face started to turn red.

Karen looked closely at the unopened boxes of equipment, bending over to check the labels on those on the floor.

"It wouldn't be hard to get this stuff hooked up and working."

Tom rolled his eyes toward the ceiling. "I just haven't had time to look at all the manuals and read all that stuff. Liz might help me when she gets time."

"I have a booking agent, but I do all my own business stuff. I use this kind of equipment. It wouldn't be hard for us to get all these things out of boxes and hooked up. Wouldn't take too long, either."

He tried to dismiss the offer with a wave. "You should just rest and enjoy your time. I'll get to this eventually."

"I'd be happy to help you, make me feel useful. It really wouldn't take that long." She looked at him. "Besides, it'll give me something to do, something to make me feel useful."

"Well, if you want to. But, why not just relax?"

"Oh Tom, I'd like to be useful...do something...okay?"

Tom blushed. "Thanks, I'm not very handy at this stuff."

Karen smiled and started to open one of the boxes. Once they got started opening boxes and looking at instruction manuals, they began to kid each other about their computer prowess, or in Tom's case, the lack of it.

Tom looked at his watch. "Wow, almost noon."

Liz appeared, looking for them to come for lunch. "Good grief. This stuff ever gonna work?" She stood in the doorway, hands on her hips.

"Sure," said Karen, "Tom's getting the hang of it." She poked Tom in the ribs. "Aren't you, Tom?"

"Uh, yeah...I think." Tom gave Liz a perplexed look.

Liz shook her head. "You guys better come eat."

76

In mid afternoon, Tom, Karen and Bandit hiked into the forest along the old logging road, ascending to the cliff edge behind the ranch. Tom left the main road and led Karen on an almost hidden path that was a short walk to a cliff offering a view of the pastures to the south and the ranch buildings that were now several hundred feet below them. It was a picturesque place, one where Tom went occasionally to spend a quiet hour. He had been there a few days earlier looking for telltale signs of anyone spying on them, but had found nothing. He looked again for any sign of someone having been there but everything appeared normal. The rock shelf afforded a comfortable place to sit. They ate from a bag of snacks and talked. Bandit found a comfortable spot, lay down, and put his head between his paws.

Tom succumbed to Karen's subtle prompting and talked about his early marriage, of the diverging careers, of their eventual divorce. He mentioned that there had been no children, and frowned.

"Liz really likes you."

"She is special."

"She's got a crush on you," suggested Karen.

"Oh, I don't know...we're pals," Tom said, meeting her glance. "She'll come to me with questions she might be embarrassed to ask her parents or even school problems she may not want to discuss at home."

"She's what, seventeen?"

"Yes. Another year, she's headed for college."

"She's not a girl anymore."

Tom didn't smile, he looked out over the cliff. "I've always liked this spot."

Karen bit her lip. "You know, Tom, I'm really amazed at your singing talent, and with no training, you said."

He grinned. "A bunch of us guys in college got together, got a band going. None of us took any lessons. We'd perform in local places, pick up some spare change."

"What did you sing? Just country?"

"Oh no, popular stuff as well. It's just that I like Hank Williams. His singing pulls something out of me."

"You have a real talent. I know."

His color reddened "Thank you."

"I guess I'm just amazed you've never had any formal training."

"How did *you* get started?" asked Tom.

"I always liked to sing. Church choir, high school choral group, and in local college bands. It was fun, but I was getting more and more interested in doing it for a living, and I felt that country music gave me the best opportunity. I was taking business administration at the time, and I guess that was a good thing as it turned out."

"My last semester at college, an agent heard me at the local club and a month later, he had me at a screening and I signed with him. He's been good to me. He's had some major names in his portfolio. After graduation, I worked clubs every week, four to five nights. I was making pretty good money, or at least I thought so then."

"How about recordings?" Tom asked.

"My agent had me cut several demo discs, even been to Nashville with them. However, so far...nothing."

Tom looked at her seriously, "I can't imagine why not."

Karen smiled warmly. "Thank you. But maybe not unlike you, I have to do my songs in a way that allows me to put my soul into it. I can't do all that flashy and noisy electronic stuff that sells these days. Studios have been reluctant to go along with me. Anyway, my agent thinks I just need more exposure, personal appearances."

"That's why you were on your way to Reno," said Tom.

"Yes," she looked at him pensively. "I couldn't pass up the chance."

"I guess your agent can get you another shot there or someplace even better," Tom suggested.

"We'll try again. I have to get back home. My parents need me, too." She wrung her hands.

"I'm really sorry about your mom. It's a sad situation. Do you have friends for support back home?"

"Uh-huh, there are several I can count on."

"Anyone special? I mean..." Tom stumbled over the question.

"No, not in a while." Karen looked at her lap. "I was going with a guy for a while, but everything had to be on his terms."

Tom shook his head. "A lot of guys are like that unfortunately. More so when they're younger, I think."

"I can't let someone else run my life." Her eyes flashed.

"You shouldn't have to."

"In my career, I see it all the time. I'm sure that my independent attitude, doing my songs the way I think they should be, not always according to the recording studios...I guess I'm paying for it, since I haven't been to Nashville yet. I just have a hard time with it, it's *my* soul." She looked away wistfully.

Tom stayed silent.

"I'm sorry. I didn't mean to put that on you." She looked at him with some sadness.

Tom smiled warmly. "I was a little bit like that when I was younger. I think I know what you're feeling."

"I didn't mean to...to..."

"It's okay. It took *me* a while to realize how alone one can be, if everything, everyone, has to be the way you want it. I hurt a few people before I came to understand it."

Karen placed her hand over his. They both looked off into the meadows below. She laid her head against his shoulder. He kissed the top of her head, inhaling her perfume. She turned her head up, and Tom felt himself sinking into her eyes. His mouth found hers.

Karen idly looked over the side of the rock ledge they were sitting on and noticed with alarm several cigarette butts on the ground. A black smear was streaked on the rock surface just above the cigarette butts. "Tom...look...cigarettes," she barely whispered.

Tom jumped to his feet and went to her side and saw the cigarette butts and the smear of ashes on the rock surface. Visibly worried, he looked at her. "Good catch, Karen. We had a shower early this morning. These have to be fresh."

Bandit growled, a menacing sound from deep in his throat. Tom turned to him and saw the hair bristle on his back as he got onto his feet. "Bandit, what's wrong...what is it, boy?"

Bandit stared in the direction they had come and gave another deep growl. It was then they heard the crunch of a boot behind them. Bandit lunged, but Tom managed to grab his collar and pull him up short. Tom stood up to face two men walking towards them, from about seventy feet away.

"Good move, cowboy. Hate to have to shoot it," growled the man in the lead, a pistol visible in his hand.

77

HE WAS SHORTER THAN THE other, but built like a brick. Tom guessed that he was at least 220 pounds. Both looked to be 30-40 years old and were dressed in blue jeans, hiking boots and canvas field jackets. Their clothes looked brand new, fresh off the rack.

Tom and Karen stood next to each other, Tom with a firm hold of Bandit's collar. Karen gripped Tom's arm as they watched the two men approach to within ten feet.

"Who the hell are you? This is private property and posted."

"Yeah, we can read. So sue me. We've been kinda keepin' an eye on you from here. Nice spot, see who's comin' and goin' down there," the heavy guy nodded his head indicating the ranch below.

"Who the hell are you? What are you doing here?"

The tall thin man kept his eyes mostly on Bandit who was straining at his collar with intermittent growls. It looked like he might break and run at any moment. The heavy man, the apparent spokesman, kept the scowl on his face, and held the pistol at his waist.

"Listen up cowboy. We can be out of here quick and not be back if you come clean with us. Otherwise, you haven't heard the last of it. Now, I know who you are. I know, too, that the lady here was on that plane that crashed back up on the mountain. You followin' me so far cowboy?"

"Yeah, yeah…what the hell you want?"

"Well now, I'll tell ya. I know you got the lady off the plane. Yeah, regular freaking hero, they say you are. I also know that it was you found the dead guy at the foot of that rockslide, and it was you got the sheriff and all up there to haul him out."

His demeanor turned ominous. "Now what I want to know is what happened to the shiny aluminum briefcase that was on the plane with the dead guy? This property belongs to us, and we mean to get it back, one way or another."

The eyes of the spokesman bored into Tom. The imminent threat in the hard steely gaze was not lost on him. He sensed that it wouldn't take much to see violence erupt. The silencer-equipped pistol was pointed right at his stomach. Tom was both angry and frightened. He knew not to mention anything about the briefcase, and the ongoing investigation by the sheriff and FBI. He had kept that bit of information from Karen as well. Being accosted on his property by a couple of thugs both angered him and hurt his pride. But he didn't want to provoke any violence and place Karen in danger. She clung to his arm and he felt her trembling. Tom decided to keep a civil tongue and string them along.

"The sheriff's team and the NTSB took everything out of the airplane and searched the area. I don't think they found any briefcase. At least I didn't hear about it if they did."

The heavy man let out a breath of exasperation and took a step forward. Bandit growled and lunged against his collar. The man levied a threatening scowl at Tom. "Listen up, cowboy. I don't think the sheriff has it. I don't think he even knows about it. You see, I'm figurin' you have it hidden somewhere. But we mean to get it back."

"I don't know anything about any damn briefcase. Now get the hell off my property," Tom replied with more bravado than he felt.

"You hid it somewhere, cowboy. Hid it from the sheriff *and* from us. Well, it's not yours to keep."

"I don't have any goddamn briefcase. Now screw off and get out of here."

"We can be reasonable, let you have a finder's fee."

"Get out of here!" yelled Tom, his face reddening.

"If you want to play this stupid game, you will end up dead. I promise you, people are going to get hurt. Hear me? I mean to get our property back." He glared angrily at Tom.

They all heard two vehicle doors slam from below them. The thin man went to look over the cliff then turned to his partner.

"Looks like the sheriff's car, couple guys got out."

"This must be your lucky day," said the spokesman. "You may not get another." He waved at his partner and they moved quickly down the faint path to the road.

When Tom made a motion to follow them, Karen tightened her grip on his arm. "Tom, no...please...let them go." He put his arm around her. She was trembling. They heard a vehicle engine start and in a few seconds the noise had faded. Tom released Bandit and he tore off through the brush towards the road, but returned within a few minutes.

78

"**Tom, who are these people?** Where did they come from?" Tom saw the fear in her eyes and decided to tell her some of what was happening.

"They're mob guys, Chicago probably. The FBI guy I told you about said that ProAir is owned by the mob through a business based in a Chicago nightclub. These guys are looking for something they say was on the airplane, a briefcase. It probably has drugs or money in it."

Tom felt uncomfortable and guilty, withholding the details from her. But he knew that he couldn't break the confidence he had with the sheriff and FBI.

"Where did they come from? Where'd they go?" Karen held onto his arm and nervously looked around.

"They had to come from Camden on the National Forest road. It comes into a gate to this property about six miles up this old logging road. They probably have a Jeep or something."

"I was on that plane. Tom...I was on that plane," she exclaimed. "I remember a guy with a strange briefcase. He kept it on his lap."

"These guys are looking at me, since they know I was there before anybody else. They think I have their briefcase, but I don't. Probably the guy that wandered off and died out there took it with him and maybe hid it somewhere."

"Oh, Tom. They'll come back. They'll hurt you." She looked at him, her lower lip clenched.

"It'll be okay. The sheriff and the FBI guy are working on some way to figure this out. Sheriff might still be at the lodge when we get back."

Karen held tight to his arm. He felt her tremble. "I'm afraid. I'm afraid for you."

Tom and Karen picked up their snack bags and started back to the ranch. She asked questions about the night at the wreckage and at the cabin, questions she had avoided before. She wanted to know more about this man. Her own feelings frightened her. She hadn't wanted to be so close to anyone, so vulnerable. She had another life back home. She stopped suddenly on the road. Tears filled her eyes. Surprising him, she came into his arms, hugging him. She looked up at him, eyes glistening, and kissed him. She held the embrace for a moment before she darted off ahead of him playing with Bandit.

79

ON THEIR RETURN TO THE RANCH, Ralph mentioned that Wayne and Allen had come by. They hadn't left any message. Tom went to his own cabin to call.

"Sheriff's Office, Allen Richards."

"Tom here. Heard you and Wayne came by."

"Yeah. Wayne wanted to let you know that we really are taking this seriously and working to put the sting together. He wanted you to hang in there, that it'd be a bit longer."

"Gee, and here I thought you guys were just taking turns running to the doughnut shop."

"Gimme a break. What's got you so cranky?" asked Allen.

"When you gonna let me in on it?"

"Not before it becomes real, can't be talking about it yet. We'll see. It might take a month yet before we get the go-ahead from the Feebs."

"A month? You got to be goddamn kidding! It's already been a freaking month since the crash." Tom paused. "Allen, listen. I'm really getting worried. Someone is going to get hurt. I know it. I ran into two of those assholes this afternoon up on the ledge...remember the place...above the ranch?"

"Yeah, I know where. What happened?"

"A couple of goons accosted Karen and me up there. The one prick, the bigger guy, had a pistol. He wanted to know where the briefcase was and accused me of hiding it somewhere. He was serious. He's going to make trouble. He threatened to hurt us; threatened to kill me. He might have hurt us if they hadn't heard your car doors slam shut. They took off then. I'm afraid for the Stehlings and Karen."

"I'm sorry, Tom. The sheriff has a patrol on the Forest Service road out of Camden, but there's a lot of country out that way. What did you tell them?"

"Nothing. I didn't say anything about the briefcase. Said I didn't know anything about it; that probably the sheriff's team recovered it, or it's still up there somewhere."

"Good, good. We need to stall them until we can get the sting organized. I don't want to roust them just yet."

"Damn it Allen! They mean business. Someone is going to get hurt. They want that briefcase. If they *knew* that the sheriff and FBI had it, they might leave us alone."

"Listen, Tom. Hang on a while longer. We'll up the patrol on the back road. I'll talk to the sheriff and see if we can move up the operation. It's all that bureaucratic interagency bullshit. They can't know we have it, or we can't do the sting."

"If anyone gets hurt…"

"We'll do all we can. I'll get on it right now."

"Let me know?"

"Yes, be talking to you."

Tom hung up the telephone. He felt agitated and fearful. He knew that for the amount of money in that briefcase the two goons would probably do whatever they had to. It was a long while before he fell asleep that night.

80

JAKE SLAMMED THE DOOR as he followed Sam into the motel room. "That goddamn hayseed asshole! He's got that fuckin' briefcase, I just know he does." Jake was angry and not at all used to having the likes of some cowboy denying him anything.

"You shoulda put one into the dog, he'da talked then," said Sam nodding his head for emphasis.

"The boss wants a low profile. You know that."

"Yeah, well…if you'da plugged the dog, I bet he'da talked his fool head off. Christ, we'll be here 'till Christmas before we find the damn money. We've been here a month already."

"Shut up. Go get yourself a beer and let me think. I'll call and see what they'll let me do about this."

"Alright, I'll be down the street at that Mexican joint." Sam grabbed his jacket and left the room as Jake picked up the phone.

81

Karen and Liz were rapidly becoming friends. The two spent many hours talking about Liz's plans for school, college and career. Liz volunteered anecdotes about Tom's life, and it became apparent to Karen that Liz worshiped the ground he walked on.

"You like Tom a lot, don't you?" Karen asked casually.

"Yes. He's always there for me. I can't talk to my parents about some things. They're pretty protective so I can't always ask things that might give them a wrong impression. Sometimes Tom's a little uncomfortable with what I ask, but we both stumble through it. He doesn't lie to me. He doesn't take me for granted. He's always respectful." She paused. "Yeah, I really like him."

"He impresses me as being really easygoing. He doesn't fly off the handle, least I haven't seen it." She raised her eyebrows in a question.

"I've seen him angry. It was with some useless guy we hired last year to work on the corrals and gates. Tom was really ripped, but all you saw was the seething on his face. He didn't get vocal or physical with the guy. He just paid him off and fired him. But I heard in town that last year, he and Larry worked someone over one day. The guy was a real jerk who beat his wife and sent her to the hospital a couple of times. I guess he showed up at Larry's where she worked, looking for trouble. Well, he found it. He doesn't bother her anymore."

"I would never have guessed," Karen said.

"Being his friend...it means he cares about you." Liz raised her eyes to meet Karen's. "You like him, too. Don't you?"

Karen hesitated, "I...I...yes. He's so much older than I am though. It kind of scares me."

"He likes you, too."

"Oh Liz, I don't know..."

Liz gave Karen a knowing grin. "I'm not blind."

82

Tom looked up from his brushing when Dakota nickered. He saw Karen walking towards the corral. He admired her elegant stride, one that would turn heads anywhere. He stole a look through the corral fence. "God, she's beautiful," he said to himself.

"Good morning. It looks like Dakota appreciates all that attention."

"Hi. Yeah, he does. I have to do Sioux as well. They roll in the corral dirt and I like to brush it all out every couple of days or more often if I ride them. Did you have breakfast?"

"Sure did. Liz and I sat down for some blueberry pancakes that Susan was making. They were really good."

"I like the early hours."

"I'm going home, Tom, in a couple of days. I've been away from Chicago for so long."

"A couple of days? Are you well enough?" He wasn't able to hide his disappointment. He knew all along that she would be leaving. She had said so when she arrived. But hearing it now was a shock.

"Well, my parents are there, my mom is dying. All my club engagements have been cancelled. I'll have to work with my agent, maybe get some of my old spots back again. My apartment... it's been empty."

"I...I'm going to miss you, not seeing you here." He dropped his eyes and petted the horse.

"We'll see each other again."

He nodded and looked into her face. He felt short of breath. His heart pounded. He touched his lips to hers and she melted into him. They held each other, not saying anything. Tears ran down her face. She hugged him.

They spent the day together, working the horses, raking the barn and in the evening, walking through the meadows.

83

AFTER BREAKFAST AT THE Stehling's the next day, Tom stepped outside the kitchen door with his coffee cup and sauntered to the fence at the meadow. The sun was heating the heavy dew; steam rose from the field. He heard the screen door close, but dismissed it until he heard a footstep behind him. Karen came up to him and wrapped her arms around him. He felt her body tight against him. He turned to face her, pulling her against him, his hands running down her back. He felt her tremble as she turned her face up to him.

"Tom, can we ride the horses up to Timberline Cabin? Stay there overnight?" Her voice was just above a whisper. She looked into his eyes. "Please?"

He didn't want to refuse her anything, but he hesitated. "We met those bad guys up that way the other day; it might not be safe."

She pressed herself to him, her arms tight around him. "Susan said that maybe you wouldn't want to go. But I want so much to see where you and I were that first night, that cabin where I met Bandit. Can't we please go? Would they bother us again? Bandit would be with us."

"They are still around, Karen, still wanting to get whatever it is they lost, and they're attention is on me now. There is a real danger they might come after us again." Tom was serious, his voice firm. "I don't want anything to happen to you."

She looked into his eyes. "I know, but it would mean so much to me," she said softly.

Slowly a grin formed at the corners of his mouth. She suddenly smiled.

Tom shook his head. "How can I refuse you? I hope I don't regret this."

"Oh thank you...thank you." She kissed him.

"Okay, okay. I'll pack and get the horses ready." He looked at her and shook his head.

"I'll get a few things. I'll be right back." She smiled as she darted off to her cabin. He saw the look and demeanor of contentment come over her. He smiled inwardly, glad he could make her happy so easily.

Tom had Sioux and Dakota saddled, and food packed away in extra big saddlebags by the time Karen returned to the corral. He decided that it would be prudent to take his Winchester carbine, and he had slipped it into the scabbard.

"What's that?" asked Tom, pointing to a canvas bag that bulged.

"It's a laundry bag. I put my stuff in it, thought it would be easier to take with us. Don't scowl, a girl has to have her stuff."

Tom rolled his eyes. "Sure. We'll tie it across your saddlebag. Here, let me get it."

He took the bag from her and was startled at the weight. "Good grief, what all you have in there?"

Karen smiled, "Just a few things."

"Probably the kitchen sink, too," he mumbled as he shook his head and swung the canvas bag across the saddlebags on Sioux and secured it with the leather thongs. When they were ready, Tom went to help Karen mount Sioux, but she swung into the saddle in a smooth form and movement. Tom admired the way she filled out her jeans, and let his eyes linger on her thighs.

"I haven't been on a horse in a couple of years, but I rode western saddle out at a friend's farm in Iowa many times." She grinned at him. "I'll be able to keep up with you."

"It's a really nice ride up on the ridge. You'll like it."

"I'm sure. It's a beautiful morning."

Karen stared at his saddle. "Why do you have that?" nodding toward the carbine.

"In case we run into trouble."

She looked at him, her brow wrinkled. "You really think...?"

"Just a precaution," said Tom cautiously. "Bandit will let us know if anyone is up there."

Karen glanced at Tom, then shook her head. "I'm not going to worry about it, not until I have to. I really want to see that cabin."

Tom whistled for Bandit, who tore around the side of the barn and, with a couple of barks, was off up the logging road. He seemed to know where they were going and was soon out of sight in the forest.

They rode side by side up the old road, chatting about life on the ranch, about what he expected during the next season and the impending arrival of guests. Tom admitted some apprehension on his part, but with the help of Ralph and Susan, felt that everything would go fine, "I hope," he added. Karen agreed; she couldn't think of any reason why the ranch wouldn't be a huge success. She praised the work that had been done to make it into a rustic and beautiful place.

"You know, it may not be for everybody," Tom said. "I wanted a place of beauty and serenity, a place where people could come and enjoy horseback riding and chasing cows."

"I guess some will come expecting more of a resort," suggested Karen. "They'll be hard to please."

"Well, I hope those people stay home. I'm going to be explicit in my brochure and Internet site. I'm going to emphasize that this place is best suited to those wanting horseback experience or just some peace and serenity, without the trappings of a resort. You have a point though. I guess I should be ready for those who don't see what they want when they get here."

"You can't make everybody happy, but I bet most people that come here won't want to leave." She looked at him. "I think I know how that might feel." She quickly turned her head away.

From slightly behind, he looked at her. He admired her svelte form and smooth movement. She had beauty and poise. He felt an ache in his heart when he thought of her leaving. He wanted her with him, to stay.

Karen turned and looked at Tom. "What do you think about putting in a hot tub? I think many of the guests would welcome that at the end of the day if they're sore from riding."

"You know, Susan brought that up a while ago. I just haven't given it a lot of thought."

"They *are* expensive and cost money to keep heated."

"Yeah, I know. But you might be right. I should ask Ralph about having one installed. I'll bring it up tomorrow."

Her eyes, as well as her voice, caressed his senses. What magic was she working in him? How could he let her go? And yet, he knew that she had to go home, and he couldn't stop her from that.

She turned toward him again. "What are you going to do for horses? You have to have a good string of them, don't you?"

"Ralph has a friend out by Billings who raises and trains horses. He'll have them bring up a string with a couple of wranglers. They'll stay here over the season."

"Well, that sounds like a good way to go."

They rode quietly for a few minutes, lost in their thoughts. Then she turned toward him again "Say, is there any news from Allen on those bad guys?"

He shook his head vehemently, "Haven't heard a word. I don't know what he and the Feds are up to…if anything. They sure know how to irritate me." Tom scowled.

"Do you think anything will come of it? Maybe they'll give up and go away." Karen sounded hopeful.

"I think those guys are mob muscle, sent here to retrieve what was on the airplane. They're probably afraid to go back without it. They will be dangerous if they don't get what they're looking for."

"You know, I remember there was a guy on board, had a metal briefcase with him. Is he the fellow you found, the dead man at the bottom of the hill?"

"Yes, he's the missing guy. The sheriff's men recovered the body and took him into Camden."

"And these guys are looking for that briefcase?"

"That's what they say. No one's seen it. It may still be up there." Tom averted his eyes and avoided looking at her.

"Drugs?" Karen asked.

"Could be," Tom shrugged. "A briefcase could hold a lot of it, worth a huge amount of money. The sheriff's team scoured the place. I can't imagine they would miss something like a metal briefcase. I'll have to ask Allen about it."

"Those guys were looking to blame you the other day... scary guys." She bit her lip.

"Don't think about it, Karen. It'll all work out. The sheriff and the Feds, they'll figure out what to do with these guys."

84

They stopped their horses at the Forest Service gate. Tom dismounted and discovered the locks were broken again.

"I guess this is from our visitors the other day,"

"I hope they're gone." Karen looked around and began to fidget in the saddle.

When they arrived at the cabin, the first thing they noticed was that the blanket closet had been rifled. The storage pantry for dry goods and cans had also been disturbed, with things on their side. An empty whiskey bottle and numerous cigarette butts were on the table.

Karen looked at Tom with concern.

"It'll be okay. Bandit will be sure to let us know if company is coming. I'll take care of the horses and bring the stuff in. Be back in a few minutes."

Karen turned to go outside but stopped to look around the cabin. She saw the rustic furnishings, the bunk beds, the potbelly stove, and realized that she had spent her first night with Tom here. A flash of memory recalled Bandit's face looking at her and Tom sitting by the bunk bed. She went to the nearest bed and sat on it. She began to shiver. She wiped away a tear, got up and went around the room touching things.

85

OUTSIDE, SHE WENT TO TOM, who was unloading a saddlebag, and wrapped her arms around him, pressing her face against his back.

"Karen?"

"I'm okay. Here, let me help with that," and she took her canvas bag from him and went into the cabin. Tom hobbled the horses and brought in the saddlebags. Bandit started to come into the cabin when Tom opened the door.

"Bandit, stay. I need you out here." He reached down to pet him. Bandit settled into the soft grass growing along the cabin wall where the sun reached for at least a few hours each day.

Tom put the bags on the far bed and then retrieved a folded tarpaulin that had been left on the upper bunk. That was Ralph's contribution to a hunting party of mixed company where a curtain had to be improvised between the couples. Karen watched as he moved a chair around to stand on, and hang the tarp on old nails protruding from one of the beams.

She looked up at him and smiled while he hung the last eyelet. "Cute, kind of stylish."

Tom seemed a little embarrassed. "I had forgotten that there wasn't a wall between the bunks. It's a good thing this tarp was still here."

"I'll say. We can't have people talking, now can we?" She was smiling gleefully at him, amused at his blushing.

He got off the chair and moved it back to the small table by the window. He didn't say anything for a couple of minutes. She came up behind him, grabbing his arm with both hands.

"You're a funny guy, but I like you." She gave him a quick kiss, and went to arrange her things from the canvas bag. She pulled out a small bottle of wine and set it on the table and placed a corkscrew next to it.

"Wine. Wow, that is nice. I wondered why the bag was so heavy."

Karen smiled, "I talked Susan out of it. I borrowed these, too." She put a tablecloth and two silver place settings on the table. She turned to him. "Whaddaya think, huh?"

"That's really nice."

She blew him a kiss before turning to unpack her toiletries.

86

TOM WENT INSIDE AFTER LOOKING to the horses.

"Are the horses okay, tied up?" asked Karen.

"I hobbled them. They won't wander far in these thick woods, but they'll be able to move around and find grass. Bandit is a good watchdog. He won't let anything bother them…or us."

"How did you find Bandit? Did you raise him from a puppy?"

"Oh no. He came into the ranch a couple of years ago, stealing chicken eggs out of the barn and getting the cat food. I tried to get him to come to me but he wouldn't. I could see that he was hurt bad. His neck and haunches were bitten and looked infected. After a week he couldn't run away from me anymore. Ralph helped me capture him. I took him to the vet in Camden. After a week I brought him home and started to tame him and train him. It took a lot of work, but he became a real friend. I think he was run off from his clan. The vet said that he's part wolf and part shepherd."

"I love Bandit," she said.

Tom busied himself picking up the bits of trash left behind by unwelcome visitors, then started a fire in the stove. He laid out the food that he had brought onto what served as a kitchen counter. Karen walked over to look at what he had.

"Susan didn't want us to starve," Tom said.

"Wow, slices of ham, home fries, baked carrots, and there's breakfast stuff, too. What a doll she is." She smiled and squeezed Tom's arm.

"Are you getting hungry? It'll be a little bit yet."

"Oh, I'm fine for a little while. I'll have some of that coffee when it's done though. It sure smells good."

"Cowboy coffee," Tom commented.

"Is that the kind where you have to chew the grounds?"

"Not the way I do it. You'll see." He smiled. She rolled her eyes at him.

87

THE EVENING LIGHT PLAYED the shadows onto the small table by the window. Karen and Tom sipped from the Merlot while enjoying the food Susan had prepared.

"Bandit won't be getting much of this," Tom said

"Oh, don't we have anything for him?" She looked up with real concern.

"Oh, he won't starve. I brought some of his dry food and I'll mix in the rest of these carrots. He'll like it."

"Do you have more of that coffee? It's not bad."

He nodded, got up and went to the stove. He checked the fire and then came back with the coffeepot. He filled both cups and set the pot on the table.

"See, no grounds," he beamed at her.

"I'm impressed."

"My mom taught me how to make it when I was a kid. It stuck with me." He got up. "I'm going to give the horses some grain and water. I'll fix something for Bandit."

"Okay. I'll clean the dishes."

It was dusk as Tom stepped out of the cabin. He placed Bandit's bowl by the door and went to the horses with the water. He placed the feed bags over their heads, and let them eat the grain before letting them take turns at the water bucket. Suddenly, Bandit came up to him growling and stopped, his fur bristling. He was looking into the dark woods.

"What is it boy? What's out there?"

He stared in the direction that Bandit was facing, but couldn't discern any movement or shape in the darkness. He reached for Bandit's collar; he wanted the dog with him. Suddenly Bandit lunged and almost slipped away from Tom's grip. Tom saw what looked like a flashlight beam moving some distance away and receding rapidly.

"Bandit, stay." A low and almost continuous growl came from his throat. Tom kept his grip on his collar. The light had disappeared.

"Someone's been snooping around. Damn, I don't like this. You're definitely staying outside tonight. Keep your ears and eyes open Bandit. Come." He let go of Bandit's collar and after a short hesitation, Bandit followed Tom back to the cabin. Tom picked up the water bucket and feed bags and took them into the cabin.

"Bandit, stay." He sat down by the door.

On entering the cabin, Tom remarked, "We had company. Bandit spotted them."

"What? God, really? Where are they? Who?"

"Whoever it was is gone now. They heard the dog growl and took off. I saw a flashlight beam, but only for a few seconds. They're long gone by now. It's likely the same two we ran into the other day. I don't think they want to meet Bandit on a dark night."

"Are we okay, Tom?" Worry lines were evident on her forehead and around her mouth.

"We're okay. They're gone. Bandit is right outside the door. He'll stay there. Those characters are probably a mile away by now ...headed back to their safe motel in Camden."

"Oh." She bit her lip. "What is going on?"

"I think they're getting desperate to find whatever was on that plane. I just hope Allen and the FBI come up with something soon, give them something else to think about. We'll be okay here tonight. They're long gone." Tom was sure they wouldn't be back that night, but he knew trouble was brewing for him, and it wasn't far off.

88

TOM LIT THE KEROSENE LAMP and put a few more pieces of wood in the stove. They sat at the table for several hours, finishing the wine, nibbling on crackers and cheese they had found in the food sack, and talking. She wanted him to understand that she *had* to go home. Her mom needed her, especially now since she would likely die from the cancer ravaging her body. "I have to restart my career," said Karen. Her friends and family were in Chicago. There were periods of quiet, when she held tightly to Tom's hand, silently begging him to understand. She told him that the past week would always be part of their lives and never forgotten, that they would always be special to each other. She feared that their relationship might well be tattered and that there would be no putting it back together again. When Karen couldn't hold back the tears, she got up from the table.

"I'm getting ready for bed, Tom." She went to the sink and looked through her bag for her toothbrush.

Tom stepped outside to pet Bandit and take another look at the horses.

"Keep your ears open, Bandit. We don't want any surprises." The dog had made himself comfortable in the grass and leaves along the edge of the cabin. He didn't get up.

89

STEPPING INTO THE WOODS, he saw Dakota and Sioux grazing on tufts of grass between the trees. He looked at their hobbles, petted them, and returned to the cabin.

Karen was in her bunk with the blanket pulled up to her neck. Tom turned off the kerosene lamp, and then started toward the makeshift curtain.

"Good night, Karen," he whispered.

"Good night, Tom. Thank you for today."

Tom barely heard her; she lay facing the wall. He went to his side of the curtain, hung his clothes over the back of the chair, and laid his folded jeans on the chair seat. He slipped into bed in his boxer shorts.

Karen lay in the dark thinking about Tom, realizing she had never met a man like him. *So different.* Most of the guys she'd known would have ripped down the curtain and jumped in bed with her. *Were most guys like that?* In the lounge and show business world they sure seemed to be. She heard Tom slip out of his jeans. She smiled, certain he was folding them. *It had been so long since she'd been with a decent man and felt a warm body pressed against hers.* She couldn't believe what she was feeling, the warmth that thoughts of this man brought to her, and the wetness. She ran her hand down her abdomen and trembled.

Tom's head rested on the folded-over blanket he was using as a pillow. He was dead-ass tired, but knew he wouldn't be able to sleep. Not with Karen so close to him. She'd been through so much. It wouldn't be fair to take advantage of her. He shivered and closed his eyes, resigned to a sleepless night. He heard noises outside. Owls and the soft moaning of the wind as it pushed aspen branches softly against the cabin; then another sound, Karen's soft voice.

"Tom...are you sleeping?"

"Not yet."

He heard her get out of her bed, the soft footfalls of her bare feet as she approached the curtain.

"I'm cold," she whispered.

"Want me to get you another blanket?"

"Not if I can get in with you."

Tom hesitated. "I'm not wearing much." His heart raced. *What was happening?*

"I'm glad," she said and lifted the blanket and slid in next to him.

"Karen..."

"Shhh," she put her finger to his lips. She pressed her body close to his. Her breasts brushed against his chest and he felt her nipples begin to harden. Her mouth found his and they kissed, softly at first.

He ran his hand along her side to the roundness of her hip. She was wearing less than he. Their mouths parted and their tongues explored. Karen's hand reached down to the elastic of his shorts.

"Let's get these off," she said and began tugging down on the waistband.

Tom helped her and soon kicked his shorts to the bottom of the bed.

Karen's hand explored where the boxers had been. "Oh, my," she said and began kissing him again.

Tom gently pushed her onto her back. His mouth began exploring her; her neck, her breasts. Her breathing was coming in short puffs.

"I need you...inside me," she gasped.

Tom kissed her lips again as he moved over her. She took him in her hands and guided him between her legs.

"You feel wonderful," Tom said and then neither of them was able to speak for a while.

90

They lay there listening to the owls and the tree branches. Karen's head nestled in the crook of his arm. She was making soft, almost cooing sounds and he knew she was asleep. And then he closed his eyes and sleep took him.

91

Tom's eyes opened in the dim light of dawn. Karen lay propped on an elbow, looking at him. She didn't say anything. Her mouth found his. His arms pulled her against him. The rekindled fire swept through them. This time, they took their time and the love making was slow and tender.

92

Tom awoke again with the sun well up in the morning sky. He quietly slipped out of bed, dressed and went outside. Bandit stood up and stretched. Tom reached down to pet him.

"I guess you had a quiet evening, huh?" Bandit looked up at him momentarily then nuzzled against his leg.

"How's Dakota and Sioux?" Tom started walking toward where he had left the two horses. He found them only a few dozen yards from the cabin. He returned to spend a few minutes with Bandit, petting and talking to him.

Karen came out of the cabin, walked quietly to Tom, and hugged him. She caressed his face and looked into his eyes. "I like sleeping with you," she said, a slight smile played at the corners of her mouth.

He nodded slowly, "It was incredible."

She pulled at his hand and started back toward the cabin. "What's a girl gotta do to get some breakfast around here?"

He grinned. "I'll get right on it."

Tom stirred the fire in the stove to life, and soon was able to heat a couple slices of ham. There was still some bread and coffee to complete their meal. Karen looked at him across the table.

"This is such a beautiful little place. I love it." She reached over and placed her hand on his, looking at him. "I will see you again."

He smiled thinly. "I'm glad."

She stood up, put her arms around his neck and kissed him, then started to pick up the dishes.

Tom got up. "I'll water the horses and get them saddled up. I'll be back in a few to pack up."

93

KAREN WAS SUDDENLY GLAD to have a few minutes alone to get a grip on her emotions. It was agonizing having to part from Tom, and she felt guilty with the thought of hurting him. She knew she had to go back, that it was the only thing she could live with. Her mother was not likely to live out the year.

"I have to be there. I have to," she murmured.

How could she not be there with them, with her father in such deep despair? She had received several calls from her agent, and knew that she would have to rebuild her career. But yet, pulling herself away from the ranch, from Tom and Bandit, and the other people who had entered her life, would be most difficult.

"God, I'm going to miss them." She wiped her eye with the back of her hand.

Karen realized just how much everyone had come to mean to her.

94

THEY DIDN'T TALK MUCH as they started back toward the ranch. Tom's eyes were watchful, alert for danger from intruders. They stopped at the Forest Service gate, where Tom dismounted. The gate was hanging open, broken padlocks discarded on the ground. Tire tracks led into the forest beyond. He was glad that Bandit had been with them during the night.

Tom tried his small radio, not sure that it would work. "Ralph? Ralph, you copy?"

He called a few more times before Ralph answered. "Go ahead, Tom. I was just splitting some wood. I barely heard you call."

"We're starting back now, Ralph. There are still weird things going on up here."

"What? Did you have trouble?"

"I'm at the gate now and the locks are broken again, lying on the ground. Tire tracks, going off into the Forest Service land. Last night when I was out taking care of the horses, I saw a flashlight beam back in the woods. I didn't let Bandit go after them. They hightailed it out of here, though. Someone had been in the cabin also. They left crap lying around."

"I'm glad they didn't bother you. I'm going to call Allen right away, not that it'll do any good."

"Yeah, call him. You're right though. I don't know what, if anything, he and the Fed are up to. It's pretty frustrating."

"Okay, see you when you get back."

95

"Tom," she hesitated, "Are...are you going to be in danger now? Are they going to come after you?"

Tom shook his head. "It's hard to tell. These characters seem pretty determined to get back whatever they lost."

Tom felt some relief that Karen would not be here and in danger while the situation played itself out. He knew he was going to miss her, more than he had ever thought possible. He looked at her. She met his eyes. He reached over to her, and she took his hand, squeezing it momentarily. She smiled, and then coaxed her horse forward. He didn't try to keep up with her. He would give her the space she seemed to need.

96

KAREN WAS AT THE CORRAL when Dakota and Tom trotted into view. He stopped his horse next to hers and loosened the cinch on both horses. Karen was at the corral fence, looking out toward the meadows. As he came up behind her, she turned and came into his arms. Ralph came into the corral, and quietly took the two horses to feed and water. She kissed him, tears wetting her face. He held her tightly.

"God, I'm going to miss you," she said softly.

"I wish I could keep you here."

She looked into his face. "I'll see you again. I believe that."

"Just to know you; it's been so wonderful for me...and Bandit, too."

Tears ran done her face. "You'll always be part of me, and this place, too."

"I love you, Karen."

"Oh Tom, that's what makes it so hard. I love you, too."

97

It was almost a half-hour later that Karen and Tom arrived at the Stehling's kitchen door. Susan and Liz had prepared an early supper so that Karen could get into town in time for Jeff to drive her to the Camden airport. Liz tried to keep the mood upbeat, but parting had brought sadness to each of them. The forced smiles didn't help.

Ralph looked up. "Karen, we are immensely happy that you were able to spend a week with us and that we got to know you."

Susan added her sentiments. "You are very special to us. Please come back."

Liz looked at Karen. "Yeah, don't stay away. Come back."

Karen spoke, her lip quivering. "I'll never forget you folks, and all that you've done for me." She wiped a tear with the back of her hand. "Leaving you is very difficult. Part of me wants to stay here. But, I have to do this…I don't know what else I can do."

Susan and Karen hugged each other, tears flowing from both. She hugged and kissed Ralph and thanked him for the hospitality. She embraced Liz and promised to write. Tom picked up Karen's few belongings and they walked purposefully to the truck. Bandit jumped into the truck and they headed away from the ranch.

98

THE DRIVE INTO ELK CREEK was sad for both of them. They tried to make some small talk to ease the tension, but soon gave up. There were no smiles. Karen's cheek glistened with tears.

"What are your immediate plans, when you get back?"

"I have to sit with my agent, figure out where to start to get some bookings." She stared out of the window.

"Are you okay to fly again?" he asked.

"I am nervous about it. I think I'll be okay though...I'll just have to be."

"You don't have to get on that plane."

"Yeah, I do."

99

JEFF WAS WAITING IN HIS CAR in front of Larry's.

"Karen, we have to get going if we're going to make that Chicago flight," said Jeff, picking up Karen's bag.

Karen wrapped her arms around Tom. "I will write, I promise."

"I will, too." He held her tightly.

"We have to get going. Sorry, but we don't have much time," said Jeff, looking uncomfortable.

Karen and Tom hugged and kissed each other. Karen then bent down and hugged Bandit. She dashed for the car, and Jeff pulled away.

Tom and Bandit watched the car disappear down the street toward Camden. He looked at Larry's doorway. "Let's go home Bandit."

100

TOM PULLED HIS TRUCK IN front of the fuel pumps at Al's Automotive. He got out as Chris came from the service bay smiling broadly.

"Hi, cowboy. Fill it up?" She reached in the window to pet Bandit.

"Sure, it's about empty."

"How ya been, stranger. Haven't seen you around." A curious look played on her face.

"Keeping busy. Jeff brought Karen out for a visit the past week." He avoided looking at her as he slid out of the truck cab. He started toward the ancient soda cooler at the side of the building.

"Chris, want a soda?" he yelled back to her, as he reached for coins in his pocket.

"Sure. An Orange Crush would be great." She finished fueling the truck, put the fuel cap back on and jotted down the gallons and cost in her note pad. She hurried up to him.

"Soda? That the best you can do?" she grinned warmly at him, enjoying the look of discomfort on his face.

"I don't know why I even stop here..."

"Because you love it...and we're the only service station around." She bumped him with her hip. "So where's my soda... huh?"

He saw an Orange Crush part way up the stack and pulled it out, opened the top, and handed it to her. "Here you go. What are you up to? How's your dad?"

"Dad is on the phone ordering some stuff we need. I'm finishing off a tune-up for one of the Sullivan boys. Staying busy."

"I came in for some fence hardware. I'm on my way to see Jeff."

"He was here the other day, even got him to take me to lunch." She gave him a teasing grin.

"He's a good guy." Tom nodded.

"He thinks a lot of *you*. Kinda why I went out with him."

"He's a good friend."

"What do you hear from Karen? I guess she got home okay." She looked at him with lowered eye lids.

Tom shook his head, "I haven't heard from her since she left for Chicago. I left a message on her answering machine. Probably been real busy, maybe a little upset. I don't know."

Sadness showed on his face for a moment and then it was gone.

"Well, she's got to be hurting. You certainly are. Give her time; she doesn't want to be crying on the phone with you. My God, you are such a big dummy."

He put his arm around her shoulders and hugged her. "Thanks, Chris. I kinda like you, too."

"Yeah, yeah....Get the hell out of here. I've got work to do." She smiled and pulled away from him. When she got to the garage doorway, she turned around and blew him a kiss.

101

TOM DROVE THE SHORT distance to Preston's Lumber and Equipment and parked nearby. He lowered the windows halfway and got out of the truck. He scratched behind Bandit's ear. "I'll be back soon." Bandit looked at him and then dropped his head on the seat.

There were no customers in the store and Tom didn't see anyone behind the counter. He knew where the fence hardware was and soon had a bag full of gate hinges and latches. Tom dropped the bag on the counter with a loud clunk, went into the yard and found Jeff who was headed toward the store. They shook hands.

"Good to see you, Tom. How you been?"

"Oh, okay, I guess. What do you hear from Karen?"

Jeff shook his head. "Not much. One phone call. And that was when she landed in Chicago."

Tom shook his head.

"You got to be patient. I don't know what all she has on her plate these days, but I'm sure our parents are a big load on her. And then there are her appearances; she's almost starting over, as far as bookings go."

Tom nodded, "Yeah...I'm sure. Say, have you seen any strange characters prowling around?"

"You know, I haven't. I've asked the boys here, but they haven't seen anything. Do you think they're still in the area?"

"Oh yeah, count on it. Until they find whatever they're looking for."

Tom and Jeff walked into the store. Tom signed for the hardware. They shook hands again and Tom left.

102

It was near noon as Tom's stomach reminded him by growling. He had parked in front of Ken's Diner and his mouth watered at the thought of a bowl of Ken's hot chili and some coffee. First, he opened the truck and gave Bandit a drink of water and lowered the windows all the way. In the diner, he sat at a booth along the window, so he could keep an eye on Bandit. Ken arrived at his table with his customary grin and wiping cloth, cleaned and positioned a place mat and cutlery before him.

"How've you been, Ken?" Tom looked up at him and smiled.

"Oh, no complaints. Business is a little slow right now. Having that highway repair crew in here every day at lunch for a couple of weeks spoiled me. But they finished the job and went elsewhere."

"Something else will come along. You don't do bad here. It's a steady stream."

"I'm not complaining. Here..." he handed Tom the morning Camden newspaper. "Take a look at page three."

"Okay, thanks. I'll have a bowl of chili and some coffee."

He found the small article buried on page three.

Chicago Mobster Arrested

Camden, MT - Deputy Sheriff Stewart Anderson stopped a car with three occupants in Camden last night when he observed the driver making a right turn on a red light without stopping. A driver's license check showed that the driver, Vince DiAngello, who was cited, had been identified with an alleged Chicago mob run by the DeCosta brothers. DiAngello had an outstanding Chicago warrant for aggravated mayhem and was taken into custody. The other two occupants of the car were not charged and were released.

Tom enjoyed the hot chili with Ken's own sourdough bread while he finished reading the newspaper. He reread the article of the mobster arrest. He was sure that they weren't going to leave without their money. Either that or they would make their new home in some landfill somewhere. He decided to stop by the sheriff's office, hoping to catch him there. He left money and the newspaper on the table and left the diner before Ken had a chance to come out from the kitchen and start chatting.

The deputy's SUV was parked in front of the firehouse and Tom swung his truck across the street to park next to it. He let Bandit out and they entered the building. Tom walked to the back and saw Allen in his corner office, studying his computer screen.

He looked up in surprise. "Hi, Tom. Didn't expect to see you, Bandit too."

"Oh damn, I forgot the donuts!" Tom exclaimed.

"Yeah, yeah, up yours. What brings you in here? There's nothing new."

"Oh, really? Well the newspaper says that your buddies in Camden were busy yesterday. What's that about?" retorted Tom, not trying to hide his irritation.

"Yeah, they pulled over three guys, all with Chicago IDs. The one guy we arrested, the others we let go. You hadn't filed a complaint with us on the characters you met on the ridge, so all I could do was take names and release them."

"Well, did you question them? What about the guy that was arrested, what happened to him?" The irritation was still in Tom's voice.

"We questioned the guy we had locked up, but he wouldn't tell us anything -- wanted his freaking lawyer. We're sending him back to Chicago today. Their detective arrived this morning."

"Marvelous. So you got shit?" Tom slapped the desk.

"We don't use a rubber hose..."

"Maybe you should."

"Hey, the Sheriff's office and FBI are working up the sting operation. It should happen pretty soon."

Tom looked at Allen, eyes boring into him. "Allen, they want their money. I'm sure they're serious. Christ! It's been what, over five weeks? They think *I'm* in the middle of all this. They're going to come down on *me*! I'm really worried about the Stehlings, too. They're alone a lot, sometimes, just the girls. I don't like this at all." Tom didn't try to hide his anger.

"You should get up to Camden and file a complaint. It'll give us *something*. I know this is maddening, the damn bureaucrats. I don't know why it takes them so long to come up with a plan."

"Okay. I'm headed home."

"Tom, if there's anything going on up there, anything unusual, call me. It rings at home on the fifth ring."

"Yeah, yeah, be talking to you," he said rather brusquely as he left the office.

When he started for the door, Bandit jumped up to follow him to the truck. Tom sat in the cab for a moment, exasperated with the conversation with Allen. Then he started the engine, made a U-turn, and headed out of town. In a few minutes he turned into the ranch gate.

103

LIZ PUSHED THE VACUUM CLEANER down the hallway in Tom's cabin. It made a loud noise. "*Maybe I should ask mom about getting a new one,*" she thought. The cord was plugged into the outlet in the living room, just about at the end of its reach. The vacuum suddenly stopped operating, and Liz thought she had tugged too hard on the cord, and pulled it out of the outlet. She turned to go back into the living room and stopped. She gasped. She wanted to scream, but the sound froze in her throat. A man stood in the living room. In one hand, he held the power cord; in the other, a pistol.

"Don't make a sound! If you do...if anyone comes in here...I'll shoot 'em. Get over here. Now!" he commanded.

A chill went through Liz's body and fear clutched at her heart. She took small steps toward him, glancing often at the gun in his hand.

"Please! What do you want?" She was barely able to speak. Tears came to her eyes.

"Stand over here. Keep quiet and I won't hurt you. Hold your hands out...straight out. Yeah." He slipped a plastic restraint over her wrists and tightened it until she winced.

"Please, what do you want? I...I...I don't have any money," she whimpered.

"I want to know where Bauer is. Tell me!" he said. He pointed the pistol at her midriff. His cold dark eyes bored into hers.

She could smell the sour odor of sweat, could see that his shirt was wet with perspiration. She felt cold fear in her stomach, fear of being hurt or worse by this brute of a man. He was built like a brick, a chest like a bear. What was going to happen? She feared for her parents if either one should come through the door.

"Tom...Bauer...he...he is in town. Went to Elk Creek this morning. What do you want with him? What are you doing here?" Her voice trembled despite her effort to remain calm.

He took a step towards the window and looked out, and then went to the other window to look out. He turned back to face her.

"Listen, kid. Tell me where the suitcase is and I'm outa here. Where is it?"

She looked blankly at him. "What? What are you talking about?"

"Don't play games with me, kid. Tell where it is and I'll be gone. Otherwise, we do it the hard way."

"I...I don't know what you're talking about."

He pushed her towards the kitchen. There he opened the cabinets and the pantry, throwing things on the floor, while he kept one eye on her. Cursing, he pushed her toward the bedrooms. He looked under the bed and ransacked the closets. He pulled open drawers and let things drop onto the floor as he quickly checked the contents.

"Where does that son of a bitch keep it? He has it somewhere." He kicked some of the clothes on the floor to one side. "Get over by the door. I guess we have to do it the hard way," he growled.

"Please, I don't know about any suitcase."

"Listen and listen good. I'm not going to hurt you *if* you do exactly as I tell you. If anyone tries to interfere with me, comes after me, I'll kill 'em and then I'll kill you. Do you understand me, girl?"

Liz gulped, trying to keep her panic under some control. "Yes, yes. Why me, why? I don't have anything."

"Shut up. We're going up on the ridge. We're leaving right now. Do I have to gag you or will you stay quiet? Remember, I will shoot anyone comes after us. What's it gonna be?" He spoke while glancing out of the windows.

"Please, just let me go. Please, I don't know anything. I don't have anything."

"Listen you stupid kid. Do I have to gag you?" He again checked the windows.

"No, please. I'll be quiet. Please, don't hurt me," she pleaded.

He pushed her towards the door, looked through the window, and opened the door. He prodded her with the pistol and they stepped onto the porch. He reminded her again to keep quiet. In only seconds, the forest swallowed them up. He pushed and tugged her into the woods, but she saw no trail. *Where is he going?* She fell a few times as he tried to hurry her. She couldn't balance herself with her hands tied together and she fell often scratching and bruising herself. He pulled her onto her feet each time and pushed her forward. Fear overwhelmed her, but she was glad that her parents had not been about; sure that he would have shot them. And Tom...*what does he want with Tom?* She tried to think, tried to conceive of a way to escape or to warn her parents and Tom. He prodded her again and again, keeping her on a steady climb in front of him, up the lower slope of Bauer Ridge.

When Liz spotted a clump of dried stalks from the past season, she faked a fall into the old growth, falling and rolling.

"Oh! Ouch!" she whimpered feeling a new bruise on her knee.

The man cursed in irritation. He reached down and roughly pulled her back onto her feet. The place that she had fallen was now a mass of crushed stalks of old plants. Her heart pounded. She was relieved that he hadn't sensed her deception.

"Look where you going," he hissed. "Don't try anything or I promise...I *will* hurt you."

He shoved her forward, steering her ever upwards, angling eastward along the slope. She couldn't see where there was any trail or any markers, but continued where he told her. She tripped often over tree roots and stumbled on loose rocks, constantly being hurried along. *Does he know where he is going,* she wondered? Once he stopped and looked intently into the forest. After a moment he seemed to know where he wanted to go. It was then that Liz saw the scrapings on the bark of an aspen, and on more of them as they ascended. He was leading her ever upward behind the ranch, climbing eastward. Liz knew that eventually they would come upon the old logging road, but it would be a long tiring hike. Her sense of foreboding increased as she realized this man would have a vehicle there. Fear knotted in her stomach.

104

SUSAN AND RALPH WERE standing in front of the barn; they seemed to be yelling. Fear suddenly gripped Tom. He stopped the truck near them and quickly got out.

"Ralph, what?" he yelled as he ran to them. He saw the panic and tears on Susan's face.

"Tom! Oh God, Liz is gone. She's gone!" cried out Ralph. He put his arm around Susan.

"Our baby is gone," sobbed Susan.

"What? You look everywhere? Where was she?" Tom tried to understand what had happened.

"She was cleaning your cabin. Vacuuming, dusting. She's not there," Susan said with trembling voice.

"Where'd you look? All through my cabin?"

"Yes, yes. I was just in there. The cabin is all torn apart, stuff laying everywhere." Susan was crying steadily now. Ralph held her, his face masked with fear.

Ralph added, "She wouldn't just walk off without telling us. She's never done that."

"Stay here! I'll be right back."

Tom ran off to his cabin. He leapt up onto the porch and quickly entered. He stood at the door and looked around. He could see the vacuum cleaner in the hallway, the cord lying across the living room floor, but far from the nearest electrical outlet. He quickly went into every room, and saw the disarray. Boxes and clothes lay strewn on the floor. Drawers were left open, their contents spilled. Fear gripped his stomach. He knew they had come looking for the money, and now they had Liz. He left the cabin and ran to where Susan and Ralph stood by the barn.

"Ralph...Susan...you checked everywhere? Barn? Cabins?" he asked.

"Yes, yes, we did, yes," he replied. Fear and panic was on his face. He held Susan's shoulder.

"I think someone took her, Ralph. You take my truck and go up on the logging road. If there's any vehicle up there, stop them. Do what you got to do, but *stop* them."

Ralph grimaced. "Okay."

"Susan, go call Allen." She hesitated. "Call him now. Tell him what happened. He's in his office, I just left him." She nodded.

"Liz, and whoever took her, left here on foot. I'm taking Bandit and we'll go look for her. Susan, tell Allen. Okay?" Susan nodded again and hurried toward the lodge. Ralph dashed toward Tom's pickup truck, started it, and headed up the slope and onto the logging road.

105

Tom called Bandit and they went back into his cabin. He spoke quietly to Bandit, pointed to the vacuum cleaner handle, and let Bandit sniff along it. He pointed to the bucket handle and Bandit sniffed it as well. He saw Liz's jacket lying on a chair and he offered it to Bandit. The dog sniffed it thoroughly. Tom tied the jacket around his waist with the sleeves. He might need it again, he thought, for Bandit to keep the scent. Then they were out the door. Tom stood at the porch, trying to decide where someone would have taken Liz. He had no doubt as to why she had been taken. The criminals, searching for the suitcase of money, had kidnapped Liz. He suddenly thought: *They'll want to make a trade for the suitcase*; the suitcase he did not have.

He couldn't imagine what Liz was going through. He felt rage at the thought of her at the mercy of these thugs. He would have to find her quickly, before they left the area. He only prayed that they wouldn't hurt her. Tom looked about, but the only escape that made sense was up onto the ridge. Anywhere else and they would be seen.

Tom pulled the leash out of his pocket and attached it to Bandit's collar. Bandit sniffed the ground, back and forth, then suddenly pulled Tom towards the forest, towards Bauer Ridge. Bandit wanted to move fast, Tom held him back.

"Slow down, big boy; don't want to run into them. We can't give ourselves away."

He wanted to get close and ascertain some means of stopping the abduction, and wanted to catch up to them before they made it to the old logging road. He felt certain there would be a vehicle waiting. That they had kidnapped Liz was unbearable to him. "Bandit, I want us to get close, but I'm not quite sure what we'll do when we find them. Damn it, Bandit," he bit his lower lip, "we're going to get her back... no matter what."

He was armed with only a hunting knife. He thought about going back for his 22-caliber pistol, but decided to keep going and not lose any time. He hoped Ralph would be able to slow down the criminals on the old logging road. Tom hoped that Ralph's presence on the road would give him more time to reach Liz and plan some sort of action. *They will pay dearly*, he promised himself.

106

"What? Mrs. Stehling, slow down. Slow down. Start over. What happened?" Allen was trying to make sense of Susan's hysteria.

"Liz…Liz…she's gone. Tom thinks someone took her," she cried into the telephone.

"Mrs. Stehling, are you at the ranch?"

"Yes, yes. We can't find her. Ralph and Tom looked everywhere. Oh, God…"

"Is Tom there? Let me talk to him."

"He's gone. He went with Bandit to find Liz. Ralph took the truck up the old road. Tom wanted him up there. Tom told me to call you. Please, she's gone." Susan tried not to cry, but the sobs came.

"I'll be there as fast as I can. Just wait for me. Wait for me. I need you there," Allen pleaded with her, hoping that she would not fall apart any more than she already had.

He hung up the telephone, then connected again and called Sheriff Wayne Johnson in Camden.

"Wayne, Allen Richards here. I just received a call from Mrs. Stehling out at Timberline. She says her daughter is missing. I told her that I'd be right out."

"Missing? Wandered off? What?"

"I guess Tom arrived there a short while ago and told her that he thinks she's been kidnapped. He's taken his dog and went after her. I told Mrs. Stehling that I'd be right out."

"Okay. Yes, go there. Give me an assessment as soon as you can," said Wayne. "If you think you'll need help, you tell me right away."

"Okay. Leaving now."

107

ALLEN HURRIED TO HIS VEHICLE and gunned the engine, roaring toward Timberline Ranch. The somewhat strained conversation with Tom an hour earlier rushed into his memory. If the criminals had kidnapped Liz, things had turned a dangerous corner. Allen realized that the only ready access to the ranch was over the road he was coming to or the old logging road that connected with the Forest Service road high on the ridge The Forest Service road eventually connected with a county road that went into Camden. Allen reached for his radio.

"Camden Dispatch...Mobile 3."

"Camden...Go ahead 3."

"Deputy Richards in Elk Creek. Let me talk to Wayne."

"Stand by." In about ten seconds, the sheriff was on the radio.

"Allen...Wayne here."

"Can you spare anyone to sit at the intersection of the Forest Service road and the county road north of Camden? If the kidnappers get to a vehicle...well, that's the first intersection to stop them in our jurisdiction."

"Roger that...good idea. I'll get a couple of officers out there and stop anything that comes on the Forest Service road, either direction."

"Thanks. I just hope she isn't hurt."

"I guess we know what they want," said the sheriff.

"I had a conversation with Tom just an hour or so ago. You know what I mean?"

"Yeah, I do. Shit! I'll get hold of Oberman; see if he's still in town. I'll get back to you."

"Roger. Mobile 3 out."

Allen hammered his SUV up the rough dirt road to the ranch. Several bumps sent all four wheels off the ground, but he held the pedal down.

108

RALPH INCHED ALONG, LOOKING for signs on either side of the old logging road. His heart pounded. He fought back tears. He could hardly bear to think that someone had kidnapped his little girl. He mumbled prayer after prayer. He thought of Susan back at the ranch alone and his heart went out to her. And what could Liz be enduring? He bit his lip, wiped his eyes with the back of his hand. He looked for tire tracks or damaged brush that would indicate a hidden vehicle. *What is Tom doing,* he wondered? *What will he do when he catches up with them? They have to be armed. What can Tom do against them?* Ralph tried to stay focused but kept thinking of Liz and Susan. *We have to find Liz before anything happens to her.*

109

ALLEN'S SUV SLID TO A STOP in front of the barn. He got out as Susan ran up to him. Tears stained her face. She grabbed his arm.

"Allen, you've got to find her," she trembled as she pleaded. He put an arm around her shoulder.

"Slow down, Susan. Tell me exactly what happened?"

"Liz...Liz was cleaning Tom's cabin, as she does every week. She was supposed to help me clean in the lodge when she was done there, but she didn't come. I...I went looking for her." Susan sobbed. Allen embraced her until she quieted.

"I went to look for her but she wasn't there. I called Ralph. We looked everywhere...everywhere...and then Tom came home."

"What happened then?"

"Tom...he...he looked in his cabin again. He said she had been kidnapped...kidnapped." Her body trembled as she sobbed against him.

"Tom said for me to call you, and for Ralph to take the truck up on the old logging road and stop anyone. Tom went with Bandit, looking for her... or them. Went into the forest behind his cabin."

"How long ago did he start out?"

"It was when I called you, I don't know." Susan looked at Allen. She bit her lower lip. "Maybe a half hour ago?"

"What time was it when you went looking for Liz?"

"I think it was around 3 o'clock."

"Okay, sit here in the back of my car. I want to look around and then I need to check in with the sheriff. Please, sit down here. I will be back in a few minutes."

Susan sat down in the back seat of his SUV. She daubed her face with her handkerchief and cried softly. Allen rushed through all the buildings and guest cabins and satisfied himself that Liz was not there. He saw nothing that offered any clue to who had taken her. When he got back to the SUV, he glanced at Susan, saw that she was sitting quietly, and picked up the microphone.

"Camden Dispatch, Mobile 3."

"Camden, go ahead 3."

"Richards at Timberline Ranch. Plug me in to Wayne again, please." In a few seconds the sheriff responded.

"Wayne here."

"I'm sitting here at the ranch with Mrs. Stehling. I did a quick search. There's no sign of violence. Susan said her husband, Ralph, took the truck up on the old logging road to stop anyone he saw. It looks like Tom took his dog and went after Liz on foot through the forest. The kidnapping happened around 3 o'clock and Ralph and Tom probably took off about 3:30 or maybe a little later."

"She there with you?"

"Yes, here in my vehicle."

"Okay. I'm sending my wife, Jeanie, out there right now to stay with her as long as needed. You stay with Susan until she gets there. I want to hear from you every fifteen minutes."

"Roger that. Have you heard from the Fed?"

"No, he hasn't called me back. I'll drive over there right now and see where he is. I sent a couple of guys out to that intersection. They'll hold that position. You stay there until you hear from me."

"Roger. I'll be here. I'll keep an eye out for Jeanie."

"Okay, Wayne out."

110

Liz wondered how much longer her abductor could keep going. He had called a stop several times. The climb was strenuous and the footing difficult. He leaned against a tree gasping for breath. Liz could smell the sour odor of his sweat, even from a distance. She looked at him, hoping he would collapse. She could see the pain and exhaustion on his face. He labored at inhaling deep droughts of air. He reached down and rubbed his calves, grimacing.

"You don't look good, better rest some," suggested Liz, in an effort to slow them down to help anyone following. *Somebody should be following*, she thought.

"Need to keep going. Got to get up to the road. No resting." His chest heaved as he tried to get more air.

"The road is a ways up yet. You ain't gonna make it." Liz shook her head in emphasis.

"Shut up. Get going. Go on, move ahead." He pointed to where she had already seen the scrape mark on the tree trunk.

Liz noticed that the shadows were lengthening and knew that the forest would darken quickly once the sun crossed the ridge top. The scrape marks on the trees would be impossible to see in the dim light of dusk. She felt a renewed sense of hope, that maybe she could escape from this man. He didn't look too good. How long could he go on? Liz wondered what was happening at the ranch. She knew that her parents would be beside themselves in grief and worry. She knew too, that Tom would do everything possible to find her. She wondered where he was.

Their advance had slowed significantly. Liz wasn't sure how far ahead the logging road was because she had never hiked this part of the ridge. The occasional glimpses of the surrounding country suggested to her that the road was at least 500 feet above them, and at least another hour at their current rate of travel. She knew that the steep and rocky trail the man had marked on the way down had not been done with ample consideration to having to climb back up to the logging road. The slope was very steep with countless large rocks. When she looked back at him, she could see that the big man was visibly struggling to maintain headway. *This guy is no Boy Scout,* she thought. *He didn't bring any water, just that stupid pistol.* They had stopped by a small brook earlier and he had drunk from it. He offered her a drink only once, and that was after she had asked. The plastic ties on her wrists had begun to hurt badly, the skin raw in several places. She tried putting saliva on the wounds, but it didn't help much. She had fallen many times and her knees and hips hurt from the scrapes and bruises.

"Stop. Hold up there," he leaned heavily against a tree. He struggled to get his breath. His face was flushed.

"You better sit down a while. You look bad."

"Shut up and don't get any smart-ass ideas." He patted the gun tucked under his belt.

Liz looked at him in silence. *The asshole doesn't look so menacing now,* she thought. But she feared the pistol he carried and sensed that he wouldn't hesitate use it. Suddenly she heard what sounded like rocks tumbling. The sounds came from below, but close enough to be heard. She looked at the man, but he had not heard it. She hoped the gasping breath had masked the sound. She knew she had to stay alert. There was someone following their trail and not too far behind.

111

BANDIT HAD PICKED UP THE scent on the trail almost immediately and kept tugging at the leash, anxious to give chase. Tom stopped often and listened for unusual noises. Only when he was satisfied did he allow Bandit to pull him along farther. Bandit stopped at the previous season's dried grasses and plants, which lay smashed against the ground. He darted back and forth smelling the ground, then lunged ahead, almost yanking the leash from Tom's hand. *Did they stop here?* Tom wondered. He didn't want to come up to them suddenly. But, he was determined to catch up with them before they had a chance to get onto the old logging road; the abductor might have an accomplice.

Tom was feeling the strain of fear and anxiety in the stealthy chase through the forest. He cursed the thug for the difficult path he had chosen, with rock outcroppings and steep climbing. Fallen trees, boulders and rock-strewn streams forced a circuitous route, one that didn't faze Bandit, but was exhausting to Tom. He surmised that the abductor hadn't given much thought to his route. Instead, he had chosen a zigzag path to climb 4000 feet to the logging road. Tom redoubled his determination to catch up with them. He thought that maybe the difficult terrain would be in his favor, if the thug really didn't know where he was going or was ill prepared for the strenuous exertion.

"Take it easy Bandit," he said softly. "We don't want to charge in on them."

Bandit looked back, his tongue hanging from his mouth, breath coming fast.

"She's a spunky girl; she'll try to slow them down." Tom bent over, his hands on his knees. His breath was labored.

Bandit turned his attention toward Tom.

"I hope they haven't hurt her." He knew she wouldn't give up and would try to escape if she saw a chance. She felt like a daughter to him, and the thought of her terror or possible injury enraged him further. He knew her mother and father would be terribly distraught. He had to find her soon.

"Come on boy. We gotta keep going."

Bandit stood up, tested the ground, and lunged ahead, tugging hard at the leash.

112

SUDDENLY, HE SPOTTED SCRAPE marks on a tree, and a few seconds later another about fifty feet in front. He looked back, to see still another fifty feet behind. He inspected the closest one. *Had he marked his passage down through the forest so that he could then retrace his steps? Why?* Tom wondered if indeed the thug had intended to arrive at a particular place on the logging road, for it seemed that they were heading toward the National Forest gate. He nodded knowingly, sure there was an accomplice waiting in a vehicle. He began to fear for Ralph, and wished he hadn't sent him out alone on the logging road. Alarm and anxiety triggered the urge to move faster. Carelessly, he misjudged where he landed on a rock ledge. He lost his footing momentarily. Bandit froze, holding against the now taunt leash. Several rocks clattered down the slope as Tom struggled to keep his balance. Bandit held tight while Tom regained his balance with the leash tight in his hand. Additional rocks clattered away as Tom stepped back up to Bandit's side. He reached down to pet him. *That must have sounded like an avalanche*, he thought. *Hope they didn't hear it up ahead.*

"Thanks boy." Bandit nuzzled Tom's leg and then looked up at him.

Tom froze and listened. There was only the sound of Bandit's rapid breathing and his own heart pounding.

"That wasn't too damn smart, was it boy?" Bandit just looked at him, patient, his breath coming rapidly.

"Come on Bandit, we've got to get closer to them and soon. It's gonna get dark here in the woods." Bandit strained on the leash. His nose tested the ground as he took up the chase again.

113

RALPH'S LIPS QUIVERED. **HE** fought back panic and tears. He drove the truck slowly searching for tire tracks leading off into the woods, but daylight was fast fading. When he arrived at the Forest Service gate, it was wide open, padlocks lying on the ground. He got out of the truck and examined the tire tracks, fresh tracks that had turned right out of the gate and went in the direction of the ranch. Ralph turned the truck around and headed back the way he had come. He pointed the spotlight onto the ground adjacent to the driver's door and kept the truck at a slow crawl as he examined the ground closely. He cursed at himself for having missed the tracks which he felt must surely be somewhere along the road. They wouldn't have had time to hike up to the logging road and disappear, and he vowed he wouldn't let that happen. *I'll kill any son of a bitch that hurts my little girl,* he promised himself.

114

SAM SPREAD A CAMOUFLAGE net over the rented Jeep. He went back over the tracks on the logging road and swept them with a pine bough for some distance, hoping to obliterate any sign of the tire tracks turning into the woods. He also removed the broken brush and limbs, further evidence of their passing. Sam now sat alongside the Jeep, his back against it. He was well away from the logging road. He was sure no one would see him. He pulled the zipper of his jacket closed against the rapidly cooling evening. He didn't expect Jake to be back for some time and his instruction had been to stay hidden and not leave the spot, no matter how long it took. *Maybe I can catch a few winks,* he thought.

115

Jake kept Liz moving ahead, staying just a few steps behind her. He occasionally said to turn left or right, but otherwise hadn't spoken. Jake's lungs hurt from the strain, and the pain in his calves was excruciating. He knew he'd better not fail. But, he would soon have to stop because he could no longer make out the scrape marks on the trees. He might have to wait until dawn to continue. He thought about his accomplice, hopefully tending to the well-hidden Jeep. He didn't know Sam that well and hoped he would follow orders.

116

LIZ WAS CERTAIN THAT SOMEONE was following them, hopefully Tom, although she hadn't heard any more noises. The previous sounds had alerted her to some pursuit. She was determined to foil any attempt by her captor to get her into a vehicle and she tried to remain alert for an opportunity. They moved ahead for some time before Jake called a halt.

"Hold it kid. We're stopping here for a while. Can't see where I'm going." Even in the dark she could see the fatigue and pain on his face when he got close to her, the grimace with each body movement.

Liz sat down with her back against a tree. Her wrists hurt and were raw from the chafing of the plastic restraints. "Hey! How about taking these off? They hurt."

"Yeah right. They're staying on, and before I fall asleep I'm putting your arms behind you and around that tree. Tough luck, you're not going anywhere."

"Please, they hurt. My wrists are raw," she pleaded.

"Shut up." He pulled the pistol from under his waistband and reached into his pocket for the silencer. He screwed it onto the front of the pistol and then laid it on the ground next to his leg. Liz stared wide eyed at the pistol. She knew this man would not hesitate to shoot anyone who interfered with him. She thought better of pushing him further for any relief.

Jake checked the time on his watch with the aid of a small flashlight.

"What time is it?" she inquired, more for something to do than of any real curiosity. Also, she wanted to make sounds so that anyone pursuing them would be warned of their presence.

"Almost 8 o'clock. Go to sleep. I'm fastening you to that tree in a little while, before I doze off."

"Yeah, thanks. You are a real gentleman aren't you?" Liz asked in a sarcastic tone.

"Shut up."

"Why am I here anyway? Why are you doing this to me?" She hoped anyone following would hear both their voices. She wondered if Jake suspected her motive.

"You're becoming a pain in the ass, kid."

"So let me go. I'll just go home. You can get away." She tried to sound hopeful, as if she wanted to help him avoid trouble.

"Keep your voice down. You're staying with me until that Bauer guy returns what's mine. We'll be out of here at dawn. No one will hurt you unless you become more of a pain to me. You make noise, try to get away...I will hurt you real bad. Understand me, kid?"

"Yeah, I get the picture." She sagged against the tree. The pain in her wrists was distracting. She couldn't find a comfortable position.

117

JAKE WAS TROUBLED. HE HADN'T been in favor of snatching the girl. The risks had seemed too high, and even now there was no guarantee that he could get her away from this place. Also, the idea had been predicated on Bauer having the briefcase. Suppose he didn't. Suppose it was still up on the ridge somewhere, or did the sheriff have it? The FBI agent was still in town, over a month after the plane crash. What the hell was he doing here? Jake was sure it didn't bode well. It seemed to Jake that Frankie was now getting desperate and willing to gamble with Sam's life. The $20,000 that each had been promised for retrieving the briefcase now didn't seem so worthwhile. On the other hand, he wasn't yet ready to throw in the towel.

Jake had been unable to offer his boss any alternative plan that would have a good chance of seeing the return of the briefcase with their money. He had wanted to get his hands on the Bauer guy and just beat it out of him, sure that eventually he would have told him what he wanted to know. Frankie hadn't liked that idea. His 'consultant' had indicated that Bauer was too well known in these parts. Furthermore, there was no indication that Bauer would have talked. So, the plan had been set to snatch the girl and bargain for the briefcase. He worried about what the ranch people and sheriff would be doing. He knew that they would be pursuing them and trying to find them on the logging road. The getaway with the hidden Jeep would have to be timed perfectly, the deputies stationed on the National Forest road, and there must be some of them, would have to be diverted, but that had been planned. He hoped that Sam and the guys in Camden would do exactly as they were supposed to. If anything went wrong, he knew both he and Sam would be captured, and in for a long stretch for kidnapping.

118

"Mobile 3...Camden Dispatch."

"Mobile 3."

"Mobile 8 and 11 are on the way. ETA 10 minutes."

"Roger.."

"Mobile 3, Jeanie should be there at any moment."

"Roger. I see headlights approaching. Mobile 3, out."

A small car pulled up to the barn and stopped. Jeanie Crawford hurried to the deputy's patrol vehicle. Allen greeted her and they shook hands.

"Wayne brought me up to date. Where are the parents of the girl?"

"Well, Ralph, the father, he's in a truck up on the logging road. I'm not exactly sure what he's doing, keeping an eye out for any escape vehicle, I imagine. Susan, that's her mother, she's sitting in my car. She's really upset. Maybe you could take her into the house, help her out there while we figure this out."

"Sure. I'll go get her now. Where is the rancher, what's his name?"

"Bauer, Tom Bauer. He went off into the woods looking for the girl and her captor. This whole thing is a little crazy. I'll wait for Mobile 8 and 11 and then see what Wayne wants to do."

"Okay, I'm going to see Susan."

"Thanks, I'm glad you could come."

119

TOM SHORTENED BANDIT'S leash. He stepped deliberately and carefully to try not to make any noise that would give them away. Since his earlier slip, he realized that walking in western boots was not ideal. He could barely distinguish the tree trunks in the darkness. Then his heart leapt; he heard Liz's voice. Then he heard it again. He dropped to his knees, placing his hand over Bandit's muzzle, his signal to stay quiet. He saw a brief flash of light, a small flashlight beam. He fixed the location in his mind. *Now where is Liz?* he wondered. He heard her voice again and suddenly the small flashlight beam lit up her face some forty feet away. The light went out. Tom heard Liz's captor mumble something, which he couldn't understand. With his hand around Bandit's muzzle, they inched their way forward. He again heard the mumble of voices. Again he fixed the location in his mind; he still could not see them clearly. He stopped and kept Bandit still. He was sure that Liz's captor was armed, also sure that it was the beefcake he had bumped into that day on the cliff with Karen. *What can I do?* he wondered. Suddenly an owl hooted nearby. It startled Tom, but Bandit didn't seem to care. His ears and nose were pointed to where he had heard the voices. Tom kept a grip on his collar.

120

"**What the hell was that?**" asked Jake in just above a whisper.

"Just an owl," replied Liz, with a smile.

"It's time to get you intimate with that tree behind you, so don't give me any trouble." He stood up and she saw the pistol tucked in his waistband.

"Get up."

"My wrists hurt, they're sore. They're raw. Look at them," moaned Liz, hoping for some relief.

"Too bad. I'm taking them off now and retying them around this tree. Don't do anything stupid. If I have to, I will shoot you. Do you understand me?"

"Yeah, yeah."

It was then that Tom burst out of the trees, swinging a heavy branch with all his strength and contacting Jake on the back of the head. Bandit was at his heels, barking excitedly. Liz, now free of the wrist manacles, gasped and stepped back as Jake fell to his knees with a groan.

"Tom," she exclaimed. "Thank God."

The heavy branch that Tom swung at Jake had broken on impact, it's interior mostly rotted. Jake was on his hands and knees, trying to clear the pain and cloudiness from his mind. Suddenly he swung around and grabbed Tom's legs in a vise-like grip. He pulled Tom down to the ground and, in a surprisingly swift move, was on his feet reaching for the pistol in his waistband. He yanked it clear and pointed it at Liz. He reached for her arm and yanked her close. His other hand held the pistol at her midriff. He swung a hard kick at Tom who was trying to stand up. The savage kick to his calf sent him reeling again.

"You goddamn asshole," he hissed at Tom, and swung the pistol against Tom's head.

As Tom went down, Bandit leapt out of the darkness and seized Jake's pistol arm in a vicious grip. Jake cried out in pain and dropped the pistol where it clattered on some rocks. Jake fought to free himself from the dog's grip. Jake seized a rock and swung it against Bandit's head.

Liz kicked the pistol into the shrubs where Jake couldn't see it. She saw Tom trying to get back onto his feet. She heard Bandit's yelp of pain as Jake hit him with a rock. Bandit, dazed, let go, and stood off a few feet.

Tom was on his feet as Jake started to get up. He kicked hard against Jake's ribs, sending him sprawling. But Jake was quick, belying his size and weight, and went after Tom with a roar of rage. Tom didn't see the fist that hit him on the side of the face. He only felt the sharp pain and mind-boggling force as he tried to stay on his feet. Another fist smashed him on the side of his head. Tom reeled from dizziness and pain. Blood ran down his face and from his nose. A fist hit him again and Tom fell to his knees.

Bandit jumped back into the fray. His teeth sank into Jake's calf. A cry of pain and rage came from him as he tried to get the dog loose from his leg. Bandit held on.

Liz picked up a heavy stick, and went after Jake with a vengeance. The blow hit him squarely on top of his head. He staggered; fighting to stay on his feet. Bandit was still clamped onto his leg. Tom, still on his knees, his face bloodied, tried to clear his vision. Liz, now angrier than she had ever been in her life, came back behind Jake and swung again and again, landing the stick on top of his head. He dropped to his knees. Again Liz came at him, the heavy stick landed on the back of his head with a dull thud. With a roar of rage, Jake, with a superhuman effort pulled Bandit from his leg, and swung the dog away from him with his left hand. He staggered to his feet and turned to face his attacker. Liz stood six feet away pointing his pistol at his midriff.

"You son of a bitch...I'm going to kill you," she screamed at him.

Behind Jake, Tom was getting onto his feet and Bandit stood nearby with the hair bristling on his back.

"Goddamn bitch," he hissed and started to move toward her. Bandit lunged for his calf again and sunk his teeth. Jake roared in pain, turned, and tried to reach for the dog's head. It was then that Tom came at him, his fist smashed into Jake's face. Liz went to Tom and thrust the pistol into his hands.

"Take it! Take it!" she gasped. She had no idea of how to use the pistol, but Tom quickly chambered a shell and had it pointed at Jake when the big man straightened up.

"Bandit...no!" Tom called him off. But the dog stood nearby, growling. Bandit did not appear to be finished with what he had in mind.

Jake stood erect, shaking his head as if to clear his vision. He started toward Tom. Tom fired a warning shot into the trees. Jake stopped, and backed up several steps.

"It won't be a warning next time. Stay where you are."

"This isn't the end, asshole...just the goddamn beginning for you," he hissed. "They'll be coming for you. You're a dead man."

Tom was unsteady. He had trouble seeing clearly, and his head ached as never before. He turned slightly toward Liz. "You okay?"

"I'll be fine now," she gasped and stared at the bloodied face, reaching up and touching him tenderly.

Tom turned his attention to Bandit. "Hey, boy. How you doing?" He reached to pet him, and then hearing a noise, swung around raising the pistol.

"Where the hell is he?" Tom stared into the darkness. Jake was gone.

"He was right there a few seconds ago," said Liz. "You're not going after him, are you?"

Tom shook his head. "No. I just want you safe. I need to get you home. The hell with him."

121

TOM'S KNEES BUCKLED AND he dropped. He pulled himself to a sitting position, leaned against a tree and placed the pistol by his side. He wiped at his blood-streaked face with the back of his hand. His face was raw in places and his nose still bled. Liz sat down next to him, and put her arm around his neck. She started to cry. Tom held her until she stopped shaking. Neither said anything for a few minutes.

"Tom, Tom," she sobbed.

"It's okay. I'm pretty sure he's gone, for now anyway."

"I knew you would come. I heard you once; a while ago, some rocks."

"Yeah, that was me. Almost gave myself away."

"I'm so glad you came." Liz was crying softly.

"I wasn't going to let that bastard take you."

"You're bleeding, your. God, that must hurt."

"He did a job on my head didn't he? It hurts a lot right now. Your wrists. That bastard."

"I wanted to kill him!"

"But you didn't."

She rested her head against his chest.

122

"**D**ispatch, Mobile 3."

"Dispatch. Go ahead 3."

"Mobile 8 and 11 just arrived. I need to talk to Wayne."

"Standby, Mobile 3"

It took only a few seconds. "What's the situation there, Allen?"

"Jeanie went in the lodge with Susan. Bill and Andy just arrived. I haven't heard from Mr. Stehling. He's supposed to be out on the logging road along the ridge. I haven't heard from Tom Bauer either. Strange goings on. He went chasing after the girl some time ago."

"Okay. Have one of the guys stand guard at the scene. Preserve the evidence. The other will scour the area for sign and mark it. Let's make sure that whatever evidence exists is not disturbed."

"Okay. Bill and Andy are right here."

"You take your vehicle up on the road. Find Stehling and patrol that area. There has to be a hidden vehicle up there somewhere. Look for it, but watch your back. These guys mean business."

"Copy that. Mobile 3 out."

The radio went silent. The three men looked at each other. Allen spoke first. "I'm headed up the road. Listen for me on your portables."

"Yeah, sure, We'll be listening. If we don't hear from you, we'll go to the mobile radio," replied Bill.

Andy shook his head in agreement. "Be careful," he added.

123

RALPH HAD FINISHED HIS third sweep of the road and was headed up the ridge once again.

He looked carefully at the ground as the truck crawled along. He stopped occasionally at a suspicious looking spot, but each proved to be nothing. He had to admit that the kidnappers could have waited to see him pass and then departed for the Forest Service road. However, he hadn't seen any new tracks on the road as he retraced. They were here somewhere, he reckoned. He could hardly bear to think that he had missed them, and that his daughter had been taken.

Suddenly he saw headlights coming up behind him. He stopped and positioned the truck where no one could pass him easily. He got out of the truck, and thought he saw Allen as the approaching vehicle came into the area lit by his headlights.

"Allen! That you?"

"Yeah, Ralph. See anyone?"

"Nothing. They got my little girl..." he started and tears formed in his eyes.

"Yeah, we know. Sheriff's wife is with Susan. I got a couple guys at the ranch with them. Did you see anything?"

"Just some tire tracks up at the gate," Ralph said. "I hope I didn't miss them. I don't think I did though."

Allen saw the trembling on Ralph's lips. He gripped Ralph's arm. "Hang in there. We'll find them. But, listen, Ralph. They could be anywhere. Shit, we got six miles of road up here."

Shaking his head, "I'm starting my third trip up. I've been checking every damn foot along the edges. Haven't seen anything so far."

Allen nodded. "Let's do this. You go on up to the Forest Service gate and stay there. Keep your radio on. I can reach you with one of mine in the vehicle. I'll get my night vision gear out. I have it in the back; got a pretty good idea what it can do. If these guys are not too far into the woods, I might be able to see them. Maybe we'll get lucky and get these bastards before they get away."

"I'm so afraid that they'll hurt my Liz." He was close to tears again.

"Have you heard from Tom yet?"

"No. He went with Bandit into the woods hours ago. He must be following them. I don't know."

"Okay. Go ahead. Keep the radio on."

"Thanks...thanks."

"Don't worry, we will find her."

124

WHILE RALPH CONTINUED along the road toward the Forest Service gate, Allen rummaged in the back of his SUV patrol car and retrieved a small carrying case that held his night vision equipment. He attached the sensor to a special helmet fitted for correct positioning of the IT6000 Series night vision sensor to his right eye. He checked the operation of the equipment and then got behind the wheel. The headlights overwhelmed the night vision goggles so he drove with only the small running lamps on. He looked into the forest on both sides of the road as the SUV crept along. A half-hour later, he was startled by an image of a large man at the edge of the road about 30 yards away. When he stopped the vehicle the man darted across the road and disappeared. Allen let the vehicle creep forward to where the image had disappeared in the trees. He looked for several minutes but could detect no sign of movement.

Where the hell is he, he wondered. *Did he run off or is he waiting to ambush me?* Allen stared into the trees for several minutes, but decided to not pursue alone. It was just too risky. He backed the vehicle very slowly while staring into the forest on the down slope side of the road. He didn't see anything unusual.

"Damn," he said aloud, "If that was the asshole, where the hell is the girl and Tom? Maybe he hurt them, left them in the woods?"

He stopped the vehicle and turned off the engine and running lights. He opened the door and got out, listening intently to the noises of the forest, but heard nothing unusual. He looked back up the road to where the man had disappeared into the trees. All was still.

He came out around here. I should try to back track a bit, he thought.

Allen reached in through the window and picked up his microphone. "Mobile 8, Mobile 11, you copy?" There was no response. He called again, but the radio stayed silent.

"Shit. I gotta be in a bad spot," he mumbled to himself. He tossed the microphone onto the seat. "Well, here goes."

He unhooked the safety strap on his pistol and stepped carefully and slowly into the woods. He turned on his small infrared penlight to better illuminate the darker areas for his night goggles. He kept to a track perpendicular to the road and slowly made his way quietly into the forest as he swept the goggles from side to side. Just as he decided to return to his vehicle he saw movement near the ground only a few yards ahead and to the left. He reached for the pistol. *It's probably a damn raccoon,* he thought.

125

LIZ WAS LYING WITH HER HEAD on his chest. He kept his arm around her shoulder.

"You okay, Tom?" she asked softly.

"Uh-huh. Just thinking how happy your mom and dad will be."

"Oh, I know. I am so worried about them."

"I'm going to have to get up. We have to get to the old road. I need to get you home."

She tilted her head up and saw raw flesh on his face and dried blood on his nose and chin. "But you're hurt; you need to rest a bit." Liz clung to him, as if to keep him from moving.

Suddenly Bandit scrambled to his feet, hair bristling. A deep growl formed in his throat. He faced the direction that Jake had gone, toward the old road. Tom grabbed his collar before he was able to dart off. With his other hand, he picked up the pistol.

Liz's arms tightened around him and she began to tremble.

"What is it? Is he back?"

"Shhh, let's wait."

Bandit strained at the collar but Tom held tightly.

"Maybe it's an animal," she whispered.

"Bandit wouldn't be this upset at an animal."

126

THE HAIR STOOD UP ON THE back of Allen's neck. He heard a dog growling. *Who was there? Could this be the kidnapper or was it Bandit he heard?* He didn't see anyone in the night vision sensor. Suddenly he detected a movement. Then he spotted two people on the ground against a tree. Brush prevented him from identifying them. He didn't want to turn on his light and possibly draw gunfire.

He crouched close to the ground. "Sheriff's Department! Who's there?"

"Sheriff?" Liz whispered.

"Shhh" cautioned Tom. He pointed the pistol in the general direction of the voice.

"Who is it?" he asked aloud.

"Deputy Sheriff Richards. Identify yourself."

Tom recognized Allen's voice.

"Allen? Tom and Liz here."

Allen burst through the brush. He flipped up the visor of his night vision goggles and turned on his big flashlight. Tom and Liz sat huddled together against a tree. He saw the pistol in Tom's hand and stopped.

"It's me Tom. Put the safety on and lay the gun down, please."

Bandit quieted and sat down on command. Tom put the safety on and tossed the pistol a few feet away. Allen immediately picked it up, checked and pocketed it.

"Jeez, you look like a spaceman," Tom commented, nodding at Allen's equipment.

"Did you break anything? You look like shit."

"I'll make it. My nose may be broken, not sure. Everything hurts."

He glanced at Liz. "How are you? Were you hurt?"

"I'm okay. Wrists hurt where he tied me."

"Where is the jerk? Is he around here? I saw a big guy in my night vision out on the road, but he disappeared into the trees on the other side."

"That's him," Tom replied. "He slipped away from us about thirty minutes ago."

"Damn. Does he look as good as you?"

"We gave him all we had, Liz, me and Bandit. Bandit got a piece of him."

"Tell me the details later. I've got to call in and let Susan know. Ralph is up on the road somewhere, probably near the Forest Service gate. I've got to bring him back. He'll want to know that Liz is okay."

Allen reached for his lapel microphone and activated the portable radio.

"Mobile 8, Mobile 3 here." A few seconds went by and then a response came.

"Mobile 3, this is 8. Can hardly copy you. What's happening up there?"

"Tell Susan we have Liz and Tom. They're here with me. Both are okay. Then get to Wayne and fill him in. Tell him the perp escaped. Last I saw of him he darted across the road and disappeared up the hill. Copy?"

"Roger. We'll stand by here."

"Okay, 3 out."

Allen turned his attention back to Tom and Liz. "I have to get to the radio in my vehicle so I can contact Ralph. I can't do it on this setup. Can you two make it up to the road alone? It's probably 300 feet. I have to get to the radio in my vehicle."

"Go on ahead. We'll follow you," Tom replied.

Liz helped Tom to his feet and held on to his arm. "You going to be okay?" Tears welled in her eyes. "I wanted to kill him after what he did to you."

"He isn't worth it, Liz. I'm just glad you're okay."

She squeezed his arm.

127

ALLEN HAD JUST GOTTEN off the radio when Tom, Liz and Bandit arrived on the road.

"Liz, your dad is coming now. He just left the gate and should be here soon. He sure was happy to hear you're okay."

"That must have been so hard on my mom and dad," she said softly, wiping her eyes.

"Okay, Tom. Tell me what happened down there." Allen tilted his head, toward the forest below. "How'd you find Liz?"

"When I found out that Liz had disappeared from the cabin, I sent Bandit after her scent. We tracked them along the slope for a long time before I figured out he had marked the trail. I figured he was headed for this road. I'm guessing someone was up here, or coming here, to pick him up."

"What do they want?" Liz looked at Tom with searching eyes.

"I don't think we should talk about..." started Allen before Tom broke in.

"Allen, Liz has earned the right to know what is happening," said Tom with certainty.

Allen lowered his head, nodded in agreement. "I suppose so."

128

TOM SAT DOWN IN THE passenger seat of Allen's vehicle, kicking his feet at stones on the road. "Liz, there was something on that airplane that belonged to a bunch of mob guys from Chicago. It's a suitcase with a lot of money, probably drug money. We found it with the dead guy. The sheriff and FBI are planning a sting operation to try and catch some of them. Hopefully they will give up their bosses. It's a big operation, at least from Reno to Banff, maybe farther."

"We wanted to keep it quiet," Allen added. "We couldn't afford a leak. They figured Tom had hidden the money somewhere. They threatened him and were already casing the ranch. Don't be too hard on him; we forced him to keep quiet."

Liz nodded.

Tom continued telling his story to Allen. "It was dark when I caught up to them. They had stopped and were resting. When the kidnapper got up and untied Liz, he said he was going to tie her to a tree, that's when I jumped him. It was a free-for-all. Bandit bit him hard a couple of times. Liz whacked him with a big stick. I landed a few of my own, but he got a few in on me, too. It was Liz got him to back off. She picked up his pistol and threatened him with it. She gave it to me and I fired it once to scare him off. He took off into the night when I turned my back."

"You guys could have been killed," exclaimed Allen.

"He needed us alive. He was getting mad, though," replied Tom with a wry grin. Allen just shook his head.

"There has to be a vehicle up here somewhere. Liz, do you have any idea from what he said?"

Liz was thoughtful before replying. "He wouldn't talk much. But I got the sense that someone was waiting to pick us up. We only stopped because he couldn't see where he had to go in the dark. It was really dark. He had a little flashlight, but was afraid to use it."

"Well, Ralph went up and down this road several times looking for any sign of a vehicle, but he didn't see anything," Allen commented. "He should be back soon. The sheriff posted some auxiliaries on the Forest Service road entrance down on the other side. I don't know, I guess, with a Jeep or a 4-wheel drive, one could find some other way around these parts. Hey! Here comes Ralph now."

Ralph came into view driving fast, slid the truck to a dusty stop and jumped out. "Liz," he exclaimed, and rushed to her. She ran to him and they embraced tearfully. She gave him snippets of her story. He hugged her.

He came up to Tom, wiping his tears with one hand and holding the other arm around Liz. "How can we thank you, Tom? We owe you…big time." His voice trembled with emotion.

Tom tried to lighten the moment. "I'm just glad that Liz is back and okay."

Liz put her other arm through Tom's. "Thank you," she whispered.

"We have to figure out where that guy went," Allen declared. "Does he have a truck or a 4-wheeler? Is there another guy up here somewhere?"

Tom nodded, "Probably, but where? This road is six miles end to end. There are all kinds of places someone could hide a small vehicle. They just wait for us to drive by and then they can leave by way of the Forest Service road, or even some old log-drag trail through the forest. There's got to be dozens of them." He didn't sound too hopeful.

129

"Listen. You three go on back. I'm going to use my night vision gear and go up and back on this road. Maybe nothing, but I'll get some practice with this equipment. It *is* how I found you guys. I started looking in the woods where the guy had come out. I saw Bandit first, then I saw you two against the tree."

"Well, we're grateful. I won't make fun of your spaceman gear anymore. Go ahead…but if you find anything, you better call for backup. These guys are getting desperate. They could ambush you," Tom cautioned.

"I'll be careful. Besides, this is my first real chance to use this equipment," Allen smiled.

"We'll head back." Tom stood up and closed the door of Allen's SUV.

"I'll head up the road. I'll stop at your place on the way back. By the way, Wayne's wife, Jeanie, is with Susan right now. Got a couple guys walking around the place. I'll catch up with them when I get back."

"Okay. Ralph, you drive."

"Sure. What the hell happened to you? Jeez, that's gotta hurt."

"Yeah, it does. I'll tell you in the truck. Let's go."

Ralph got in the driver's side. Liz got in the other side and Tom squeezed in next to the door after he had put Bandit in the back. Liz told her dad about her experience and what had happened when Tom found them. Ralph asked questions, but Tom couldn't contribute. He stared out the window, aching and tired. Liz caught her dad's eye to caution him about his questioning.

130

WHEN THEY ARRIVED IN FRONT of the barn, they found the area crowded with two sheriff's cars, an ambulance, and the car belonging to the sheriff's wife. Frank Oberman was leaning on the front fender of his rental sedan and came up to Tom as the truck stopped.

"Hey, I just heard about it. Sheriff got hold of me. I was out. What the hell happened? You guys all right? Damn, look at your face."

"Liz is okay. Ralph, you and Liz go home. I'll be fine."

"Sure?" asked Ralph.

"Yeah, I'll talk to Agent Oberman, and then I'm going to bed."

Ralph replied, "Liz will check on you later."

Tom nodded and then turned his bruised face to the agent. "Goddamn it, this didn't have to happen. Your bureaucratic bullshit gave them time to come after us. You and the sheriff ain't helping at all."

"I'm sorry, Tom. I talked to my boss and the sheriff tonight. We will get this going in a week or so. Getting the locals to work with the FBI can be frustrating. The impediments are all from people not even involved in this operation, freaking desk jocks. I am really sorry. I should have pushed them harder."

Tom nodded, didn't say anything, but the veins in his forehead bulged.

"Damn, Tom...your face. Here, walk over to the ambulance. Let the EMTs clean you up. I mean they're here and all, you might as well."

Oberman tugged on Tom's arm and they walked silently to the ambulance. Tom was introduced to the two guys in the truck who immediately went to work.

They leaned against the ambulance while Frank gently coaxed Tom to tell what happened on the ridge.

Tom's frustration was still evident. "If we don't do something, these assholes will be back. They'll be coming back, and people are going to get hurt. I couldn't bear it if Liz or her parents got hurt. Shit! I don't want to get hurt, either. These guys are pissed now."

"Okay, Tom. I'm sorry. I'll get to my boss right away. We'll get this show on the road. It's still going to take at least a week to set it up properly. The sheriff will have patrols on the forest road keeping an eye out for those guys."

"That's what you said last time. Those guys are getting right by your patrols, they ain't stupid." Tom stared hard at Frank.

"We'll get them soon."

"Yeah, soon," Tom replied with some exasperation. "I'm hurt and tired. I'm going to bed."

"Sure. I'm sorry for all this."

"Yeah, yeah. Tom walked off into the darkness, headed for his cabin and the comfort of his bed.

131

A FEW DAYS LATER, TOM FELT better. He sat at his desk and tried to concentrate on his office work, but the scenes from the night on the ridge played through his mind. He picked up the phone after the second ring. It was Allen.

"Where you calling from, the donut shop?"

"Funny, real funny. No, I'm in my office. I just wanted to bring you up to date. Anything new out your way?"

"No. It's been quiet around here since we got Liz back."

"Well, the sheriff and the Fed have finally worked up a plan to get these criminals. Oberman is trying to get his boss to sign off."

"I won't hold my breath," Tom remarked. "It's only been six damn weeks."

"I don't think there will be any problem. Frank said it was approved already."

"Well, the bad guys haven't given up. I'm sure of that," said Tom with a note of exasperation.

"By the way, I was talking to the owners of the Baldwin spread yesterday, a rinky-dink operation over in Randolph. They run a few head and board horses for some rich guy in Camden. They told me they had rented a horse to a guy in the past week for the second time. Anyway, the guy had been gone overnight, said he was on a camping trip, scouting out places for elk hunting."

Tom shook his head. "Like I said, I'm sure we'll hear from them again."

132

Tom arrived at the back of the Camden courthouse early Monday morning for a meeting called by the Sheriff's Office and FBI to get the sting in motion. Sheriff Wayne Crawford and deputy Allen Richards were at the conference table along with Frank Oberman of the FBI and Larry Johnson, from Larry's bar and Grill. Tom took a seat near the plate of donuts and the coffee pot. Smiling, he looked over at Allen and nodded at the donuts. Allen scowled, knowing Tom's penchant for harassing him.

Wayne stood up. "All right, fellas. Let's get this meeting started. There's a lot of ground to cover."

Everyone turned to face him. "The kidnapping of Liz by this fellow known as Jake has obviously heightened the urgency. We have not found where this guy, Jake, is hiding, but he is alive and well, I'm sure, since his buddy, Sam, is still hanging out at the Camden Motel. Earlier, we wanted to trick these guys into going for the money in some way where we could nail them, and get them to roll on their bosses. Now, this has become a kidnapping with Jake as a fugitive. We suspect that Sam was in it with him, but we have no proof. We questioned Sam without getting anything useful except for the name, Jake. We now have him under 24-hour observation."

Wayne paused; no one said anything, so he continued. "This Jake fellow is hiding out around here and waiting for help from Sam or someone else. Agent Oberman and I agreed on a plan to get Jake to show himself, along with his buddy, Sam. It is a way to arrest them both and start squeezing them."

Wayne switched on the overhead projector showing a hand drawn map of the crash site and the shale slide area on the screen.

"Tom, I think you'll find this drawing to be fairly accurate. I put it together from the topo map and from the photos that Allen and Agent Oberman made a while ago. We've organized this operation pretty much around you. If, when you hear us out, you think it won't work or that you'll be in unreasonable danger, then say so. We'll then try to come up with another approach."

Tom nodded in agreement and Wayne continued. "The kidnapping of Liz was fortunately thwarted by Tom and his dog. However, the perpetrator, Jake, is now wanted for a felony. We can't connect Sam to this just yet, but we think we'll be able to soon. What we have planned, and got approval for, is a scheme to get Jake and Sam to think that they can get their hands on the suitcase. After all, that is the reason they're here. I think the fact that they've been here so long, scheming to get back their money, is our chance to nab them now on felony kidnapping."

Oberman raised his hand. "We were having trouble coming up with a solid plan with only the money. There was a good chance they would have gone free. Now, however, with a felony charge, we'll have them both."

Wayne continued to describe the plan. "Larry has agreed to help us out. He sees this guy, Sam, come into his place almost every night and he's beginning to loosen up. Larry is going to let slip to this guy that the presumed missing money that "everyone" is looking for has been buried at the bottom of the shale slide area near the crash site, that Tom buried the briefcase where he found the dead man. We're counting on their original motivation to get them together up at that site. Our team will be waiting for them."

He looked at Larry. "It will be up to you to pull this off. You have to make this guy believe you."

Larry looked around the table and then smiled. "It should work. This fellow has been hitting me up for tidbits of information every time he's been in during the last few weeks. I think I can handle it okay. He's already had a few before he shows up at my place."

"Yeah, we've seen him going in and out of the Camden Hotel bar every evening," said Wayne.

"All right, Larry is going to let slip that Tom will be going to "find" the money on Saturday morning and that he's going to claim a sizable finder's fee. Of course, what Larry won't be telling him is that the FBI and Sheriff's team will have the area staked out. That's here and here." Wayne pointed to the places on the map that was projected onto the screen. "Tom, of course, will be faking looking for the briefcase until the bad guys get into position; that is, close enough for us to apprehend them. Tom, you'll just have to play it by ear."

"I can do that." Tom nodded.

Wayne sat down as Oberman got up to speak. "The FBI will be supplying the team with scrambled two-way radios that won't permit eavesdropping by anyone else. Each team member will be using a headset so that the radio will not be heard and inadvertently alert the targets. Also, it'll ensure that neither the perps nor the inquisitive press will get wind of the operation before it is completed." He then looked over at Tom. "Tom, however, will not be taking a radio. We can't risk him being seen with one. It'll just give it away."

Tom shrugged. "I'm comfortable just relying on my dog. I just don't want him getting shot."

The agent continued. "We will do our utmost to keep you and the dog from getting hurt. The team will have men positioned as indicated by these circles on the map. Tom, you can see that there will be someone very close to you at all times, but you won't see them. Can you keep your dog from getting spooked and giving us away?"

"Yes, Bandit will be quiet."

"Okay. That will be important." Oberman nodded and continued. "Tom, you'll be seen by our targets to be digging at the bottom of the slide, and we'll carefully mark the place when we go there and bury the briefcase. It will be a similar metal briefcase to the original; only this one won't have money in it, just newspapers." He smiled. "Don't forget to bring a spade with you."

Tom nodded in agreement. "Okay. I'll be watching for the bastards to appear. Bandit will let me know when he sees them. When they get close enough to see me clearly, I assume that's when you want me to lift the briefcase out of the ground."

Wayne got up. "Allen is going to place the briefcase at the slide area the night before. He'll use his night vision equipment and another deputy will stand guard. He'll mark the place where the briefcase is hidden and then let you know, Tom, how he has it marked."

Tom nodded.

The sheriff continued. "The team members will close in and arrest the suspects as soon as they have committed to being there for the money. In any event, they'll be close enough in case things get sticky. Tom, don't give them any resistance; let them have the suitcase. It'll be locked, giving us a few more seconds to apprehend them."

"I'm worried," Larry spoke up, "Tom is at great risk here if anything goes wrong. I mean, these guys already had trouble and have it in for him.

Wayne looked at Tom. "It's your call. We don't have to do it this way. We can maybe come up with something else."

Oberman remarked, "These guys want the money above all else. Afterward, yes, they may want to shoot Tom and his dog to get rid of a witness or maybe just for revenge. We can't let that happen. The team members positioned close-in will have to be very alert and put a stop to anything getting out of hand. We'll go over this very carefully with the team before we set out. There is some risk, no doubt, but I think we can minimize it. It's your call, Tom."

Tom looked across the table at the concerned faces. "Guys, I'm gonna have to put my trust in your team. I don't know of any easier way to do this. I can accept the risk; I'll do my part to minimize any trouble."

Wayne continued by projecting pictures of the area on screen and discussing the vegetation and terrain. In about fifteen minutes, they all shook hands and left the courthouse. Agent Oberman caught up with Tom in the parking lot at the rear of the building.

"I just want you to know that our team will include some FBI guys. They know what they're doing."

"I don't know who the goons are. But if it's the same big guy that snatched Liz, he may want to kill me and Bandit on general principles. We hurt him pretty bad and his bosses can't be too happy with him either."

The agent looked at Tom. "We will be doing everything possible to keep those guys from hurting you." He paused. "One of our close-in guys will have a video camera on his helmet; hopefully we can capture the action and sound and then use it in court. Be talking to you."

"Okay, see ya." Tom headed toward his truck.

133

ALLEN CALLED TOM THE NEXT day and informed him that the operation was set for Saturday. The team would be through his ranch and onto the ridge Friday night. Tom only glossed over the plan with Ralph, because he knew that Ralph would strongly object to him putting himself in danger. *Unfortunately, there doesn't seem to be any other way,* he thought with a shudder.

134

SAM BROUGHT JAKE BACK from the failed kidnapping on the mountain. They had hidden in the forest until the following afternoon when Sam dropped Jake off at a rundown motel with a bag of groceries, enough for a week. The proprietor could barely focus on ringing the cash register, let alone be likely to remember Jake's face. A near empty bottle of gin sat on his desk. Jake dismissed Sam's suggestion to see a doctor about the wounds inflicted by the dog. He knew if anyone recognized him, he would be arrested. Of course, he hadn't called Frankie yet; maybe soon. What was he going to tell him? Maybe being arrested would be the least of his problems.

Sam made a circuitous route back to his motel room. The unmarked car across the street didn't escape his notice, but no one approached him. He stayed in his room during the day, as Jake had told him and waited for Jake to call. He only left at night, stopping first at the Mexican restaurant, then driving to Elk Creek and having a few drinks at Larry's Bar and Grill. He engaged the barkeep and listened to the conversations. The kidnapping was mentioned a few times, but he learned nothing new until the previous evening. The subject with the barkeep had turned to the rumor of missing fortune that had been on the wrecked airplane.

He had resisted temptation to call Jake on the cell phone, fearing Jake's anger. Jake had wanted to let his wounds heal, as well as have time to call Frankie and figure their next move. They hoped the sheriff would focus more on Sam, since he had the Jeep with him.

Sam sat propped up on the bed in the motel room watching CNN on TV when his cell phone rang.

Sam muted the TV and flipped open the cell phone.

"Yeah," answered Sam.

"Alone?"

"Yeah. They're following me everywhere. I don't know why they haven't picked me up. I guess they're waiting for you to show up. The bozos are so easy to spot. You okay where you are?"

"Yeah, for now. You been down the rube's bar? What'd you hear down there?" asked Jake.

"Yeah, been there every night like you said. Only yesterday I heard from the owner, he was tending bar, that this Bauer guy knew where the briefcase was, but hadn't admitted it to anyone. It seems like it's common knowledge amongst his friends, though. Anyway, the owner guy said FBI told him they were gonna post a reward for the money and that Bauer was gonna claim it for retrieval of the money. He thought Bauer would go up on the mountain tomorrow and get the briefcase. It sounds like the finder's fee will be a bunch. Bar owner is expecting a big reward party at the bar next weekend."

Sam heard the venom in Jake's voice. "Asshole ain't getting nothin' but a hole in his goddamn head. We'll be up there waiting for him. You lose those clowns before dawn, come get me, and we'll head up to the Forest Service gate."

"Yeah, we can wait for him near the gate and watch him go by," said Sam.

"Right. Then we'll drive in after him, say fifteen minutes later. I'll make my way down the hill in the trees. I don't want him to see me until I get close. You stay up top with the Jeep."

"Do you think that this might be some kind of setup? Like, are we walking into something?" asked Sam nervously.

"Nah. That goddamn cowboy wants the dough for himself. He wanted it all for himself since he first laid eyes on it."

"I keep thinking it might be a setup," said Sam again.

"Forget it. That prick has his mind on the dough, always had. It's more cash than he's seen in his sorry life. He's getting nervous now; maybe the law is asking him questions. So now he's willing to settle for the finder's fee."

"Damn him. We could've been out of here weeks ago," groused Sam shaking his head.

"When we get up there, you stay with the Jeep. Don't leave the Jeep no matter what. Got it?"

"Yeah, I got it, I got it. Are you gonna pop him? You oughta pop him and that goddamn dog, too."

"We don't need to leave any witnesses, do we?" asked Jake.

"No goddamn way," said Sam.

"I owe that bastard some real pain." Jake hung up.

135

FRIDAY EVENING, THE SHERIFF - FBI team arrived in two Chevy Suburbans and a Sheriff's SUV. The Suburbans were hidden in the barn. Allen would wait and then drive the SUV up the mountain road well after Tom was under way, cutting off any escape through the ranch. The agents took positions at the Forest Service gate, near the airplane wreckage, and in the heavy brush and trees near the slide area. As an added precaution, the sheriff stationed a few men in a car out of sight at the junction of the Forest Service road and the small county road going to Camden. Two men were in the barn as well. Every route was being watched.

136

An unmarked sheriff's car was parked across from the Camden Motel. The deputies watched as Sam left the motel to get breakfast at McDonalds.

"Hey, this guy's a little early today."

Brian turned to look. "Okay, remember what we got to do. Let's head down to Sue's place, give this jerk a chance to leave."

"Okay, it'll be another hour before we're relieved. Sure can use a coffee," said Hank.

"I can't figure this guy," Brian mused. "He sat in that room all week. Where's his buddy?"

"Who the hell knows? They wanted us to baby sit him, so that's what we do."

Sam watched them drive away, grabbed his coffee and food and hurried to the Jeep. He turned into the alley behind McDonalds and after a few turns, was on a county road. He leaned on the accelerator.

137

Tom began the morning in typical fashion, with breakfast at the Stehling's. Afterward, instead of working with the horses, he threw a shovel into his pick-up truck, let Bandit in, and started up the ridge over the old logging road. He was a bit nervous about the operation, unsure of himself if it came to a dangerous situation, and worried about Bandit getting hurt. When he told Ralph a few scant details, Ralph had wanted to give Tom his old .38 pistol. The sheriff had promised that he would be covered by a couple of good marksmen, and they would act to protect him above all else. Wayne and Allen thought that a pistol with Tom might raise the level of anxiety with the suspect and precipitate a bad ending. Tom agreed.

"Well Bandit, this could get a little hairy for us," he said, glancing at his dog. "That one guy really was pissed. Well, hell, so was I. But he may want to put a couple holes in me just to feel better. He can't be too fond of you either."

Bandit glanced at Tom and then put his nose back to the window crack.

"These guys may not want to leave any witnesses around when they grab the briefcase. That could sure louse up our day."

Tom knew he had to keep a clear head. He drove along the logging road slowly, his eyes scanning the trees and brush to either side of the road. He saw nothing unusual, yet he knew that the team was dispersed throughout the area. He passed the Forest Service gate; there were no recent tire tracks. He stopped the truck at the Timberline Cabin. The cabin looked undisturbed. Tom could still see the trampled brush and some cut trees where the NTSB team had forced a path for their vehicle to the crash site. He started the truck again and crawled forward slowly following the NTSB path.

In a few minutes he saw the wrecked airplane, pieces of yellow tape still seen on some of the trees.

"Hey Bandit, wonder when they're going to yank this wreckage outa here? It's been a while."

Bandit's ears twitched, but his attention was on the wreckage.

"We'll stop here. You stay close to me."

Bandit stood up on the seat and nuzzled Tom's face.

"Yeah, you're a good boy. Stick with me." Tom petted him.

Tom slid out of the seat and Bandit quickly followed. Bandit began circling the wreckage, investigating the scents. Tom grabbed the shovel from the truck and started walking. He stopped and returned to the truck, reached into the truckbed and retrieved a small coil of rope.

"I think I better tie you to a tree down there, Bandit; can't have you loose."

Bandit looked at the rope, his brow wrinkled. They set off toward the slate slide area. Tom looked at his watch; 10:30. He thought about the mob guys; were they in the vicinity, or had they waited for him to drive by the Forest Service gate before coming this way? He knew they needed him in order to locate the buried briefcase, but then what? He resisted the urge to look around. He didn't want to give the plan away. Tom slid slowly down the edge of the slide area. The footing was loose and treacherous and Tom used the shovel to keep his balance as he descended to the bottom. Bandit stopped and sniffed the air.

"Bandit, come."

The dog looked at him, and then hesitantly moved next to him, but turned his attention to the trees.

Tom reached down and petted him. "It's okay, boy. I know you smell them in there, but you need to be quiet. Come." Tom moved ahead. Bandit stayed with him.

Tom stopped at the bottom of the slide area and looked for the landmarks they had agreed on. He spotted a small piece of yellow ribbon on a tree just in front of him, and he knew that the briefcase was buried on the far side of the third tree directly behind.

He pulled the tape from the tree and walked forward slowly until he saw the disturbed ground that marked the spot. He kicked away the rocks exposing a piece of yellow tape.

He looked again at his watch; almost 11 o'clock. Tom tied the rope to the ring on Bandit's collar and then fastened a slip knot around the nearest tree. He dropped the loose end of the rope next to where the briefcase was buried.

"Bandit, stay." The dog glanced at Tom, and then sat on his haunches.

We've got to give those mob guys time to get down here, he thought. *I wonder if they're coming today. Maybe they sensed a rat. I hope Larry didn't overdo it.*

Bandit stood up, smelled the air, tested the rope, and then looked up at Tom and whined.

"It's okay, boy." He reached down to pet him. "The guys in the bushes are our friends."

Tom couldn't stop worrying. *So much can go wrong,* he thought. He leaned against a tree and decided to wait a half-hour before starting to dig. Bandit was fidgeting, sniffing the air and looking around. Tom was sure Bandit could smell the agents hiding in the trees.

"Bandit, relax. It's okay." Tom reassured him.

About 11:30, Tom started to dig, going through the loosened dirt easily. His shovel struck the briefcase and he bent down to scoop the dirt away. It was then that Bandit jumped to his feet, a low growl in his throat. As he started to get up, Tom glanced to where the dog was staring and spotted a movement along the side of the slide area. Bandit's ears were erect, an intermittent low growl in his throat.

"No. Quiet Bandit. Let the guy get closer. I don't want him to know we see him."

Tom scratched the dog's ears. Bandit stood frozen, all his attention on the place where he had seen movement. Tom stayed on his knees by the hole he had dug, surreptitiously watching for movement inside the tree line. In a few minutes the man had descended through the trees to the bottom of the rock slide. Tom saw only one man and wondered where the other one might be.

He knew that the most dangerous time was rapidly approaching, and that the intruder would be at his side in just a few minutes. Bandit growled again. Tom placed a hand on his muzzle. The briefcase was now totally exposed and Tom pulled it out of the hole. Bandit growled louder, Tom quieted him again. When he straightened up, Tom saw a man only a few yards away, approaching cautiously a pistol in his hand. The man was the same brick-shaped man that he had encountered before, the one Tom had fought with when he had taken Liz. A tremor went through Tom as he realized that this man likely wanted him dead. He was dressed in the same outfit Tom remembered, hiking boots, blue jeans, and a canvas field coat. He looked like anyone else hiking in the mountains, except for the menacing pistol.

Tom looked up at him. They made eye contact. Bandit started to bark, bared his teeth, and lunged against the rope.

"Hold your dog or I'll kill him."

Tom reached down and grabbed Bandit's collar. "What do you want?" Tom feigned.

"Don't screw with me, cowboy. Step away from that briefcase. Move over to the mutt."

"Look, I'm the one that found it. I want to claim the reward," Tom exclaimed in as genuine a hayseed manner as he could muster.

Bandit kept up his barking and lunged repeatedly against the rope.

Jake raised the gun to shoulder level and pointed it directly at Tom's head. "You get over by the mutt like I told you, asshole, or you'll get your reward all right, right here and right now. It's your choice. I owe you plenty from before. I haven't forgotten. The money better be in there."

Tom held tightly to Bandit's collar. Bandit tested his grip with intermittent lunges. Jake glanced nervously at the threatening dog, but then took a step closer to the briefcase.

"Hey, man, I found this. I want the reward," said Tom in a voice of feigned confidence.

The man turned back to face him, visibly annoyed. He raised the gun again to Tom's head. Tom's comments and the lunging dog were distracting and irritating him.

"Shut the fuck up, asshole! This isn't your money. Forget about it!" he growled at Tom.

Tom wanted to keep him talking and keep his attention diverted from the suitcase filled with newspaper. If he opened it, it would be all over, and only a quick shot from one of the officers would save him. He decided to keep pressing him as long as possible.

"What the hell you mean? I found it. Whose money is it? It ain't yours!"

Jake turned toward Tom. His left hand gripped the briefcase handle and, in a few quick strides was directly in front of him.

"Asshole!" and in an explosion of anger he swung his pistol in a powerful arc which smashed against Tom's temple.

As Tom fell to his knees, he grabbed the loose end of the rope and pulled as hard as he could, untying the slip knot. In a second, Bandit was free and leapt at Jake seizing his gun arm in powerful jaws. The gun fell to the ground. Tom was on his knees, semi-conscious, in pain and bleeding. Bandit's teeth punctured the canvas sleeve and entered the flesh of the man's arm. The man bellowed in rage and pain, trying with his free hand to pull the dog from him. Then he seized the fallen pistol and raised it to aim at the dog. The gun went off, discharging into the ground. An FBI agent crashed through the brush, assault rifle at the ready.

"Drop it! Drop it now!" roared a command from the camouflaged agent. Jake dropped the pistol to the ground, and a deputy appeared quickly to pick it up. Cursing, Jake continued to try and dislodge Bandit from his arm.

"Tom! Tom! We got him. We got him. Call your dog off!" yelled a deputy.

Tom called to Bandit, but had to reach for him and pull him off Jake's arm. He held tightly to the collar, trying to stay focused through the spasms of pain in his head. The dog lunged toward his nemesis again and again while Tom held on. Suddenly Bandit sat down, turned to Tom and licked his face.

"You're a good boy. Stay." He petted him, hugged him and talked softly to him.

138

SAM SAT IN THE JEEP AND watched Jake disappear into the trees. He couldn't stop the nauseous feeling that had crept into his stomach. He felt sure this was a setup. It just didn't feel right; it was too easy, too contrived. If they were caught, he, too, would go to prison for kidnapping. He had no doubt about it. He had just completed a stretch; he wasn't going back again. Then he heard a noise behind him. It sounded like a twang from something metal. Was it a radio antenna hitting a branch? There it was again, and then he heard the sound of breaking branches. He leapt out of the Jeep. Keeping the Jeep between him and the approaching vehicle, he slipped into the brush and was soon swallowed up by the forest. Branches tugged at his clothes and whipped against his face, but he ran toward the National Forest where he thought he would be safe. The sound of a pistol shot quickened his stride. He wasn't going to stick around. He'd settle with Jake later if it came to that, but he had a sick feeling in his stomach.

139

WHILE ONE AGENT CLEANED and bandaged Tom's head, the other two handcuffed Jake, who refused to say a word. They read Jake his rights, while a deputy photographed the scene, rapidly clicking off shot after shot. Another spoke into his headset radio and advised those up on the ridge that they had apprehended one of the suspects. Then word came back that although they found the suspect's Jeep, the other perpetrator was not in the area. It seemed that he had fled, likely when he heard their approaching vehicle. Tom could hear several voices arguing, and then recognized Agent Oberman's angry voice on the radio.

"You let him get away?" he asked.

A few seconds passed and then Oberman responded. "He's got to be close by." Another pause, then "Get Wayne on the radio. Tell him what happened. I don't believe this."

The agent approached the small group gathered around Jake and Tom. The scowl said it all; Tom knew Jake's accomplice had escaped. The deputies and FBI agents took Jake and started up the side of the slide area. Oberman looked at Tom and shook his head, still trying to contain his anger.

When Tom's head injury had been cleaned and wrapped, he was able to stand. His head was clearing and the pain subsiding somewhat. He put a leash on Bandit, unsure what the dog would do if unattended.

While the deputies and the FBI agents took the sullen and injured prisoner up the steep hillside, Oberman stepped closer to Tom.

"Sorry you got hurt. I hope it isn't a concussion. You did good."

"Yeah," said Tom. "What happened up top?"

Oberman wrinkled his face in frustration. "I guess the other suspect heard Allen's vehicle coming through the woods and hauled ass out of there. He's on foot, but who the hell knows which way he went."

"We got the main guy, the one that grabbed Liz," exclaimed Tom.

"Yes, I am glad of that. We'll squeeze him; see what he gives us. In the meantime I hope Wayne can get some deputies out on the other side of this ridge."

"He's got to turn up somewhere," Tom said.

"This asshole is a lot more desperate now; can't go back to the motel, doesn't have his support. Come on, I'll help you up this hill." He took Tom's arm.

"Would you mind taking Bandit? I can use the shovel for a crutch." He handed Oberman the leash.

Bandit went quietly, but turned back to look at Tom every few yards. Tom made the strenuous climb despite a pounding headache. At the top, he took the leash and hugged the dog. He sat down against a tree and watched the deputies and FBI agents connect the tow hitch on the Jeep to Allen's SUV.

Oberman waved at Tom as the group took the prisoner back to the old logging road where an FBI Suburban waited to transport them. Tom saw Bandit wagging his tail and turned to look. Allen was approaching. Tom strained to get up.

"I'll have one of my guys drive you home," said Allen.

Tom shook his head, "No. I'll be okay. It just hurts like hell."

"Yeah, we're sorry that happened. I apologize."

"Not your fault. Did you talk to Wayne about the other suspect?"

Allen nodded sheepishly, "Yeah. He's sending some guys out, but he could be anywhere. Hell, he might be a hundred yards or a mile away by now. I just wasn't thinking. Shit, he had to have heard me coming and took off."

"Don't beat yourself up about it. He'll show up." Tom tried to sound conciliatory.

"Thanks. Wayne is going to have me for lunch when I get back," said Allen.

"Oh hell, he'll get over it." Tom tried to force a grin.

"Let me walk you to your truck. You sure you don't want a driver?"

Tom shook his head. "I'll be okay."

140

TOM LEANED AGAINST HIS TRUCK. He could feel the blood pounding in his head. He tossed the shovel into the back, opened the door, let Bandit jump in, and then sat down in the driver's seat and closed his eyes for a moment. His head throbbed.

Allen came up to him and placed a hand on his shoulder. "Well Tom, it's over. We owe you a lot, couldn't have done it without you."

"You guys did good. I couldn't tell you were in the trees near me, but Bandit knew."

Allen smiled, "I'm sorry you had to get banged up again. I hope it's nothing too serious. You might want to get an x-ray though. The county'll even pay for it."

"It sure hurts. I'll see how I feel later."

"Okay. We're hauling the Jeep on the forest road to Camden. The evidence people can go through it. There is a mountain of paper work we need to do before we go home. You sure you're okay to drive?" Allen looked concerned.

"Yeah. You guys go on. I'll be fine." Tom started the engine.

The two lawmen drove off with the Jeep in tow. Tom sat there for a while, his eyes shut, letting the tension drain from his body. He felt that eventually the Sheriff and the FBI would get the prisoner to talk and the FBI would be able to "follow the money." He wasn't too sure about the missing suspect; he would have to keep an eye out for him. He was still a threat.

141

Tom arrived back at the ranch mid afternoon to find vehicles from the local TV station and newspaper parked in front of the barn. A large antenna dish pointed skyward. A video cameraman, still photographers and news reporters milled around in a group until one of them saw Tom's truck coming into the yard. Everyone turned in his direction, and when he stopped the truck, they all moved toward him in a mass.

"Goddamn horde of locusts," Tom mumbled. He was tired; his head throbbed, and he didn't want to be interviewed; only wanted to sleep. When he stopped the truck, Ralph quickly went up to him and leaned in the window.

"You look like shit. You want to see a doctor, or maybe an undertaker?"

"No, not yet. Just let me get some sleep. My head is killing me."

"Oberman told me what happened up there. God, you sure took a big chance." Ralph shook his head in disapproval.

"Well, it's over now. If Oberman can get the guy to talk, he'll have his case made. Anyway, they now know that the FBI has their money. They'll just have to write it off."

"What a nightmare," exclaimed Ralph.

"You know, those guys might have an easier time with the FBI than the thugs back home. That was a lot of money they lost."

The press crowded toward them. Questions were being yelled out. The TV camera appeared over Ralph's shoulder.

"Come on, give him a break. Stand back," pleaded Ralph.

Tom got out of the truck and let Bandit jump out. He kept the dog on the leash, not sure how he would react to the hordes. Cameras were whirring and clicking around him. The reporters yelled questions over each other. Tom attempted to answer a few, then asked Ralph to stand in the way while he escaped to his cabin. The video cameras captured everything Tom said, while focusing their lenses on the ribbon of gauze bandaging his head.

Tom walked away with questions still being yelled at him. Ralph finally entered the cabin as Tom was getting into bed. He turned to Ralph.

"I just gotta sleep, Ralph. This damn head really hurts."

"Okay. I'll have Suz come by and look at you," he insisted. "You might be better off if you don't sleep; concussion and all."

"Leave me alone. I'm sleeping."

In the kitchen, Ralph picked up the telephone, punched in the extension for his home and asked Susan to bring some clean bandages and first aid ointment. Ralph could see that the TV people were still milling around. He closed the window blinds, went outside, and insisted that they depart.

142

SUSAN ACCOMPANIED BY LIZ, who was spending a few days away from school, arrived quickly at Tom's cabin, knocked and went in without waiting for a reply. They found Tom in his bed starting to doze off.

Susan spoke, "Damn, Tom. What'd you do now?"

"Oh, I'm okay. Just let me sleep awhile."

"Baloney, sit up, let me have a look. You took a hard knock."

"It'll be okay, just sore," protested Tom.

"Liz, open up some clean bandages and give me that tube of ointment."

They ignored his protestations and removed his soiled dressing, cleaned his wound, applied first-aid ointment and re-bandaged his head. Susan looked carefully at his wound.

"Tom, this should be X-rayed."

"If I don't feel better in the morning, *then* we can go to the hospital," he mumbled.

"All right, but we'll be keeping an eye on you," said Susan.

Susan went back to her home, while Liz curled up in a chair in the living room and pulled a blanket over herself. She looked in on Tom from time to time. She lingered at the door each time.

143

Tom woke the next morning to the smell of coffee. He still had a dull ache in his head. He wrapped himself in his robe and went into the kitchen, startling Liz who was at the stove. She could see that he was better. She turned to him and hugged him.

"I'm glad you're up and around. We weren't sure last night."

"Oh, I'll be all right, I've got a hard head," and he smiled warmly at Liz. "What're you doing?"

"Making toast and coffee. Want some?"

"I sure would, thanks. Were you here all night?"

"Yeah, stayed in the big chair...mom wanted me to. We were worried."

"You didn't have to do that, but thank you." He put his arm around her shoulder.

She blushed and turned away. "We wanted to be sure you didn't spike a fever."

They sat at the kitchen table and had coffee and buttered toast. "Tell me everything that happened on the ridge," she said.

He related the story again.

"The Fed said one of the guys got away."

Tom nodded, "Yes, he apparently slipped away when he heard Allen coming through the trees with his SUV."

"What a nightmare." She shook her head. "Mom and dad are still upset about the kidnapping."

"I would think so, but I'm glad it's over. What are you doing out of school by the way?"

"I got ahead on the work, and decided to take a few days off. I'll take a bus back to Billings tomorrow."

"It's good seeing you again, kid."

"Same here." She kissed him on the cheek and turned to pick up the dishes.

144

Tom settled himself near the fireplace, and began to doze when the telephone startled him. He reached for it on the third ring. Bandit, in front of the fire, twitched his ears when Tom began to talk.

"Hello."

"Hi Tom. It's Karen. How are you?"

"It's great to hear your voice. How are you?"

"Were you asleep?"

"Oh, just dozing in front of the fireplace."

"I thought so. I had to call. I saw the news on TV. How bad did they hurt you?"

"I got whacked on the head. It hurts some, but it'll be okay. Bandit did real good though, sunk his teeth into the guy's arm."

"I was so worried about you."

"It's over now. They arrested one of them, other guy got away. Sheriff is looking for him, though. The money is gone, so it's really over.

"I'm glad."

"How have *you* been? How is your mom?"

"Holding her own, but it's really just a matter of time. The medicine just helps with the pain. Dad isn't too good. He's functional, but that's about all."

"I hope they can keep your mom comfortable."

"Yeah, me too. It's hard to watch the decline."

"And *you*, how are you doing?" Tom asked, his voice softening.

"I'm doing okay. I told you about the places I've performed at. Well, they had me back again. The money isn't too bad either."

"How about Nashville? Your agent doing any good there?"

"I'll be cutting new promotional CDs in a couple of weeks. I'm hoping to get some favorable response. My agent is hopeful and encouraging, but I don't know."

"You still want to go there - to Nashville - don't you?"

"Part of me does. I love to sing. I like to sing in front of people, to feel the interaction. That's why I love the smaller clubs. But I could use some record sales to help my concert bookings. I need to be in Nashville and get better known."

"Do you have faith in your agent?"

"He's been in the business a long time, has some big name artists. He's okay. I think it's me, figuring out what's inside of me. It's a little confusing at times."

Then her voice brightened. "So what have you done at the ranch lately?"

"Well, I think you're up to date. All the cabins are finished. All the equipment is in everywhere. I should be ready to open up in the spring. Should be fun, huh?"

"I am really happy for you. It will be wonderful. It's your dream."

"It certainly is a dream come true."

"I better let you go, got to get ready for bed."

"I miss you, Karen. I wish you were still here."

"I wish I was there, too," she whispered. "Good night, Tom."

145

IT HAD BEEN NEARLY A WEEK and Sam was hungry, dirty and cold. He was afraid to go back to the motel despite everything he left there. He had eluded capture by walking, mostly at night. It had taken him two days to get out of the forest and two more to get to Camden. The two trail-mix bars he had in his pockets were long gone. Hunger was an ever-present torment. Water hadn't been a problem because of the many small brooks along the way. He hid in a barn at the edge of town. The property seemed abandoned and he hoped no one would discover him there.

He cursed his situation; the lack of a shower and shave, the smelly clothes, the ever present hunger, and the not knowing what to do. He looked at his possessions; a wallet fat with cash he couldn't spend, a 9-mm pistol with an extra clip, and a cell phone. He checked the phone and was surprised to see the battery had retained its charge. He should call Frankie, but he dreaded it. He wondered, *what is happening to Jake*. Had he talked to the law to save his own skin? *Jake might be out of Frankie's reach, but what about me?* he thought. *Would Frankie let me hang out to dry?* He didn't want to go back to prison.

He couldn't think straight. He was preoccupied with the need to find food. It was almost dark. A trip into town might relieve his hunger. He would slip into town again in a couple of hours and see what he could find for food. He ran his fingers through his scruffy beard, wondering if it would offer him any anonymity.

Sam looked out the dirty window onto the sunny street below. It was a seedy part of town. He saw abandoned cattle corrals and wooden sheds at the far end of the street. There were more signs of life in the other direction. He would look for a quiet place to eat and some obscure place to sleep.

146

HE GOT LUCKY; THE MANAGER at the Livingstone, an old run-down hotel, usually rented rooms by the hour. All the girls were out, he said, but some would be back that night. He jumped at the chance to let Sam have a room until Monday for the hundred dollar bill he laid on the counter. The grizzly manager asked no questions, merely handed Sam the room key.

He was asleep almost immediately, lying on the bed in his clothes. Later, after a long shower, he felt better. He looked at his soiled clothes; they would have to do. He had to get out of town quickly, but to where? Should he try to go to the airport? No. Surely someone would be looking for him there, as well as at the bus station. He would call Frankie from a pay phone when he was far away from here. He had to find a car, though. Stealing one would be risky. He had a long way to go to a city large enough to remain unnoticed.

147

SAM NEVER THOUGHT HE WOULD have to eat in such a pigpen. He sat at the counter and felt his sleeves sticking to the grubby counter top. The few people sitting in booths ignored him. He looked outside and spotted a used car lot through the grimy windows. But first he would eat. How bad could breakfast be?

A sullen waiter stood before him, pad and pencil in hand. Sam recognized the look -- a long time in prison.

"What'll it be, buddy?"

"Let me have the four-egg omelet," replied Sam looking up at his face. The waiter didn't meet his gaze.

"You want potatoes 'n ham or something else?"

"Yeah, that'll be fine. Toast and coffee, too."

The waiter poured a brackish liquid into a heavy mug, plunked it down in front of him and dropped several prepackaged creamers next to it.

"Be a few minutes," he mumbled and went back to the kitchen.

Sam looked at the coffee but took a sip anyway. He poured all three creamers into the cup along with several sugar packets. He sat quietly, eavesdropping on conversations around him.

148

HE PULLED THE BASEBALL hat down on his face as he approached the used car lot. The sign read *Duane's Used Cars, Rent to Buy*. *This is definitely the poor section of town*, he thought, *nothing but old relics.* He heard the door close on the sales shack and spotted the salesman walking toward him.

"Good morning. Duane's the name." He extended a hand. Sam forced a smile and they shook hands. "What do you need; some basic transportation?" Duane was all smiles.

"I'd like to explore the area for a few days. I've never been out this way," Sam responded.

"Where you from? Just off the morning bus?" Duane looked at Sam with more interest.

"Yeah. Outa work. Traveling around, seeing what I missed. Maybe find a job." Sam shrugged.

"Got money?"

Sam nodded.

Duane swept his arm in an all encompassing gesture. "These cars are mostly repossessed. Plenty of life left in them. If you need something over the weekend, any one of 'em could suit ya."

Sam looked at an old Ford Taurus, ordinary enough, just what he wanted. "What do you need for this Ford?" asked Sam.

"I usually get twenty bucks a day to rent it. This is Thursday; if you want it through the weekend, I can let you have it for sixty bucks plus insurance. Insurance will run you another seven bucks a day."

Sam looked around at some of the nearby cars, and didn't respond to his offer.

"You want to drive it, check it out? It's a good running little car," Duane looked at Sam hopefully.

"I don't know..." Sam looked unconvinced.

"Look, it doesn't have much gas in it; kids around here steal it. Tell you what, you can have it for fifty bucks. Let me hold onto a hundred buck deposit and I'll give you back change on Monday morning. I get here around 9 o'clock." Duane smiled and started toward the sales shack.

Sam followed along. This was easier than he had thought.

Inside, Duane led him to a desk and indicated a chair. He started filling out the rental form, while Sam reached for his wallet. He pulled out two fifties. Duane looked up at his face momentarily, then back to his paperwork.

"Cash, huh?"

"Yeah, while it lasts." Sam tried a face of sadness, hoping that Duane wasn't getting suspicious. "Have to find some work soon, credit card is tapped out."

"I need to see your driver's license," said Duane, looking up briefly.

Sam pulled it out of his wallet and laid it on the desk. Duane picked it up, looked briefly at the picture and back at Sam. Then he wrote the license number on the agreement. He handed the license back to Sam.

"Okay. Just sign here. From Chicago, huh?"

"Yeah."

"What kind of work you do?" asked Duane.

"Drove a truck most of the time, different outfits." Sam wanted to get out before the salesman got too inquisitive. Sam signed the rental form and handed it back.

Duane rummaged through his desk drawer and pulled out a set of keys.

"Here you go. Have it back here Monday morning."

Sam nodded.

149

TOM SLAMMED THE HOOD of his truck, swearing under his breath. The radiator cap seal wasn't holding, and he had been losing coolant. He opened the door, looked around for Bandit, then whistled. The dog ran toward him from the barn, and leapt into the truck.

"Good boy."

Tom slid onto his seat, closed the door and started the engine. He reached over to Bandit and petted him.

"Off we go. We'll stop at the gas station to get a new radiator cap. I'm sure Chris will be happy to see you."

Bandit flicked his tail, but his attention was at the window as the truck started to move.

In a few minutes, Tom slowed to look at the cattle grazing on the dried grass. "Those cows will be gone soon and the elk will be dropping down from the hills. Sullivan's boys should be through here next week gathering up this herd. There are some fat calves out there." Tom scratched the dog's ears. "Yeah, autumn will be here before you know it."

Tom moved the truck along the ranch road; his thoughts became focused on Karen. He thought of her often. She had left a feeling of emptiness, a hollow spot that even the ranch and the Stehling family could not fill. He wondered at the magic of her presence, the faint trace of perfume, the soft touch of her eyes, and he missed her. He thought about the night they had spent together and wished for her to be in his arms again.

The truck bounced over the unpaved bumps as he pulled into Al's Automotive. He parked alongside the building and got out with Bandit at his heels. Looking into the double bay, he didn't see anyone. He pushed open the door to the office as Chris hung up the telephone.

"Tom!" Her face lit up in a smile.

"Hi Chris. Bandit wanted to visit you."

She wrinkled her nose. "Glad to see you, too." She bent down to hug the dog. "Good to see you, Bandit." She scratched his head. "I heard about your adventures up on the ridge. Allen came in the other day and told me all about it." She shook her head. "Got hurt some, huh?"

"Little bit," he reached up to touch the still tender spot on his head. "We got the guy that grabbed Liz. His sidekick got away. No one's seen him since. Say, where is your dad?"

"He went into Camden, had a dental appointment. I'm here alone. Think you can behave?" Her eyes twinkled.

"Well, I'll certainly try," he grinned. "Say, you wouldn't have a radiator cap for my truck by chance?"

"I didn't think you came just to visit me." Her lower lip puckered. "I've got caps in the store room, be right back." She disappeared through a small door into a storage area.

Tom saw the light come on, heard her moving boxes around. "Chris, you see much of Jeff these days?"

"Yeah, he's kinda growing on me. We went into Camden last week for a movie."

She came back into the office holding a small box in her hand. "Here it is. It's a universal replacement; book says it'll fit your truck." She started to write down the purchase in her accounts book.

"I'll put it on tonight after the engine cools off," he remarked.

"Have you been talking to Karen much?" Chris looked into his eyes.

"She called a few days ago. It's kinda hard though; we don't talk long."

"You miss her, don't you?" Chris looked away.

"I didn't dream I'd miss her so much," he said with a catch in his throat.

"She's really lucky. So are you," she said softly.

"Chris?"

She turned to him, tears in her eyes. She put her arms around him. They hugged.

"Chris, I..."

The bell rang twice as a car pulled in front of the fuel pumps.

"Oh, shut-up..." she said hoarsely, wiping away a tear. She hurried toward the fuel pumps. Bandit ran after her.

150

Sam folded his map. He would keep to the back roads until he was south of Butte, less chance of meeting a highway patrol cruiser. He wasn't too worried about the sheriff; he'd deal with him if he had to. The pistol was under his jacket, uncomfortable but reassuring. He started west on County Road. It would take him through Randolph and Elk Creek, but after that, he would be in open country. *I should be able to make Salt Lake City by midnight. I'll call Frankie from there; get the lay of the land.* He didn't feel hopeful, he wasn't a made guy, just a soldier, a grunt.

Wonder what happened to Jake? He won't tell them anything. He'll wait for Frankie to bail him out, get some fancy lawyer. Yeah, Jake, a made man. He'll survive. Shit, they'll hang me out to dry. He looked down at the speedometer as he entered Elk City, letting his foot up from the accelerator. *I've got to get gas, and then I'm out of this town. It'll be a while before Duane gets his car back.* He was nearly through town when he spotted Al's Automotive. He slowed and came to a stop in front of the fuel pumps. The place looked deserted, but then he saw a young woman walking rapidly toward him. He spotted the dog.

151

SHE QUICKLY WIPED HER EYES with the greasy rag from her pocket. She hadn't meant to fall apart in front of him; now they would both feel bad. She looked at the driver as she came up to the pump island. It wasn't anyone that she had seen before; *rather odd for around here*, she thought. He had a scruffy beard, more like a two-week shadow. Bandit pressed against her legs.

"Good morning. Fill 'er up?" she asked.

"Yeah, regular." Sam avoided looking at her, and didn't want to look at the dog. He fumbled aimlessly with the radio. He was startled when the dog began to bark.

Chris pumped fuel into the car. She glanced at Bandit; the fur on his neck was raised. He was staring at the driver and barking.

"Bandit, quiet down." Bandit kept barking.

"Come on boy, back inside." She grabbed his collar and tugged him toward the back of the car.

"Sorry, sir. I'll take him inside." She tugged at the dog's collar.

At the back of the car, she glanced purposefully at the license plate, and then tugged Bandit toward the garage office. Bandit stopped barking but turned his head toward the car and growled. She tugged him into the office, letting the door close behind her.

"Chris, I'm sorry..." began Tom. He heard her mumbling something repetitively.

Chris fumbled on the counter top and grabbed a pencil. She scribbled the license number on a scrap paper and handed it to Tom.

"Something's wrong!" exclaimed Chris. "Did you hear Bandit? He knows that guy in the car."

Tom's eyes were wide. "It could be the fugitive; they've not found him yet." He turned to stare out the window.

"Tom, that license, it's weird, not a regular plate. What should I do?" She looked at Tom. "What if it's him?"

"Can you stall him? Don't make him suspicious. I can't let him see *me*. He'll know me. He probably remembers Bandit. I'll call Allen right now. You just be careful."

She squeezed Tom's arm, kissed his cheek, and was out the door. He reached for the phone, getting Allen on the second ring.

"Allen, it's Tom. I think the fugitive might be at Al's gas pump. Chris is trying to stall him. Can you get here quick?"

"Yeah. I'll head right over."

"Just a second, listen." Tom read the number from Chris's note. "What the hell kind of license is that?"

"Might be a rental. I'll call it in. Be there in less than two minutes." Allen hung up.

152

A **SUDDEN TREMOR OF FEAR** ran through him. The dog just stood there barking and staring at him. *Oh shit! It's got to be the same dog! Where is that Bauer guy? Hurry up, goddamn it. Where is she?* Sam pulled his wallet out of his jacket and on impulse un-clipped the strap on his pistol holster.

He saw her coming toward him, casually flipping the grease rag in circles. Maybe he was overreacting; the dog wasn't with her. He could still hear the fuel pump running; he had been near empty. She came near his window.

"Sorry. Put him inside. Want me to take a look at your oil?" She twirled the grease rag aimlessly.

He glanced at her briefly. "Thanks, no. It's fine," he said. He glanced at her again. Her jacket was open now. His eyes lingered on her tight blouse. *She's certainly a looker; a little of that would go a long way.* His eyes followed her as she picked up the rag she had dropped. *Fine, real fine.* He heard the pump click off, and saw her move toward it. He watched her in the side mirror as she topped off the tank. *When was the last time? Damn!* He saw her pull the nozzle out of the car and return it to the pump. He watched as she put on the gas cap and let the cover slam closed. He turned his head forward to open his wallet. He glanced in the overhead mirror as the sheriff's SUV pulled in and stopped a couple of car lengths behind him. A chill went through his body.

Allen saw the tan Ford Taurus at the pump. He pulled in behind it and reached to his hip to take the safety strap from his pistol. When Chris looked at him, he indicated with a jerk of his head, that she should move back from the car. Allen watched as she handed the driver his change. Suddenly the driver was out of the car with a hand gripping Chris's arm, and a pistol pointed at her side.

Allen opened his door and crouched behind it, pistol in his hand.

"Driver! Police! Let her go!" yelled Allen.

Sam put the pistol to Chris's head and pulled her in front of him. "Hey, cop. Toss your keys over here. Right now, before I put one in the head of this cute little girl."

"Don't hurt her. Let her go. We'll talk about this." Allen reached for the ignition keys.

"Throw your keys over here," yelled Sam, while waving the pistol menacingly at Chris's head.

"Please, please, don't hurt me. Let me go," pleaded Chris. She tried not to cry.

Tom felt as if his heart would stop. The guy had Chris by the arm, waving a pistol at her head and yelling. Allen couldn't shoot, not with Chris as a shield. The bastard would probably take her with him as a hostage. He sprang toward the shop door, cast about for a suitable weapon and grabbed a big adjustable wrench from the bench top. Shielded from view, he darted back into the office, through the storage room, and out the back door. There were pines close by the building, suitable, he hoped, for cover. He kept well into the trees as he quickly and quietly made a loop to come up near the car, behind the fugitive. He stooped low and watched, waiting for his chance.

"Let's talk about this. No one has to get hurt. Let her go." Allen stooped behind the door of the SUV, his pistol held useless in his hand.

"Throw your keys to me. Throw them over here."

"Don't hurt her. Here...here are the keys." Allen recalled he had another set on his house key ring and pulled the key out of the ignition and tossed them from his shielded position. They landed at the back bumper of the Ford Taurus.

"There. There they are. Let her go. No one has to get hurt."

Allen saw the vise-like grip on Chris's arm. But suddenly, he was distracted by a blur of motion as Tom came up behind the fugitive who, startled by the sound of steps on the gravel, turned his head. But it was too late. The heavy wrench landed against his arm. Allen saw the pistol drop to the ground and Sam let go of Chris. He roared in pain as he favored his injured arm, now hanging limp at his side. Allen came from behind his door and spurted toward the fugitive. Chris backed away a few steps, and then ran toward the building.

Tom dropped the wrench and leapt at Sam, putting a powerful choke hold around his neck. With all his strength he pulled the man down onto the ground between the car and the fuel pumps. Sam raged in pain and fury. Allen came up quickly and picked up the pistol that had dropped from Sam's now useless hand.

"Tom...you okay?" Allen gasped.

"Yeah."

"Let him go."

Tom stepped out from the choke hold.

Allen grabbed Sam by the neck and slammed him against the hood of the car. Sam roared in pain and tried to hold his injured arm.

"You broke it," he roared and turned his head toward Tom. "You goddamn bastard. You broke it."

"Allen...I think this guy's arm *is* broken. Look at it," said Tom, shaking his head.

"Yeah, looks like it. Stand off a little while I go through his pockets."

"What's your name? Where you from?" asked Allen.

"Kiss my ass. You assholes broke my goddamn arm," bellowed Sam.

Allen pulled what was in Sam's pockets and tossed it onto the hood. He found his billfold in his jacket packet and flipped it open to his driver's license.

"Sam McGill, huh? Where did you get this car?" asked Allen.

Sam ignored the question, uttering only a moan as he tried to shift his weight to favor his injured arm.

Allen pulled Sam up from the trunk lid and walked him back to his SUV, picking up his ignition key from where he had tossed it.

"Hey. You broke my arm. Let go of me," he raged at Allen.

"Have a seat. Just give me an excuse to blow your head off. You are under arrest. You are advised to remain silent. Anything you say can and will be held against you in a court of law. Do you understand that?"

"Screw off."

"Just answer the question. Do you understand?" Allen finished the Miranda warning from memory. He grabbed Sam by the broken arm, "I asked you a question. Do you understand what I just said?"

Sam mumbled, "Yeah. Maybe. Now get me to a fuckin' hospital."

"Sure. No problem."

When Allen pulled Sam's arms behind him to put on handcuffs, Sam writhed in pain and cursed him vehemently. Allen ignored the outburst.

Allen had Sam sit the back of his vehicle but not without more curses and cries of pain. Allen closed the door, went around to the driver's door, and reached in for his microphone.

Allen tossed the microphone onto the seat and turned as Chris hurried towards them with Bandit in the lead, tugging on the leash. Bandit sniffed the air, staring at the SUV. He tested the leash and whined.

Chris came up to Tom and grabbed his arm. "Is this the guy...the *other* guy?"

"Bandit thinks so," said Tom. "I can't be sure until they get the beard off him."

Allen grinned, "I'll check with Wayne. He'll probably want to talk to the DA before shaving the beard. This jerk's got *some* rights."

They all turned toward the sound of another vehicle approaching. The sheriff stopped his SUV next to Allen's.

"Here's Wayne. Let's see what he wants to do," said Allen.

"What do we have?" Wayne bent down to look in the window at the prisoner.

"He grabbed Chris when I drove up. He had a gun on her. I was afraid of a hostage situation with him making a break for it."

Wayne looked up, waiting for the rest of the story.

Allen continued. "Tom snuck around behind him and whacked him on the arm with a big wrench. He dropped the pistol, let go of Chris, and Tom grabbed him. It looks like his arm is broken."

"Let's get cuffs on his ankles," said Wayne as he reached for the door. Allen kept his pistol ready. Wayne looked at the prisoner. He was holding onto his injured arm.

"They broke my arm," he whined.

"Too bad it wasn't your neck. We'll have it looked at. I'm putting cuffs on your ankles. Don't make trouble," said Wayne.

Allen lifted his hat and wiped his forehead. He stepped away from the car with Wayne. "His stuff is on the hood of his car. He has a Glock 9-mm and a billfold, some loose change, a watch."

"Who is he? Is he our fugitive?" asked Wayne.

"His license shows Sam McGill out of Chicago. Tom doesn't recognize him. He didn't see him with a beard. The dog sure recognized him, wants to tear into him."

Wayne turned to Tom. "You don't recognize him?"

"Not with the beard."

Wayne smiled and shook his head. "That's one for the DA. If this is our guy, the DA will be real interested in cleaning him up. Especially, since the other guy we have hasn't said a thing to us, only to some Chicago lawyer he called."

"Go on, bag his stuff. I'll go on to the hospital and wait for the ambulance. I'll call it in. You can come later."

"I'll call a flatbed to come for the car," said Allen "Did you check on the plate?"

"It is a reseller plate. It really shouldn't be used on a rental. I've got to have a talk with this Duane guy that runs the lot downtown. He won't be happy we have his car." Wayne turned toward Tom. "I imagine the DA will be calling you to come down and give a statement and witness this guy. I'll tell him about the beard."

"Okay, just about any day will work for me," replied Tom.

Wayne headed back to the courthouse. Allen sat in his vehicle and waited for the platform truck to arrive.

"Your dad is going to be upset that he missed all the action," said Tom.

"He will be. You want to wait for him?" asked Chris.

"I need to get back. I promised Ralph I'd help load the hay bales in the barn. It's heavy work and he's not a spring chicken." He started toward his truck. "It's nice seeing you again. Take care."

"Tom."

He stopped and turned to look back at her.

Chris cleared her throat. "Thank you."

Tom smiled. "You're welcome."

"Are we okay...you and me?" asked Chris.

Tom smiled. "We're okay."

153

SUMMER HAD PASSED AND WITH autumn, a frosty chill settled in the mountain valleys. Aspens were aglow in golden splendor for a few weeks, as the snow line crept down the mountainsides. Smoke wafted from chimneys and split wood was stacked close by. Hunting season closed as the first snows dusted the valleys. With deepening snows of winter, herds of elk gathered daily in the meadows, pawing through the snow for whatever was left of the dried grass. Wolves were heard frequently. The old and weak deer and elk would disappear by spring. The first storm of the winter season arrived a few days before Thanksgiving and brought nearly two feet of snow overnight with temperatures in the low 20s.

In the lodge at Timberline Ranch, Thanksgiving Day was celebrated with roasted wild turkey and goose. Jeff and Chris brought several pies. Al and Larry came with a box of wine and spirits. Allen arrived last, after his shift was over, bringing a box of chocolates he presented to Susan.

Liz, home from school for the week, was up early to help Susan prepare the Thanksgiving feast. The dining room, normally little used, was decorated with pumpkins and cornstalks and the table was extended to accommodate both the guests and the array of food. Tantalizing aromas filled the house. Everyone had gathered at the Stehling's cabin in early afternoon for appetizers, drinks and conversation. Bandit chose a spot just outside on the kitchen stoop where odors of food sifted under the door.

Everyone talked about things happening in town and events in Camden and Randolph. Soon the conversation became a rehash of the events on the ridge, the capture of the gangsters, the excitement at Al and Chris's garage, and all the publicity in the newspapers. Tom and Allen tried to satisfy everyone's curiosity, but the questions didn't stop. Tom squirmed in his seat and tried to change the subject each time the conversation went to questions of the crash scene.

Chris glanced at Tom. He caught her signal with the shift of her eyes. He nodded.

She smiled and spoke, "Hey Tom, how about showing me what you've been doing around here? Let's take a walk."

"Sure." Tom got up from his chair and Chris excused herself. "We'll be back. I want to see what he's been doing over at the lodge." Jeff smiled at her. Al nodded. Ralph kept talking.

"Thanks," he whispered to Chris as they left the room.

They put on their coats and left for the lodge. Outside, she grabbed his arm and reached up to kiss him on the cheek.

"What's that for?"

"I don't need a reason." She smiled and squeezed his arm.

"I guess Jeff's taken a shine to you, huh?"

"Yeah, I like him," she replied. Then she became more serious. "What do you hear from Karen? Jeff calls her every couple of weeks."

"We exchange e-mails every so often, but we haven't talked in a while. It seems we both have trouble saying what we feel, and it gets awkward."

"I'm sorry," she said softly. "What *do* you feel?"

"Her voice, I miss hearing her voice. And there's the way she looked at me..."

"Have you told her?"

Tom shook his head. "I did say that in a letter. I told her that things had not gone back to the way they had been… that I missed her."

They trudged through the snow toward the lodge. Bandit had caught up to them and Chris stopped to pet him. She looked up at Tom.

"Maybe you should go see her."

"I've thought of it, but she hasn't brought it up. I keep thinking it wouldn't be right. Her life is in Chicago. Mine is here."

She looked at Bandit, who nuzzled her for more attention.

"Go see her, Tom." She didn't look up.

154

TOM PLACED HIS LAST PURCHASE in the back seat of the truck. He looked at his Christmas gift list again, assuring himself he hadn't forgotten anyone. It had taken all afternoon to find everything he wanted. Bandit paced back and forth on the back seat while Tom had gone from store to store. Tom petted and talked soothingly to him, feeling somewhat guilty. He gave him a drink of water and let him out for a few minutes.

The narrow back seat was loaded with wrapped boxes, gifts for his friends in town and the Stehlings. Bandit inspected every box as Tom brought it to the truck, but seemed disappointed.

Bandit became alert when Tom pulled into Arby's. His tail started thumping on the seat. His eyes followed Tom into the restaurant and stayed fixed on the door until he returned with a BBQ beef sandwich. Tom unwrapped the food and placed it on the ground. Bandit made short work of it and then looked at Tom expectantly. "That's it, boy. There's no more." Bandit licked Tom's fingers.

As he entered Elk Creek, Tom made a U-turn to a parking spot close to Larry's Bar and Grill. He let Bandit out of the truck for a minute and then gave him some water before putting him back in.

"I know it's been a long day, Bandit, and you've been very good. But I have to stop in here for awhile... take these gifts in." Bandit curled up on the front seat.

Tom lowered the windows a bit to give the dog fresh air. "I'll be back. It won't be too long." Bandit looked up at him momentarily and then put his head down between his paws.

Timberline

Tom picked out the shopping bag that had the gifts marked for the people at Larry's and took it with him. He heard the band well before entering the bar. This was the day Larry put on his Christmas party buffet, food which was donated by all the town's businesses on tables near the bar. Tom hung his jacket by the door and asked Jim, who was tending bar, to take the bag of gifts and give them to Larry. Jim smiled warmly and went off with the bag toward Larry's office.

Tom saw Chris and her dad at a table with a couple he didn't recognize. Chris waved and smiled at him. Tom returned the greeting. Jeff was on stage with the Rustics, singing a cowboy ballad. His baritone voice carried to all corners of the lounge and many people looked up and listened. Tom fixed himself a plate of food and found a place at the end of the bar. Jim brought him a beer. Larry waved to him from the other end of the bar. The owner had given everyone the day off and tended bar himself with only Jim to help him. Tom could tell that Larry was in his glory; he loved a warm and fun-loving crowd. He certainly had that tonight. Every table was filled, people crowded both ends of the bar, and some stood along the wall eating from paper plates. Tom felt the closeness of his friends, but somehow felt incomplete.

155

Outside, a gray sedan with the lettering *Camden Taxi* on the door went by Larry's Bar and Grill.

"Driver! Please turn around and stop in front of that green truck, the one with the dog in it."

"No problem."

The brake lights came on, and the car stopped quickly. After a pause, the driver turned the car around in the street and came back slowly to stop just past the front of Tom's truck. After a minute, the back door opened and Karen stepped out. The driver removed two large bags from the trunk and placed them on the curb. Karen checked her makeup once more with her purse mirror, and dragged her roll-along bags to Tom's truck. Her heart was pounding. She had not told him she was coming. It had been a last minute impulse, one that she hoped not to regret. She felt some trepidation and yet was driven onward by the anticipated joy of seeing Tom again. As she approached the truck, she heard the familiar barking. Bandit had his head out of the window looking at her excitedly.

"Bandit. You beautiful dog." Bandit's tail wagged furiously, his head out the window as far as he could get it.

"God, I missed you boy. I really missed you."

She hugged and kissed him, and then on an impulse she lifted her bags into the back of the truck. She then turned towards Larry's. Seeing Bandit again had lifted her spirits. She felt more assured of her impulse to come here.

156

JEFF HAD ASKED TOM TO JOIN the group on the stage and sing a number. The crowd clapped and whistled as he moved through the tables. Tom told Jeff that he would sing *I Can't Help It*, a Hank Williams standard. Jeff said something to the quartet and then the fiddle started into the introductory refrain.

As Tom went into the first stanza, the hubbub of the crowd diminished.

People were listening. Chris watched Tom with tears glistening in her eyes as he sang.

Karen, almost unnoticed, made her way to the stage as the fiddle scraped through the instrumental refrain.

Jeff's jaw dropped in disbelief as he saw his sister making her way to the stage.

Tom saw her at the same instant and his face showed the happiness that she had so hoped would be there. As the second stanza started, Karen stood next to him, sharing the microphone.

Their harmony, the sonorous sound, filled the room. The crowd was on their feet. Whistling, clapping and a few teary eyes greeted them as they finished the song.

She stepped away from the microphone, turned and hugged Jeff. "I had to come."

"I'm glad you're here. What a surprise! Did Tom know you were coming?" Jeff asked.

"No. It was a last minute thing. I told mom and dad. I hope they understand." She knew they had been disappointed at her not being there over the holidays.

Karen turned to Tom. They didn't say anything, just held each other. Then the band broke into a slow dance number.

"Hey, cowboy, can you dance in them fancy boots?" She smiled into his eyes. Wordlessly he steered her to the stage steps and onto the small dance floor. Her arms encircled his neck. His were wound tightly around her waist.

"God, I missed you," she whispered to him.

The dance number was almost finished. "I can't believe you're here," Tom whispered. "I couldn't believe my eyes at first."

"I had to come," she whispered to him.

"Don't leave..."

"Do you still want a daughter? We could go home and try," she smiled into his eyes.

He kissed her. "Yes," he whispered to her.

She knew at that moment she was home. This was where she belonged.

e n d

Printed in the USA
CPSIA information can be obtained
at www.ICGtesting.com
CBHW070549030724
11010CB00022B/393